STRANGLED BY SILK
(A Poppy Cove Mystery)

by

Barbara Jean Coast

For information, email **Cozy Cat Press**, cozycatpress@aol.com or visit our website at: www.cozycatpress.com

COZY CAT
PRESS

ISBN: 978-0-9881943-5-9
Printed in the United States of America

Cover design by Cecilia Rockwell
http://coversbycecilia.daportfolio.com

1 2 3 4 5 6 7 8 9 10

You are cordially invited to the
Opening Ceremony of Stearns
Academy for Girls
1000 Oceanview Drive
Santa Lucia, California
Thursday, August 15, 1957
Champagne Reception to
commence at 7:00 p.m.

CHAPTER ONE

Reginald Montgomery was searching high and low for Constance, his wife. Drat that woman! With only nine minutes to go before the ribbon was to be cut on the school bearing her family's name and she was nowhere to be found. *That's not like her*, he thought. *She's always on the ball for these things.*

"Where's Constance, Reginald? The trustees want to start the ceremony. I haven't seen her." Charles Stearns, the younger brother of Constance, strode up to his brother-in-law. At six-two and lean, the bachelor towered over his portly companion.

"I was just asking myself the same question. I was hoping she was with you. Now I don't know what she's gone and done. Charles, we need to find her right away. People are curious and want to get into the school. I think I just saw someone trying to sneak in the side by the Arts Building." Reginald pointed one of his stout fingers toward the cordoned-off alley between two of the buildings.

Charles looked over his shoulder and saw no one around. "I think you're just anxious, old man. Everyone's swilling the champagne and out on the lawn. You're right, though; we do need to get this event started. I'll go appease the trustees while you keep looking for her. It's bad enough that I've had to calm the waters over the headmistress not making an appearance tonight; I don't need Con to agitate them further by being fashionably late."

"Ah, maybe that's what she's doing—trying to get Larsen to reconsider. It's her career on the line; she should be here. I told Constance to be firm with her—no excuses." Reginald was miffed at the headmistress. To him, missing such an event was a direct snub to the town. Bad business.

Charles thought about it for a moment and nodded. "Yes, that's something she needed to do. That phone call last night had her very angry, she said. I'm sure that's it." With that, Charles made his way through the crowd to the front steps that led onto the gardened yard where the trustees were waiting impatiently.

A veritable *Who's Who* of Santa Lucia society had turned out on the warm, late summer evening for the opening of the Stearns' Academy for Girls, the new private school named after the Stearns family—founders of the first building supply and mercantile of Santa Lucia. Constance and her brother Charles, now the president of the family building empire and the architect who designed the school and grounds for their namesake, were the only remaining heirs in the county. The academy was situated on thirty acres of prime waterfront property—1000 Oceanview Drive. It had been in the Stearns family's possession for the last twenty years. For much of that time, it was wild, open land. Now it was handsomely landscaped, with gardens containing hedge labyrinths, seating areas and fountains, tennis courts, track and field pitch, outdoor and indoor swimming pools, a gymnasium, and riding stables—as well as the finest school for girls aged twelve to eighteen. The buildings were done in contrast to the Mediterranean style of the town, in red brick and stone that reflected the eastern preparatory schools that all of the Stearnses had attended. Being of natural materials, they fit in nicely with the landscape of the harbor.

There were three main school buildings. The first one housed academics and sciences, including languages and mathematics. Another building was dedicated to the arts. The first floor was for music, theater and dance; the second to teach the domestic arts of cooking, sewing and deportment; while the third floor had light-filled art studios for painting and sculpting. In the middle of the grounds was the third and most public building which contained the administration offices, auditorium, library, dining hall, display rooms for future art exhibits and a reception hall for social gatherings. Towards the back of the property near the hillside, quietly surrounded by trees were the dormitories, which would accommodate up to 300 young ladies from around the world. There was a house for the headmistress, a small infirmary that employed a school nurse, and an apartment block that served as living quarters for the 24 teachers and their spouses. There were trees and rosebushes everywhere. The views from all of the windows were picturesque, be they of ocean, mountain or town. Constance had worked very hard to make it perfect, but where was she?

"What seems to be the problem, Mr. Montgomery?" asked Loretta Simpson, *Santa Lucia Times*' Society Editor.

That's just great, he thought. *Now I have the society snoop and her lap dog nosing around. They don't need to know there's a problem with the headmistress. Think fast, Montgomery!* "Oh, hello, Loretta. Constance has vanished, I'm afraid. She's probably showing off the entrance tile to some poor parent. Have you seen her? It's almost time for the dedication speech."

"No Reggie, I haven't. I'll have a look around for you." Loretta scampered off, pen and pad in hand, always looking for a side angle to twist into a major scoop. As usual, her rookie photographer, Jake Moore, a young local boy who snapped up pictures at Loretta's command, followed her. *Everyone, just everyone is here*, she thought, as she pushed her horn-rimmed glasses up the bridge of her nose. *The mayor, the governor, the entire school board, as well as all the well-heeled parents—some of whom were Hollywood stars and the richest Californian elite.* "Get pictures of the crowd, Jake. There must be something we can use for the story." It was a sea of people.

She started scribbling notes in her pad about the people she saw while directing Jake. There was the newspaper magnate and his wife who brought their teenage daughter to settle in before classes started in two weeks. Years ago, Loretta had worked in Hollywood as a syndicated entertainment reporter in his stable of papers. His wife was an actress who was mediocre at best, but who became a big star due to her husband's insistence of story coverage; she was to be mentioned in the column no less than three times a week, Loretta remembered. Just arriving from the parking area was Hollywood's latest *It* girl—a buxom, blonde divorcee with a young daughter who was heading for big trouble according to rumors. "She must have figured getting her out of town would straighten her out," Loretta skeptically muttered under her breath. All the while, Jake kept taking pictures.

"Jake!" she excitedly hissed as she grabbed his arm. "Get that picture!" There was Tinseltown's supposedly most eligible bachelor with his wife and two daughters, looking very domesticated and—well— plain. "I'd heard that he wasn't the marrying kind. Things really have changed since I left town," she sighed. So intent on getting her story of the year, Loretta almost ran into Daphne. "Sorry, Daphne. I didn't see you there. Do you have any idea where Constance is?"

A waiter passed by very quickly with a tray of champagne. Daphne took two glasses—one for her and one for Margot. "I think I saw her near that building; she was taking a few minutes alone." She gestured to an area just past the waiter's shoulder. "That was about half an hour ago. I don't see her there now." The young man almost dropped the tray as Loretta briskly grabbed a glass for herself, clinking the base of the crystal glass against his cufflink.

"Careful," she said as she swerved out of his way. "This silk is very dear. Daphne can attest to that." Loretta was, of course, wearing an original design by Margot herself, accessorized by Daphne Huntington-Smythe, from the girls' dress shop. Loretta's cocktail dress was cherry-red, shantung silk with a bateau neckline and little off-the-shoulder sleeve bands. It was slim, just past the knees, with a low back and a little nipped in waist with a black belt, and silk covered buttons down the back—perfectly suited to Loretta's tall, thin, bird-like frame and her short, curly brunette hair and deep green piercing eyes. To complete her ensemble, Loretta had black satin gloves, black patent leather purse and pumps, jet earrings and a black pillbox hat.

"Oh, Loretta, you know it's worth every penny. Dear silk for a dear lady," Margot chuckled as she turned to look for Constance. The waiter turned down his head and mumbled a terse apology and vanished from sight.

"Well, you'd think he could be a little more sincere. I have half a mind to have this cost him his job!" Loretta turned as she felt a light touch at her elbow and saw a handsome face looking in her direction.

"Miss, are you all right? I saw what happened," the stranger voiced his concern.

Both women paused momentarily as they gazed upon the tall and fit figure. Loretta beamed a smile and pulled her glasses off her face and let them drop on their chain. "Uh, fine, thanks." She quickly regained her composure, and extended her free hand. "I'm Loretta Simpson, Society Editor for the *Santa Lucia Times*, the local newspaper. And you are?"

"Daniel Henshaw. I head up the equestrian program here at the Academy." He gently shook her hand and looked over at Daphne and Jake. "Who are the rest of your party?"

"Oh, right, I forgot about them. This is Jake; he's my staff photographer—great kid, never misses a shot, and Daphne Huntington-Smythe, a wonderful friend and talented young lady."

Daniel greeted them both, but directed his gaze at Daphne. "My, Miss Simpson thinks very highly of you. What is your talent?" He grinned.

Daphne beamed. "I suppose she's referring to my shop. I have a boutique with my friend, Margot Williams." She indicated her friend in the distance with her champagne glass.

"And she's a great sportswoman—golf, tennis, riding, surfing, you name it. Our Daphne's out there." Daphne considered kicking Loretta in the shins. She was laying it on a little thick. That was Loretta. Subtle as a brick.

"Mr. Henshaw, may I take your picture for the *Times*?" Jake held his camera closer to his face.

Loretta butted in. "What a great idea, Jake. Wait! Take one of them together! That'll make a great shot. Move a little closer, just a bit." Loretta motioned for Daphne and Daniel to stand closer together. "Do you mind? Just drape your arm around her shoulder. That's it. Yes, this is good, Mr. Henshaw. Getting your picture taken with Daphne's a great way to introduce you to our set. Welcome to Santa Lucia!"

Jake snapped the picture twice to make sure they had the shot, but over Daniel's shoulder he saw a frantic Reginald questioning various members of the crowd. "Miss Simpson, what do you make of that?"   He nudged Loretta in his direction.

"Oh, Constance.   He still hasn't found her?   I wonder where she could be? I guess I better help in the search. People are getting restless. Excuse us, Daphne, Daniel. Come along, Jake. She's here somewhere."

"I'll ask Margot," Daphne said over her shoulder as Loretta and Jake ran off. "It was a pleasure meeting you, Daniel. I'm looking forward to seeing you in tomorrow's edition."

As she was departing to bring Margot her champagne, Daniel added, "Yes, just one more thing. Loretta mentioned that you were a horse rider. Any chance of you showing me the local trails? I'm not that familiar with the area."

"I think that could be arranged. Why don't you come by my shop tomorrow morning and I'll check my diary. The store's called Poppy Cove, and it's right off of Avila Square downtown, where Poppy Lane and Cove Street meet."

"I'll do that. See you tomorrow."

The two parted company and Daphne caught up with Margot, who was admiring the wide ocean view at sunset from the cliff with Elaine Stinson, the mayor's wife. Elaine Stinson was a lovely and willowy ash blonde, tanned and fit from all the time she spent outdoors painting. Daphne was pleased with how her pale lavender, almost silver shantung suit complemented her graceful figure. Margot found the most flattering cut, a slim skirt to the knee and fitted jacket, with pearl buttons—and the matching pumps and clutch purse were to die for.

"Hello, Mrs. Stinson. It was wonderful to have seen David last week. Has he gone back to Los Angeles now?" Daphne greeted her as she handed Margot her drink. David Stinson was an old high school sweetheart of Daphne's and now they were just good friends. Whenever he was in town, the two got together and had a good laugh.

"Yes, he went back yesterday. Only two more years and he'll be a practicing lawyer if all goes as well as it has been." Elaine took a good long look at her surroundings. "It's just amazing what they've done with these grounds. I remember trudging up the hillside full of weeds and wildflowers carrying my easel as if it were just yesterday." Elaine was an accomplished watercolor painter and had often come up to paint the landscape when it was a meadow. "I'm pleased that they still have a beautiful viewing area for the public. I can still come up here and work." Between the main buildings and the cliff were manicured grounds, but there was plenty of room for everyone—including the school members—to appreciate the natural setting. She turned and faced the center building. "I can't wait to see the art studios upstairs. Looks like they have the windows well placed to get great natural light all day long."

"Any minute now, we can get in and have a good look around." Daphne was eager to see the interior too. "Providing they find Constance. Everyone's looking for her. Have either of you seen her?"

"I was wondering what the hold-up was. They're running a little late, aren't they? I hope she's not having second thoughts about her dress. It's so different from her usual look." Constance had commissioned Margot to create something completely refreshing for her. She was almost always in tweeds and riding gear—impeccable, but very staid. Constance's dress for this occasion was a vision in soft pastel shades of gathered chiffon, strapless with a sweetheart neckline, cinched at the waist with a wide skirt that grazed her calves. The shirred bodice appeared to hover and shimmer with the hint of ethereal color. As the pleated skirt opened up from the cinched waist to a circular mid-calf length, all of the pastel greens, pinks, blues and peaches of the fabric glowed. She also had a long silk scarf that wrapped around her neck and trailed behind her as she walked. "Maybe she's just taking a few moments to get used to her new self before everyone else does."

"If you ladies will excuse me, I really should rejoin my husband before the ceremony begins. Enjoy your evening. I'll be by the shop soon. Fall fashions are right around the corner!" The girls watched as Elaine Stinson walked away and scanned the crowd for Constance.

Not seeing hide nor hair of her, Margot took a sip of her champagne and turned her attention back to the enormous view of sky and sea. "It's so beautiful here, every color you could imagine, all laid out in perfect order."

"Yep, it's just lovely. Come on; we need to mingle and compliment our people while we're waiting. We have a lot of our best customers here and who knows how many new ones we can entice?" Daphne was wearing a linen two-piece suit with a wide, open collar and three-quarter, fitted sleeves, paired with a slim skirt just below the knees in sky blue that brought out her eyes. She was a strong California girl of twenty-five who had no problem keeping her figure trim with all the athletic pursuits that she could fit into her day. All the warm sun kept her tanned and her short wavy hair blonde and sun-kissed.

Margot's looks contrasted her friend's, but were equally as beautiful. She was wearing a light pink wool crepe sheath that was tapered to her curvy figure— sleeveless with a low scoop neckline and u-shaped back with a black satin ribbon trim just below the bust line above the waist. The palest pink set off a rosy glow in her fair skin, and her chestnut pageboy hair was adorned with a black clip on one side that complemented her clear complexion, delicate bone structure, and made her dark brown eyes deeper. "Speaking of enticing new ones, who was that you were talking to with Loretta? A real looker."

"That's Daniel Henshaw. He takes care of the horses here. I'll introduce you tomorrow. He's coming by the shop to set up a riding date with me." Daphne grinned as she sipped her champagne.

Margot laughed. "Good for you! He did look nice, tall, strong and handsome. A horse rider, huh? That's a good match for you."

"We'll see. We still should join the rest of the party though. The ceremony's bound to start soon. They must have found Constance by now."

The girls started to make their way back to the groups of other guests when they heard a chilling shriek coming from outside the main building. For a moment, time stood still. "What was that?" Margot breathlessly ventured.

"Sounds like someone screaming," Daphne turned her head in the direction of the school. "Let's go."

The girls followed the rest of the crowd moving towards the rosebushes by the left side of the center building. They could see Loretta's shocked, pale face looking down and her right index finger pointing to the ground, as Jake instinctively snapped a photo of the scene. "Oh my goodness, that looks like a foot!" exclaimed a voice from the crowd. Margot and Daphne made their way through the stunned group to be at Loretta's side. What they saw was a woman's ankle and foot in a pale blue shoe. Daphne's eyes grew wide with recognition. Just then, Reginald burst through the crowd and stopped in his tracks when he saw the shoe. "That's Constance," he blurted. The tails of her chiffon scarf were tangled in the thorns.

CHAPTER TWO

There was a hush through the crowd. Mayor Stinson took authority of the situation. He faced Reginald, held him by the shoulders and met his eyes. "Reggie, let me handle this."

He gently guided Reginald toward Charles and they leaned onto each other for support. Mayor Stinson turned to the crowd. "Men, I could use some help. Is Dr. Browning here?" A couple of the men, including Dr. Browning, a local family physician whose daughter would be attending the academy, moved forward to aid the mayor in parting the bushes to see the woman's face. He began to examine the victim, paying most of his attention to her head and neck. There appeared to be a bluish tinge around the woman's throat. Mayor Stinson stepped back to face Constance's family. "Reginald, Charles, I know you want to help her, but the best thing you can do is give Dr. Browning some room to work." Mayor Stinson gently guided Reginald and Charles to a private spot behind the roped-off doors.

"We need an ambulance and the police here immediately. Sarah, go to the car and get my bag. Where is the school nurse? I could use some assistance." Dr. Browning moved into action. His wife, Sarah, ran towards their car in the parking lot and nodded in the direction of one of the school trustees, who entered the main building to make the emergency telephone calls.

"I'm right here. Shall I check her pulse?" School nurse Carol James ran forward to help Dr. Browning with her own medical bag. She was dressed in her uniform for the evening's events. Dr. Browning instructed Carol to start recording Constance's vital signs while he paid further attention to her neck and face.

There was very little noise and movement in the crowd. They were hushed and riveted to watching every move around the bushes. Loretta looked like she was about to faint. Daphne and Margot took her to sit down at a nearby bench. Jake, who had been capturing the unfolding events with his camera, stopped and went to hover behind Loretta. "I can't believe this. Was that really Constance? What happened?" Loretta asked, trembling.

"I don't know, but we'll find out. Let me get you some cool water and just sit for a while." Daphne found a waiter and asked him to bring ice water to Loretta. She saw Dr. Browning and Nurse James leaning over Constance while some of the men held the bushes back. Charles looked on, distraught and pale, trying to restrain an agitated Reginald.

"Where's that ambulance, damnit! How could they take so long? There's an emergency here!" Reginald barked as he lunged forward, escaping his brother-in-law's grasp. It seemed like forever, but it had only been about five minutes since Constance had been discovered. Reginald was a strong and capable man who made things happen, but helping his wife right now was out of his league.

Charles gripped Reginald's arm again as he got tangled in the ropes. "Reggie, we need to stand back and let Dr. Browning do his job. I'm sure more help will be arriving soon. There's nothing we can do."

School trustee Franklin Matthews returned to the scene. "They're on their way. I brought the head greenskeeper with me to help clear the hedge." The Stearns' Academy head greenskeeper was Edward James, husband to nurse Carol. Both were in their early twenties, a pleasant and attractive couple new to the area.

"Thanks, Frank. That helps." Dr. Browning greeted Edward and was about to direct him to cut the bushes with his shears to free Constance when both the police and ambulance crew arrived.

"Stop right there. Don't cut anything. This may be a crime scene and you could be destroying evidence." Detective Tom Malone stepped onto the scene. His six-foot tall athletic stature lent him great air. A plain-clothed detective, he was a dashing figure in his grey tropical wool suit and fedora. He wore his 32 years well, with just the beginning of creases around his green eyes and mouth, and the odd silver showing in his dark brown, almost black, hair. It gave him the look of a thinking man.

"Detective Malone, I don't think you realize that is Constance Stearns-Montgomery lying there. We need to get closer to her. I don't care if she's simply tripped and fallen or something malicious has happened, she needs proper and immediate attention. We have to get her out of bushes to take care of her." Dr. Browning met the detective's eyes and both men held their ground. Dressed in white, two young ambulance attendants raced up to Dr. Browning and stood poised ready to take action. A couple of uniformed police officers stood behind Tom, waiting for instruction.

Tom assessed the situation quickly and turned to the right. "You—what's your name?"

"Edward James, Sir. I'm the head greenskeeper."

Tom motioned to the two officers behind him. "Riley, Davis, work with James here. Put aside the cut twigs." Malone quickly scanned the crowd and zeroed in on Jake. "Jake, our photographer hasn't arrived yet and I want shots of this before they move things. Can you snap photos for me as the officers work?"

Jake leapt into action. "Yes sir!" He put a fresh roll of film into his camera and started working.

Tom turned to his officers. "Good. We'll compare them to the photos later and see if we can figure out how they bent or broke as she landed." Dr. Browning, satisfied with the procedure, led the ambulance men to take over. He and Nurse James murmured to them what he had already discovered. The attendants confirmed Dr. Browning's conclusion, focusing their attention on Constance's pulse, face and neck. Then they stepped back.

"Damnit, Malone, what's going on? We have a right to know what's happening to my sister." Charles had done his best to keep a level head, but his patience was wearing thin and he was raging with fear and panic.

Tom glanced at Dr. Browning who bowed his head. Dr. Browning quietly conferred with the two medics. Detective Malone met Charles' and Reginald's eyes. Reginald crumpled. Charles barely supported him as the white sheet was draped over Constance's body. Loretta wailed from the nearby bench. Margot and Daphne huddled closely around her. Tom turned from the grieving men to address the crowd. "Ladies and gentlemen, may I please have your attention? I know this is a very traumatic situation, but I need all of you to stay calm. My men will ask you a few questions—your name, address, purpose for being here and anything you have seen in the last few hours that may help our investigation into this matter. Once you have done this, you are free to go home. Until we have talked to you, please keep to yourselves and focus on the matter at hand. Thank you for your help." Additional uniformed policemen were at the back of the crowd, with pen and paper in hand, to speak to as many people as quickly as possible.

"Detective Malone," Mayor Stinson stated, "I believe the first person who you need to speak with is Loretta Simpson. She was the one who found Mrs. Montgomery. She's with Miss Williams and Miss Huntington-Smythe over there."

"Thank you, Your Honor." The mention of Margot's name brought a smile to Tom's lips. The two sweethearts locked eyes, a flash of comfort in a terrible time. He walked over to speak to the women. He knelt before Loretta, who was sitting between Margot and Daphne, sobbing. "Loretta, I'm sorry to disturb you, but while this is all fresh in your mind, I need to ask you a few questions about what you saw tonight." Loretta nodded and sniffled.

"It's okay. We'll sit with you. You can do this." Daphne hugged Loretta a little closer. "It's Tom. You know Tom and he's just doing his job. He only wants to sort out what happened. Just answer a few questions and I'll take you home and make you a nice cup of tea." The sun was starting to go down, and the air was beginning to get an ocean chill.

Loretta recalled her tale of coming across the shoed foot from the rose bushes outside the side entrance. She did not see anyone or anything out of the ordinary prior to that. "We were looking all over for her, but no one saw her until I did. I wish I could help more, but that's all I saw. I guess I was too late," she wailed. "A second or two earlier and this may not have gone this way."

"Who was all looking for her?" Tom sparked.

"I guess everyone here, but especially Reginald, Charles, Jake and I. I asked Daphne, too, if she had seen her," Loretta recalled.

Daphne replied, "I saw her about half an hour before that. She was on her own, on the other side of the building."

Tom made a quick mental note. "Was she acting any different than usual? In your mind, did she do anything specific that stands out?"

Daphne thought for a moment and shrugged her shoulders. "No. I just caught a glimpse of her and everything seemed fine, nothing odd."

Tom looked around at the other people Loretta named. He focused in on Reginald. "How long had you been looking for her? When did you last see her?"

Reginald stated, "Around noon. We met briefly over lunch at the coffee shop near the market."

"You didn't arrive here together?" Tom watched Reginald's facial reactions.

Reginald met his gaze with resigned eyes. "No, I was busy at the market. She had her errands to run and a few last minute things to attend to at the school. We were to meet here just before the ceremony."

"And you never saw her tonight?" Officer Jenkins was making notes rapidly as Tom asked his questions. The two worked as a team. Tom fired his questions on instinct, while Jenkins recorded it all, efficiently and accurately, not interrupting his train of thought until prompted.

"No. When I got here, Charles was looking for her and so were the trustees."

Tom turned to Charles, who was still standing by Reginald, numbly watching what was being done with Constance. "Charles, have you spoken with or seen your sister this evening?"

"No. The last time I spoke with her was this morning on the telephone. We were just going to meet here around six-thirty. When I got here at twenty-five past, I started looking for her. That's when Matthews and a couple of the other trustees spotted me and asked me where she was."

Tom turned to confer with Jenkins. In a low voice, he stated, "We need to figure out who was the last person to see Constance alive. Where and when are of vital importance. We need to determine if she was alone or if someone was with her."

Reginald interrupted him. "What are you saying, young man?"

Tom paused to phrase the statement carefully to the husband of the deceased. "We need to determine if Constance died due to natural causes, by accident or at the hands of another person."

Reginald's eyes grew wide. He said loudly, "Are you suggesting Constance was murdered?"

The crowd stopped as they overheard and reacted with a murmuring shockwave. Tom did his best to restore order. "I said no such thing. It's too early to determine anything. All I ask is that people report any information that might help us figure out what has happened."

A medium built woman in a tweed wool day suit stepped forward. "I saw Mrs. Stearns-Montgomery earlier. It was just after six."

Tom saw her facing him about ten feet away in the crowd. None of the officers had spoken to her yet. "Where did you see her? What is your name?" Tom signaled to Jenkins to catch her response.

"In the school, near the Administration office. She was walking in the hallway. I'm Mrs. Rose Adams, school receptionist."

Tom focused his attention on her "So you were working?"

"Yes. I was getting my desk ready for tomorrow and having one last look around. I greeted Mrs. Montgomery."

Tom's full attention turned to Rose. "How did she seem to you? Did she respond to your call?"

"Yes, but she seemed distracted. I figured it was because it was such a big day."

"Was she alone?"

"Yes. She just said hello and continued down the hall."

"Which direction?" Tom was looking at the school, gauging her movements.

"I suppose it was towards where she was found, to the side exit of the main building."

"Anything else you can remember?" Tom looked at her, waiting.

The receptionist thought carefully. "No, not really. I think that's it. I didn't see her go out the doors, just in that direction. That's all." It wasn't much, but it gave them something to go on.

"Thank you, Mrs. Adams. Please call me at the station if you recall anything further. Jenkins handed her Tom's card.

Tom turned away from the woman and looked over the sea of people once more. "Anyone else see anything of note?" There were a few small mutterings in the crowd, but no leads. "Okay then. My officers will circulate through the crowd and resume their questioning." Tom turned to Jake, who had been capturing as much as he could with his camera—the body, the crowd, the specific witnesses. "How'd the camera work go?"

"I won't know 'til I get these developed," he said as he was unloading a roll of film from his camera. "That's my last roll. I'll get them processed right away."

"Can you get the pictures to me by morning?"

Jake replied, "Yes. I'll take them to the newspaper lab tonight."

"Good. I need all the pictures and the negatives of everything you shot at the school this evening."

Jake's skinny chest puffed out with great pride and importance. "Sometimes the camera catches more than the eye."

Tom nodded with confirmation. He felt a light touch on his elbow. "I'm sorry I didn't see anything more, Tom. I don't know if I was any help." Loretta looked exhausted and weepy.

"You did your best, Loretta. If you recall anything else no matter how insignificant you think it may be, please call my department." Tom handed her his card. "You really shouldn't drive tonight. Daphne, could you take her home and pour her a good, stiff drink? If I need information from you, I'll call you tomorrow."

"Of course. Loretta, what do you want to do with your car?"

Loretta looked lost for a moment, then Jake piped up. "Miss Simpson, I'll take your car and bring it to your house in the morning, after I take the pictures to the police station."

Loretta brightened. "Thank you, Jake, that's very good of you. I think I'd like to leave now."

"Sure thing," replied Daphne. "Tom, can you give Margot a ride home if I take Loretta?"

Tom lifted his hat and scratched his head. "I'm going to be here for some time yet. Didn't you drive up?" he asked Margot.

"I came with Daphne and I don't think Loretta's in any state to be carted off all over town." Tom knew that swinging by Margot's place would double Daphne's trip in getting Loretta home.

Jake saved the day again. "I'll take you home, Miss Williams. He faced Tom and announced with authority, "Then I'll go develop the pictures myself at the paper."

Margot smiled. "Well, that's settled then. Jake, why don't you go and help Daphne get Loretta settled in the car and I'll meet you in the parking lot shortly."

Margot and Tom watched them leave and realized they had a couple of moments alone together. "Are you all right?" he gently asked as he moved in for an embrace as he sat down on the bench beside her.

Margot rested her head on his shoulder. "I think so. It's shocking. Do you really believe that someone may have murdered Constance? I can't imagine why anyone would want to hurt her, let alone kill her. She was always so well respected in the community, especially with what their family continues to do to serve Santa Lucia."

Tom turned to look into Margot's eyes and brushed a hair from her cheek. He glanced around and sighed, "Unfortunately, not everyone shares your point of view."

She sat up straighter and faced him. "What do you mean?"

"The Stearns and Montgomery families have done a lot for this town, and their names are on everything around here. It can cause a lot of envy."

"Are you suggesting that Constance was murdered by someone she knew? That someone would deliberately want to kill her?" Margot's eyes grew wide.

Tom thought before replying. He didn't want to alarm her. He also didn't want to lie. "Strangulation is an intimate crime. Someone has to be very close to the victim to commit the act."

Margot's heart raced. "I can't believe that anyone who knew her could want to see her dead."

Tom shrugged. "Well, even the best of people can make enemies over the smallest of things. Jealousy is a strong motive." Tom's earlier police life in San Francisco taught him to understand the darker side of human nature, but he could see it was upsetting Margot and he softened a bit. He signaled to one of his men to come over. "Darling, it's been a long night. Why don't you report your account of tonight to Detective Riley here and go home and have a hot bath and a nightcap? I can't take your report, I know you too well," he said with a sly grin. "I'll come by the shop tomorrow and take you out for lunch."

"I'd love that. See you tomorrow." She gave him a quick peck on the cheek and watched as Tom walked back to what was now the crime scene. The sight caught her breath as she reported to Detective Riley that Constance had been in Poppy Cove earlier that day. She had left the shop in the early afternoon with her new dress on, all beautifully coiffed and primped. It did seem a little unusual for Constance, as she normally would have her new purchases boxed and wrapped, but she and Daphne thought nothing of it, or her excited and fluttery behavior, given the evening's events and how busy she'd been over the last few weeks. That was the last Margot had seen of her friend and client before tragedy had struck.

Margot finished recollecting her evening to Detective Riley and couldn't look away from watching the professionals load Constance's lifeless corpse onto the gurney. As they were wheeling her away, Margot could see the hem of her beautiful chiffon skirt fall gracefully from under the white sheet. She got up and made her way back to the parking lot where Jake was waiting to take her home. Her head was filled with what Tom had said and how horrible it was to think that all of the Stearns' good work had come to this.

CHAPTER THREE

After a long and arduous night, Margot got up with the sunrise and put the coffee percolator on. She was achy and stiff, not having slept very well with all the memories of Constance and what had happened. She shuffled around in her sunny kitchen in her pajamas. They were done in her favorite design, a capri-length, drawstring waist pant, the shirt with small pearl buttons and three quarter sleeves in soft white cotton, with both pants and sleeves trimmed with crocheted lace cuffs. "I wonder if other colors would sell as well as these did in the shop?" She thought out loud to her cat, Cuddles, who always approved of her business ideas no matter if they made sense or not with a low, rumbling purr. "You'd like whatever I said, as long as you got your tuna, wouldn't you?" She gave the cat a big hug and carried it to the front door to grab her milk and morning paper.

There on the front page was a photograph of Constance Stearns-Montgomery, with the headline, 'Local Heiress Found Murdered.' Beside it was a ghastly picture of Constance's body sticking out from the hedge. Margot slowly got up and closed her door. *How awful*, she thought. *Why would they put such a picture on the page? What about dignity and respect?* Saddened, she didn't know whether to put the paper down or read it. Curiosity got the better of her. She read the article, and it was pretty accurate to what she'd witnessed the previous night.

Another article entitled, 'School Opening May be Delayed,' was below it. The story went into the Stearns' history in Santa Lucia. Robert Stearns, Constance's father, was a Bostonian who moved to Santa Lucia following his tour of duty in the Great War. After spending many summers as a boy with his family at various health spas on the southern California coast, he decided to bring his young family comprised of Lillian and their children Constance and Charles, to the sleepy little village to start a new life in the wild west, supplying building materials to the hardy ranchers and holdouts from the gold rush—all determined to create their own California dream. Business was steady and brisk, but after the devastating 1922 earthquake, Robert and Lillian's vision truly shined. They, along with the town's elders, began to create the Santa Lucia that existed today. Robert turned overnight from a purveyor of boards and nails to city planner. He took the dreams of a beautiful village to new architectural heights. They restored the town square of cobblestones, terra cotta, and stucco, maintaining the Mediterranean heritage. No building, plant or sidewalk was overlooked. The style grew outward from the original center fountain courtyard which dated back to the 1700's when it was used as the town's communal fresh water source. Now it was where the Saturday morning farmers' markets were still held. The resurrection of Santa Lucia had garnered attention through civic organizations and newspaper articles across America. People fell in love with the dream and many moved to the area, building homes in the surrounding oceanside and mountains that respected and carried the Spanish influence that Robert and Lillian helped to develop.

The article carried on about the creation of Stearns' Academy. It came into being as a facility of outstanding educational and deportment services for young ladies and gentlemen. Constance and Charles had been sent to the Boston alma maters of their parents, but the family felt it was a wise move to educate future generations of Californians right here. Lillian passed away after a lengthy illness in 1954 and Robert, Constance and Charles changed their focus to create a school for girls that would reflect the grace and elegance of their wife and mother. Robert died the following year, leaving the siblings to create a school that would honor their parents' standards and bear the family name. The community was very welcoming of such a rich contribution to the state's growth and cultivation.

The story gave details of the Academy's facilities and also asked the inevitable question: Will the school open later or at all?

What was becoming clear, as the shock was wearing off, was the fact was there was a murderer loose in the town. It was now known that Constance's death was a murder. With no visible motive or criminal, was anyone safe? Margot felt a chill, as she made sure her door was locked. Would she ever feel safe alone in her back yard again? So much can change in an instant.

Margot turned the page of the paper and read some lighter news, including the society column that Loretta had turned in the day before the murder, which was thankfully filled with trivial observations about other people and happier events. She finished her toast and jam, drank her last cup of coffee and quickly did her dishes. She went into her bedroom and was deciding what to wear today, given the somber mood of the town. Over her foundation garments, she put on a nude silk charmeuse slip with lace trim and embroidered floral detail at the décolleté. Her dress was a sleeveless navy wool crepe, with a square neckline, fitted waist and slim skirt to mid-calf. It was belted with a belt of the same fabric and white trim, paired with a bolero jacket, that finished just above the waist, with three-quarter sleeves and double breasted with two metal buttons and the same white trim around the collar and edge of the jacket. Both the dress and jacket were lined. She put on her red lipstick and black mascara, a little dab of perfume behind the ears, affixed her navy hat, added white gloves and navy and white spectator pumps in the hallway and out she went. She let Cuddles in, who was waiting not so patiently, and dropped her keys into her navy clutch purse after making sure her door was locked.

Her bungalow was a short, two-block walk from Daphne and Margot's shop. Poppy Cove was their two and a half year old atelier, located on the corner of Poppy Lane and Cove Street, which was the main street of Santa Lucia. It was a very tony spot, with the entrance that came up from the corner, in a beautiful building, one of the first ones that the Stearns family designed. Margot reached the shop at five minutes to nine, went up the three little stairs leading to the front door, unlocked it and stepped in. She heard one of her favorite sounds—the tinkle of the little bell over the door, always telling her someone had come in to pay a visit. A few seconds later, looking a little worse for wear, Daphne arrived, wearing the same suit from last night. She flipped the sign from *Closed* to *Open* as she shut the door behind her.

"What a night! Even though Dr. Browning came by and gave Loretta a sedative, she was restless. I came straight from her place. No time to go home and change." Daphne began looking through the racks to find something clean and fresh to wear for the day. "I called my mother last night to tell her what had happened and that Loretta needed me to stay with her. You know how she is. If I was out all night without her knowing where I was, she'd be in a state." She held up a cotton print dress with a slight sheen, in a leafy sage green pattern. It was sleeveless with a boat neck and fitted to the waist with a side zipper and a slim pencil skirt. It matched the tint of her shoes from last night. "What do you think of this on me?"

"I've always thought that would suit you. Remember, if you take it off the rack, you've bought it." Daphne was probably the store's most frequent customer. Sometimes it was like others were shopping in her closet.

"I'll slip an IOU in the cash box and have the accountant take it out of my pay at month's end. What do you think of these with it?" She held up a necklace of many strands of different shades of green cut glass beads and a pair of matching oval earrings. She posed in front of the full-length mirror and took a look. She caught a glimpse of Margot behind her. "Say, you look like I feel. You had a rough night too, huh?"

"All I could think about was seeing her there, lying in the rose bushes," Margot sighed. "Just yesterday, we were getting her ready to debut her brand new look. She'd been so much more easy going lately. You know, choosing brighter colors and more flattering fits than her usual heavy and bulky tweeds. Con had a true glow about her."

"That's because of the lover in her life. She was keeping company with a much younger man, at least that's what I heard," said Irene Swanson, the store manager, who came in at the tail end of Margot's comment. She was a striking brunette, but had a penchant for gossip, both giving and receiving. It made her very popular with the clients.

Daphne ducked into a dressing room to change. "Irene, shame on you! You've got a lot of nerve after what happened last night."

"What happened?" Irene was busy wedging the front door open and watering the nearby hanging flower baskets.

Margot clasped her fingers and placed them up to her pursed lips. "You honestly didn't see today's paper?"

Irene met her gaze. "No. I got up late and ran out the door. Tell me. This must be big."

"Constance was strangled to death and found in the rosebushes on the school grounds, just before her speech. It was horrible," Margot stated.

Irene stopped in her tracks and visibly paled when she heard the news. "Jeez, no. I hadn't heard that. Who'd have thought that would happen here?" Irene was from Los Angeles and moved by her parents to live with her grandmother in Santa Lucia last year after getting involved in some big city adventures.

"Well, it did, and now we have a murderer loose in our town," Daphne said as she stepped out of the dressing room, looking very beautiful and surprisingly refreshed. She quickly glanced in the mirror. "It's amazing what a new outfit can do for a girl."

Irene turned on her heel and faced Daphne. "So, if it was true about Con having an affair, was it lover boy? And, how would Reginald have taken that? Where was he when this happened?" If trouble was to be stirred up, the bewitching Irene was certainly the one to do it.

Both Margot and Daphne glared at her. Daphne spoke first. "At a time like this, how could you be so cold? First of all, it's only hearsay about this other man. And for heaven's sake, Reginald, the man who was her husband for more than twenty years deserves the benefit of the doubt. Besides, he was in plain sight the whole evening. He was looking for her, too."

"Sounds like a good cover to me." Irene's views bordered on cynical most of the time. The worse the gossip, the more she believed. And, unfortunately, sometimes she was right.

For all her faults, she was a meticulous bookkeeper and an excellent sales woman. She had a way of winning people over. They would tell her the most intimate things, even though they knew her nature, and still reward her with a purchase. Margot and Daphne thought it must be the entertainment she provided to others. Plus, Irene had an uncanny knack for always looking put together—another reason the girls hired her last year when it was clear they were too busy purchasing accessories and designing clothes respectively. They needed help managing the busy day-to-day operations of the store. As with everyone else who worked at Poppy Cove, Irene wore a shop design when she was working. Her last minute ensemble for today was a crisp, white, sleeveless, surplice blouse with a wing collar, deep v-neckline, and a wide sash that tied on the right side, ending at the waist. Her slacks were cotton capris, in a lively burnt orange, the perfect transition color from summer to autumn. The pants were fitted to her legs, with a little slit on the outer calf. She paired it with ballerina flats, amazingly the same color as the capris. She had a way of finding just what worked from all kinds of sources to pull her look together. That was one of the great things about Irene in the clothing business. The accessories were ones Daphne had to match—bauble earrings and a great coral/orange bauble necklace, which brought life to her hazel eyes.

Margot turned her attention to looking over the day's appointments and design production schedule in the Poppy Cove diary. It was the store's bible. In the big, thick spiral-bound book, every incident and appointment for the store was kept. All the girls referred to it throughout the day. It was indispensable.

Margot noticed it was a full day. Mrs. Lewis was coming in any minute to pick up her custom-ordered dress, and as soon as she was finished, Margot had to go over the fall production line. They were in full swing, with the daytime fall garments and the beginning of the holiday wear, plus all the details on the ongoing custom orders. That would take up her morning. She penciled in lunch with Tom. It would probably feel all too short, given the recent crime events in town and her own tasks, but she was grateful she could take a break with him.

"Ooh, lunch with one of Santa Lucia's finest? Maybe I should tell him what I think if he hasn't solved the case by noon," Irene commented as she glided by, glancing over Margot's shoulder, while running a broom over the gleaming wood floors. Her morning routine also included a little light polishing of the racks and mirrors, as well as giving the steps a quick sweep.

Margot shot her a quick look. "I'm sure they have their own ideas."

Irene sneered. "Great. Fill me in when you come back."

Margot focused back to the day's schedule. At one-thirty, she had a meeting with a Los Angeles fabric importer to view the new spring textiles for next year, followed by a first-time client consultation for a mother of the groom. Daphne was meeting with a local handbag designer who had sold some of her clever little clutches to a couple of the most glamorous stores in Hollywood. Daphne had seen some photographs of movie stars carrying the purses and she was quite excited. If they were as cute in real life as they were in the pictures, she would want to place an order, and Margot should be in on that. They also needed to finalize the garments and models for the fall fashion show scheduled for next month. All in all, their days went very quickly and happily. This day, however, had a melancholy feel to it. Privately, everyone's thoughts would drift back to how they knew Constance in their lives.

Irene turned to greet the day's first customer as she walked in the shop while Daphne wrote her IOU. "Good morning, Mrs. Lewis. Did you hear the news?" Margot flashed a warning look to Irene that she chose to ignore.

"Of course I did. She got what she deserved. Any woman blatantly showing off her family connections and carrying on like she did, well, it's not a wonder." Mrs. Nancy Lewis had a long time rivalry with Constance. The Lewises were also among the rebuilding families of the twenties. Nancy had apparently felt that the Lewises were much more important than the Stearnses or the Montgomerys, ever since Charles Stearns snubbed her affections when they were young adults.

"Did you get the enrollment straightened out for your girls at the new academy?" Irene fished again.

"Why would I want my girls to go there? No, they will go to Lords, on the east coast and graduate as my first girl, Barbara, just did. The eastern seaboard schools are excellent. Late enrollment is normal for them. The girls and I leave next Friday. We are flying out of the Los Angeles airport, of course. It's the only way to travel now," Mrs. Lewis announced. It was their family's first flight. In the past, it was always a weeklong train trip, each way.

Margot remembered the conversation from the last fitting she'd had in the shop and didn't want the situation to get heated. "Right, then! Back to the matter at hand. Nancy, are you still going through with your party this afternoon?"

"Of course. The murder is irrelevant. We have a lot of out of town investors here that we want to entertain. If the men like our hotel and health resort plans, we'll get first class people in our town. My garden party for their wives is just the thing to show the women our best people.   Besides, Constance wasn't invited and everyone else in town knows the show must go on." Nancy was no nonsense when it came to social influence.

Practical, but cold, thought Margot. "Fine. We have your dress ready for your garden party." Marjorie Cummings, Poppy Cove's head seamstress, brought Nancy's dress from the back workroom.   Margot motioned to her and Marjorie placed the garment in the fitting room, stepped out and stood beside Margot. She was always present during client fittings—pinning, taking notes and measurements.   It gave Margot a chance to concentrate on the overall line of the garment. "On the ledge, Daphne has laid out your jewelry. Irene, please get the hat and gloves for Mrs. Lewis and place them on the dressing table. Nancy, Irene will assist you in dressing if you need her help. Please, let her know if you need a hand with your garment." Margot was tired and dealing with Nancy was a headache at the best of times. She was grateful when Mrs. Lewis slipped into the dressing room.

"I can't get the clasp on this necklace right. I need help now," came the sharp voice from the dressing room.   To Margot and Daphne, she could be Nancy. All others in the shop were to address her as Mrs. Lewis.

"Right away, Mrs. Lewis," Irene was not put off by her ways. If anything she found them amusing and played along. Daphne just laughed silently and shook her head. Irene stepped in the spacious curtained room to help.

A few seconds later, Nancy came out in her new dress of white and pastel floral print in cotton lawn. It was very refreshing and cool looking, perfect when offset in a backyard setting of trees, grass and flowers. It had a stand-up collar, soft shoulders with three-quarter sleeves, with French cuffs. The dress buttoned down the front, with a darted, fitted bodice, and a wide, gently pleated ballerina skirt. She wore cut-glass and pearl, pastel flower earrings and a necklace of the same materials, a double-stranded choker with the costume pearls getting larger toward the center, resting in the hollow of the neck and running from collarbone to collarbone, alternating the same glass beads and pearls. At the seated dressing table were the short white cotton gloves and wide-brimmed straw hat with matching chin sash waiting to complete the ensemble. Daphne adorned the hat on Nancy's redheaded curls and fitted the gloves onto her hands. Even to Nancy admitted that it was lovely and suited her wishes for the party. "Girls, you've done it again. You must have read my mind. It's exactly what I wanted. Thank you!"

There was a collective sigh of relief. As always, working with Nancy Lewis could be a trial. At least, she was predictable in her behavior. She came in with a vague idea of what she wanted, very demanding at every step, critical and particular, yet in the end, she was always pleased with the final results. After viewing every angle in the three-way mirror carefully, Nancy stepped into the dressing room to change back into her other clothes. Margot smiled at Marjorie, who nodded and went back to the workroom. The girls carefully wrapped Nancy's hat in tissue and placed it into a signature box with a painted red Poppy on the lid. Irene came out of the dressing room with Mrs. Lewis' dress draped over her arm, and carrying the gloves and jewelry. They wrapped everything with great care and attention, sealing the tissue paper with a red poppy seal and slipped it all into a Poppy Cove paper bag. Nancy came to the sales desk to pay for her items. As she left, she mentioned that she would be back to pick out a couple more garments off the rack for herself and her two youngest girls before her trip to Boston.

"Glad that's done," said Daphne.

"That was a lot smoother than her previous visit," Margot sighed. The last time she was in, Constance was also in the shop. The two women could barely remain in the same room for more than five minutes before rowing. As I understand, when they were young ladies, they had vied for attention from all the young, eligible men in town, including Nancy trying to catch Reginald *after* he had proposed to Constance. He couldn't be swayed, so Nancy turned to a slightly younger man—Charles—much to his sister Constance's dismay. The courtship was very short lived. Charles had no time for Nancy's nasty disposition, but Nancy always believed that Constance had deterred Charles from returning her affections. With her pride bruised, Nancy accepted a quick and unexpected proposal from Andrew Lewis, an older gentleman banker who had more money than charm, which allowed Nancy to this day to purchase all she felt she was lacking in her life. It was a marriage of convenience—she provided company for his social gatherings and produced a family of three girls, which he lovingly doted on, and Nancy had a high stature in the community.

Nancy was so sure of her family's place in Santa Lucia society, that she thought that her remaining, school age, twin daughters Betsy and Anita would have guaranteed enrollment in the new Stearns' Academy. Furthermore, she also took for granted that all the tuition fees would be waived because her husband's bank handled all of the finances for the Stearnses—both the family business and the new Academy. The Stearnses were one of the most important clients of the First Bank of Santa Lucia. Nancy never bothered to actually confirm her daughters' placement with any of the Stearns' Academy administration or members of the Stearns' family personally. It was quite the shock for her to find out that they were not enrolled only weeks before school was to start. It was an embarrassing situation right there in Poppy Cove.

Constance had come in for the final fitting of her dress and accessories for the opening night of the school. Just as the girls were saying goodbye to her, Nancy came in for her second appointment for the garden party dress and accessories. The two women met at the front counter. With a surprised expression, Nancy looked Constance up and down and then cast her gaze to Constance's almost completed chiffon dress that Marjorie was tending to. "Hello, Constance. Is that what you're wearing for the Academy's opening ceremony? I'd think you'd choose something more suited to your figure and stature." She sniffed and turned her head away. "I've heard your ribbon cutting is next Thursday. Your school should be sending out invitations and enrollment confirmation packages by now, shouldn't it? I haven't heard anything from you or your people. How do you expect the right clientele to attend?"

Constance stopped and looked at her for a moment. "Why, hello, Nancy. Yes, the Academy does start its first classes on September 3rd. I was surprised not to see your name or the girls' names on any of the registration forms. Didn't you get the envelope I had delivered to your home a few months ago?" Constance had wondered why she hadn't heard anything about the Lewis girls or their demanding mother from the admissions office.

"I didn't think it was necessary—just a formality that you would personally overlook. I'm sure it's fine; just sign my girls in and we'll be there." Nancy was very cool and flippant about the situation. To her, it was no problem.

"Nancy, that's not something I can do. We've been fully booked for the last month, with not one seat available in any grade. I'm sorry, but I know we haven't even received a deposit from you, so I couldn't hold places for Betsy and Anita." Things were beginning to get heated. The girls stood back. Daphne and Margot busily removed themselves from the scene with other work while Irene was all ears behind a nearby mannequin.

"Deposit? Why would we, the Lewises, have to pay a deposit?" Nancy raised her voice.

Constance remained calm. "The protocol is the same for everyone, from the families of movie stars to the children of governors. Even the children of the teachers had to be registered months in advance." Constance was very pleased with the caliber of people her school had enticed. The enrollment was a tight competition, with only the best and the brightest accepted to get the full value of the bountiful education that the Stearns' Academy would offer. "The rules apply equally to the Lewises." She was tired of Nancy always overstepping her generosity and assuming that Santa Lucia revolved around her and her family.

"That just won't do, Constance. My girls are very important in this town. Fix it!" Nancy's face was turning red.

"There's nothing I can do for you now, Nancy. There's always next year, if you get the deposit and paperwork handed in nice and early. I really have so much to do, I must leave. Good day, and thank you, ladies, for another job well done. I'll pick up my dress

Thursday afternoon." With a snap shut of her purse, Constance turned and left the store.

"Well, I never. The nerve of that woman! If it weren't for my Andrew helping out her family when they needed it and approving Reginald's first loan to get their store built, she would be nowhere today. That's fine. I won't invite her to my garden party. I'll invite all of her friends—all the important people of this town—and let her know she's been snubbed. Charles would never treat me this way." Nancy, in her heart, still carried a torch for Charles Stearns. She still believed he'd wanted to have a romance with her, perhaps even marry her. Nancy felt that Constance always stood in the way, thinking she was too old for her younger brother, but the truth was that Charles was never interested in Nancy's petty behavior.

Irene brought Nancy a cup of tea, and the women sat down to relax and get Nancy back into the garden party spirit. Things proceeded quite well, except for one remark that she made under her breath on her way out the shop door, "That's the last time that woman tries to ruin my life! I'll make her pay for what she's done to me and my family."

Irene remembered the vague threat that Nancy had muttered as she left last week. "Hey, you don't think she had anything to do with the murder, do you? I mean, she was pretty mad over the whole school situation and she didn't seem that upset today. Could you imagine? A murderer in our midst!" Irene had a very active imagination.

Margot wouldn't dignify her remark with an answer. Daphne loved to goad her on, "Really? If looks could kill, you could be next, if Margot had her way!" The remark broke the icy tension, and all three of them had a good chuckle. It helped them to relax on such a horrible day.

"I'm so glad to see everyone in high spirits. I didn't know what I'd find when I came in today," Betty Young said as she arrived. "It's so shocking to read about Mrs. Stearns-Montgomery. She was just here yesterday. I've never seen her look so happy."

Constance certainly was more effervescent than usual that day. Girlish, which was very unlike her. She was giggling at the slightest things. She looked like she'd spent the day at the salon, coiffed from head to toe. Her blonde hair had platinum highlights and had been set with a light wave, off her face, which was lit with the subtle glow of blusher, lipstick and eye shadow, all of which she rarely wore during the daytime, and as she walked, she almost glided around the room, and she left a trace of a very soft and floral perfume. She'd never looked lovelier, but it was unnerving, given Constance's everyday no-nonsense appearance. It even made an impression on Betty, who'd only known her from a distance at her social appearances and mentions in the society column, and most recently, shop fittings.

Betty Young, aged twenty-two, was born and raised in Santa Lucia, to a happy, middle class family. After graduating from the local high school, she enrolled in the Santa Lucia Community College, where she met her future husband, Dwight. Dwight Young, from Sacramento, was in his last year of studies when they met. It was love at first sight and the couple never left each other's side. They shared the dream of living in a little house by the ocean, and when Dwight received his business diploma at the college, he told his father of his plans to marry Betty, who was a year his junior and their intentions of staying in Santa Lucia and raising a family by the sea. The senior Mr. Young called upon an old arm buddy to find a professionally suitable job for his son.

Dwight became the youngest member of the new Oldsmobile dealership in Santa Lucia, which opened in June, 1954. Harold Smart, the owner of Smart's Oldsmobile, took an instant liking to the young Mr. Young and hinted to him that if he kept working as hard as he did, he would be promoted to sales manager in a short time. Everything was working out beautifully for the two young lovebirds. With a bright future, Dwight proposed to Betty and they agreed to a June wedding the following year, after Betty's graduation.

The time moved very swiftly. Dwight worked hard at his job, Betty at her studies and planning the wedding. Shortly after Poppy Cove opened its doors, a curious Betty and her mother walked in. The two women took an instant liking to the vibrant and energetic shop owners and decided to have Betty's wedding gown made there, the first custom order for Poppy Cove, instead of making it themselves with fabric and trimmings they were planning on purchasing from Martin's that day.

The wedding was a small and simple affair, on June 25, 1955. For their honeymoon, the couple drove off in their brand new Oldsmobile, a wedding present from Mr. Smart. They had a wonderful time cruising down the coast highway to San Diego. Two weeks later, they came back to their own place. With a down payment from Dwight's parents, they moved into a little bungalow off Harbor Street, a short walk from the beach and the town center. It didn't take the couple long to settle into their new home and in the afternoons, Betty would often walk to Avila Square and shop, becoming a regular customer of Poppy Cove. One August afternoon, while she was purchasing her third or fourth garment, she noticed the store were particularly busy and approached Daphne with the idea of working there. The girls talked it over very briefly on the spot and decided to hire her. Her sweet disposition and charming manner were enough for them to want to keep her around. She worked part time on their busiest days, Thursdays to Saturdays, which still left her time to keep a clean house and have a hot meal on the table at suppertime.

It was just after ten when her shift began. "You were there at the academy, weren't you?" Betty directed her question to Daphne and Margot as she put her handbag in the drawer behind the sales counter.

"Yes, we were there," Margot sighed. She looked at her watch. "If you'll all excuse me, I've got to see Marjorie. There's always plenty to do around here." All the murder talk was getting to her. Jumping into her busy routine was a perfect remedy.

Betty nodded and understood, so she busied herself with setting out the cookies she had made that morning at home and putting on some coffee and tea. She was the perfect hostess, keeping a little table neat and tidy with refreshments for their customers all day long. Daphne and Irene set to work arranging the jewelry display counter. Every week or so, they would rearrange different combinations so it looked exciting and fresh to all their frequent customers. They had just received a shipment of sweater pins, some with inlaid mother-of-pearl and others with red, amber and olive-colored rhinestones shaped like leaves. They would compliment the new cashmere twin sets that would be arriving soon for their fall stock—in camel, black and cream.

Margot went to the back workroom to meet with her highly valued sewing staff. Marjorie ran the store's team of two sewers, a patternmaker, a presser and a cutter. Marjorie was a lady in her late 50's, with sparkling blue eyes, wavy white hair and still very nimble fingers. Her experience garnered her great respect from the rest of the staff. Prior to working at Poppy Cove, she was the head dressmaker at Martin's Department Store, in the next block on Cove Street. Daphne had gotten most of her clothing there since she was a little girl and always remembered the magic Marjorie could do to make clothing fit just right for her, her mother and aunts, too. Marjorie knew almost every woman in Santa Lucia and the surrounding area. When Daphne and Margot decided to start the shop, it was just natural for Daphne to introduce Marjorie to Margot and the women got along famously. Within minutes of Margot seeing her work, the girls welcomed her into the fold by making Marjorie an offer that was a great challenge for her, but easily within her reach. Each morning, Margot conferred with Marjorie about the list of priorities to balance out the custom and ready-to-wear clothing they were creating. Things changed every day, so they all had to be alert and flexible. The team was very efficient and dedicated. Margot was good with praise, and when money ran high, the girls all got a little extra in their wages.

"Oh my, it's so sad about Mrs. Montgomery," tutted Marjorie. "She was such a good woman. How are you holding up, dear?" This was the first moment that the two women could speak privately since the murder. "I heard you were there when it happened. It must have been a horrible night for you." Marjorie was like a mother to Margot. She looked out for her girl, all alone without family in the area. Marjorie often wondered what brought such a pleasant girl out here all on her own, without more than a fleeting mention of her family or past. Marjorie liked Margot, and although she would never pry, she looked out for her whenever Margot would allow her.

Margot took her arm and patted her hand. "Oh I'm fine; it was a big shock, but I'm all right. How are you?

You've known Constance a long time." Marjorie's eyes were less bright this morning, a little watery and teary. She'd known many of the town's society ladies since they were children.

Marjorie had seen a lot of passing and sorrow in her life, living through the depression and the two wars. She was kind, but resilient. "The same as you. It's just a shame. She was just coming into her prime," Marjorie sighed.

Margot shook her head. "It just doesn't make sense. It seems to be murder and there's all kinds of rumors floating around."

"Yes, I've heard a few including talk that she had another man in her life, but I don't know if that was true. But, I must say I was a little surprised about the last dress we made for her."

Margot agreed. "It was lovely, and she definitely had the figure to carry it off, but it was such a departure from her usual tweed day suits."

"I remember hearing that she would wear them to dinner parties, for heaven's sake!" The women chuckled. Marjorie continued on, "This one was all chiffon and very feminine. Honestly, I was beginning to like the change. I thought she was finally understanding that type of dressing has a place in her world."

"Yes, it was very nice, indeed," said Margot. "It was a pleasure to create something so flattering for her. She always kept herself in great shape, what with horseback riding and tennis at the club."

"That Mrs. Lewis should be ashamed of herself, the way she talked about Mrs. Montgomery. She walks all over everyone she can. The things she said to and about Mrs. Montgomery, well, it makes you wonder—" Marjorie shuddered without finishing her thought.

"I've heard that more than once today. Do you really think that Nancy could be so vicious?" asked Margot. Hearing a judgmental tone coming from Marjorie lent it some credence.

"Dear," said Marjorie, "stranger things have happened. You never know what a woman scorned will resort to. She's still in a lather about her short romance with Charles. It seems that she'll always blame Mrs. Montgomery for his lack of interest in her." Nothing was beyond the sharp sense of Marjorie. She believed anyone was capable of anything—good or bad.

"I think that Tom should know about Nancy's visit this morning. I'm meeting him for lunch today. Her behavior was malicious, even for Nancy. Maybe she didn't mean anything by it, but it sounded like a threat and I don't think it should be ignored. I wonder if I should have mentioned the fight sooner." Nancy's attitude had troubled Margot.

"Oh, Mrs. Lewis and Mrs. Montgomery were always bickering. That's just how they talked to each other. How were you to know if it really meant anything? I do agree that it's a good idea to tell Tom about it now, Margot. Let the police sort it out." She paused and soon the twinkle was back in Marjorie's eyes. "So, how is that handsome man of yours?" Nothing made her happier than young love.

"He's fine, wonderful in fact. He's so strong, I feel very safe with him around." Margot was truly smitten with Tom.

"Maybe we'll be making a dress for you soon!" Marjorie winked.

"Marjorie, I've told you many times, I don't want to get married right now. I like things as they are. Besides, Tom's career is so busy, there are a lot of people who need his help. And I love this place, it keeps me going day and night. In a few years, maybe then I'll have the time to be a proper wife. For now, I'm happy and that's what matters, right?" She gave Marjorie a little hug, to tell her that what she said was sweet, but politely to mind her own business. "Now then, Sam Baker is coming today. He's bringing his sample trunk. I expect him in the early afternoon. Can you keep some time free around half past one? I'd love to get your thoughts."

"Yes, I will. Sam always has some great fabrics. It's so exciting to see the new colors and designs." Marjorie was very thorough with her inspection of the color, finish, weave and texture of material. She was brutally honest when it came to the standards of how a fabric would stand up to construction, washing and wearing. There were many times that Margot would love a specific piece, only to have the keen eye of Marjorie see that it wouldn't hold up to a single washing or tear with stitching. With that, the women got back to work. They briefly reviewed the garments in production for the sales floor and Margot told Marjorie that she was very happy with the success of Mrs. Lewis' dress. The two also discussed a new client—a mother of the groom coming in later that day.

Margot came out to the front of the store. It was surprisingly busy with many customers, keeping Irene and Betty occupied. All the while, there was a constant buzz. Little groups of ladies were moving the garments around on the racks, barely noticing them. Above the fitting room doors, you could hear banter from one woman to the next, full of suspense and speculation about last night's events and Constance's recent behavior. They would come out, do a quick spin in the three way mirror, and zip back in to try on the next item—all the while, not missing a beat in the conversation. Shopping was considered to be a healthy distraction in emotional times, Margot had read in a fashion trade magazine. The busy sales floor was proof of that theory. Women tried to shop their troubles away, and spending their household budgets on themselves felt good.

Daphne was at the sales counter, finishing up with a purchase for Mrs. Falconer. She handed the customer the wrapped package and turned to Margot as the woman left out the door. "You wouldn't believe all the things people have been saying. I guess Constance had really been out on the town the last couple of months. Perhaps there's some truth in the rumors of an affair. An awful lot of people have mentioned seeing her with a man other than Reginald or her brother at various restaurants around town. Evidently, she was rather cozy with a handsome man who was definitely not Reginald." Daphne's mind was spinning, recalling all the snippets of conversation she'd heard around the shop in the past few weeks and also this morning, both aimed directly to her and things she'd overheard.

"I know. It's a little unnerving. As skeptical as Irene is, she believed Constance was having an affair, and come to think of it, Marjorie commented on the change in Constance's appearance—how she was becoming more interested in her attributes. Makes a girl wonder, huh?" Margot's sorrow was beginning to give way to curiosity. Could there be a mystery man? And, if it reached him, how did Reginald react to the gossip?

No sooner had she thought about it, than a dark haired young man in a suit that seemed awkward and two sizes too big for him walked through the open door. The constant murmur immediately stopped as all the ladies froze and stared at the stranger. Daphne bristled. She had the same thought as Margot, and they looked at each other before addressing him. Daphne jumped in, "Yes, sir, may I help you?"

CHAPTER FOUR

"Michael Weathers—acting *Santa Lucia Times* Society Editor. Can you give me the scoop on the Montgomery murder? Word has it you two were there. I've got a picture to prove it." He threw down a picture of the crime scene on the sales counter, showing Daphne, Margot, Reginald, Charles and Loretta, with Constance's shoed foot peeking out from under the rose bush.

"Excuse me, Mr. Weathers, but we're unfamiliar with you. Did you say you were the *Times* Society Editor? Personally, I *know* Loretta Simpson is the editor that you claim to be." He really had a habit of rubbing people the wrong way, even Daphne who was easy going with most people. She pushed the nasty picture back in his direction, after taking a quick glance.

The black and white photo was one of the ones shot by Jake. It was very candid and close-up, so it must have been taken just as they had realized something awful had happened. There was a look of shock on their faces; the moment seemed so harsh and cruelly final. Weathers was so insensitive with such a brisk way about him, that the browsing patrons were completely silenced and slowly began to leave. They apparently didn't like their private places invaded by such a rude young man and most certainly wouldn't say one word about last night—either around or to him.

Weathers pushed up his sliding, wire-rimmed glasses and gave a frosty sigh before continuing, "I said *acting*

Society Editor. I am apprenticing under Miss Simpson. She's taking a few days off after last night's unfortunate events. I'm here to cover the story, find out what's really going on. What about the husband? Do you think it was a crime of passion? Most people are pretty sure she'd taken up with a new man in town. I'd like a quote from your shop. I've heard this was one of the last places she was seen in public yesterday. It'll be good for business; you know it'll bring people in." He eyed Irene at a nearby display and looked her up and down with a raffish smile. She was eavesdropping as usual, but even she was left speechless by Weather's cold manner and probably found his advances too disgusting even for her. She huffed and walked away.

Margot chimed in before anyone else could. "We have no comment. Please remove yourself from our premises. You're disturbing our clientele." She crossed her arms and was firm in her stance.

"Yeah, well, it's a big story, and I want to crack it wide open. A dame like that, well, who knows what you'll uncover, you know what I mean? Knew a lot of people, but not many knew a lot about her. She was a cool one, but they say still waters run deep; they usually have the most to hide. So, don't you want to help me out?"

No one answered for a moment. "I'd like to squash that persistent bug," Daphne muttered under her breath.

A strong, deep voice replied from behind Weathers. "Sir, you heard the lady. I suggest you leave now. I don't want to be forced to arrest you for trespassing. Miss Williams, are you planning on pressing charges against this young man?" Tom had this wonderful way of showing up just when he was needed. Whether it was love or cop instincts, it didn't matter—he was there. In his tailored grey suit that fit perfectly, he was twice the man this twerp was. He was so commanding; Weathers knew it and backed down.

Margot looked directly into Michael Weathers' eyes and stated, "As long as he leaves now, there will be no need for a formal arrest. Good day, Mr. Weathers." Weathers closed his notebook, gathered his picture and scurried out as fast as he came in, cowering under Tom's stare.

"Our hero, Tom, out to save the day, yet again. I swear, you'll find trouble just to save your girl." Any opportunity Daphne had to tease Tom, she seized it. It was all in good fun—both could appreciate each other.

Tom grinned at Daphne and playfully ruffled her loose curls, making her look even more carefree than usual. Margot got her gloves, hat and handbag, and gave herself a quick onceover in the mirror. "Let's go for lunch—it's been a crazy morning. I need to get some fresh air." She gave her man a peck on the cheek, took the arm he offered and looked over her shoulder at Daphne. "See you later. I won't be late. We have that appointment with the fabric agent at 1:30." It was just going on noon now, which left Margot plenty of time to enjoy a relaxing lunch and still have time to get ready for the meeting.

"That's great. I'll be back then, too." Daphne was going to the tearoom across the lane for a soup and sandwich. She grabbed a new European fashion magazine that came in the mail that morning and got ready to go. "You can go for lunch as soon as I get back," she said to Irene. They all departed for lunch.

Margot and Tom walked down Cove Street to Antonio's, a sweet little Italian restaurant run by Antonio and Maria Chelli, that had been there for many years. It was very quaint, with checkered tablecloths and Chianti bottle candles, which made it very romantic anytime of day. It was a favorite spot for couples, present company included.

It was a beautiful day, warm and sunny with a light breeze off the ocean. As Tom and Margot walked by the various businesses, people were greeting each other and passing the time of day. Flowers in baskets were in full bloom and, off in the distance, one could see the shoreline. For a moment, Margot was blissfully happy, in a place she loved, with the man she adored. Then her thoughts wandered back to the murder, and Margot realized that Constance would never enjoy such pleasures like this again and her heart sank. She sighed as she turned her attention back to Tom. "How has your day been so far? Anything you can tell me?"

Tom thought carefully before he answered her question. He took his position as detective seriously and would never compromise a case by exposing any confidential information. "You'll be happy to know that Charles has been cleared. We had him in for questioning last night. There were quite a few people who saw him around all through the evening. A couple of statements taken down at the scene from different areas and unacquainted witnesses confirm his actions. It was pretty easy to let him go. The same can't be said for Reginald, though. He's suffered quite a shock. It's really hit him hard. He's not answering our questions. He's still at the station with his lawyer. They have to give us a straightforward statement about his actions last night. So far, Reginald's activities are not all accounted for and without even his word to go on, he can't be ruled out."

Margot shook her head. "I can't imagine Reginald being a cold-blooded killer. He was running around all over the place last night, so lots of people must have seen him. What about Loretta? Did she mention him at the ceremony? She sees everything. Have you talked

to her today? Maybe she could give you something to
go on." The order of events last night kept replaying in
Margot's head. Loretta was the one who discovered
Constance.

"Two of my officers went to her place this morning
with Jake's photos. She was in quite a state and so
upset she couldn't recall any further details. Dr.
Browning has ordered her to take some time off, at least
over the weekend. You'd think someone who is always
fishing for a scoop could handle it when she gets one,
but you never know how people will react."

"Things like this don't happen every day in Santa
Lucia. They were good friends—Loretta and
Constance—and it's scary to find a dead body, let alone
someone of your own set. Honestly, Tom, sometimes I
think you forget what it's like to be an ordinary
civilian." Margot was good for Tom. She could soften
him up when he got hardboiled about situations that
required compassion.

Tom paused and sighed, "I guess you're right. If it
was my mother or aunt, I'd feel quite different." He
relaxed a little and asked, "Tell me about your
morning."

Wheels were clicking in Margot's head. "Well, all
that's been talked about by everyone this morning is the
murder. I don't know if this means anything to the case
or not, but Nancy Lewis was in. You know that she and
Constance have never been good friends, just socially
bearable with each other, being in the same crowd, but
she was very callous and not surprised about what
happened last night. She was there right on time, dry-
eyed and going on about her garden party. As far as I
know, the last time the two had seen each other was in
Poppy Cove about a week ago. They had this huge
argument about the Lewis girls not being registered at
the Academy." Margot filled Tom in on the details,

including the threats that were issued by Nancy. "As I've said, it may be nothing, but I have a hunch it might be important. She's gone so far as to spread rumors about Constance having an affair. That's mean, but do you really think she could go so far as to murder Constance?"

They reached the restaurant. Tom opened the door for Margot. Antonio met them at the door. He was an exuberant Italian and greeted them as he greeted all his friends, loudly. "Welcome, Tom and Margot! We are so glad to have you come for lunch. I bring you our specials—no menus for you! Where do you want to sit, huh? We have a beautiful table in the back or would you like to be under the leaves?" He hugged them both, and took their hats.

Margot looked over to the patio at the entrance and at Tom. "Outside, please. Your patio is so lovely this time of year. Is that fine with you, darling?"

"Sounds great, Mar. The patio it is." Tom matched Antonio's enthusiasm and slapped him on the back. They lightly chatted about the weather as they went to the loggia. The tables, just like the ones on the inside had the familiar red and white tablecloths and wine bottle candles, but outside, the air was fresh, and all around them were grapevines—big, green and leafy, with small, hard green grapes dripping all over in bunches. There were a couple of other diners, who nodded and smiled as the couple sat down.

"What can I bring you? The Chianti is beautiful. You like?" Antonio was very proud of his family's wines from the old country. His brother still had the winery and vineyards that went back many generations in his family. Theirs were the only wines he served.

"No thank you, Tony, I'm on duty. Please bring me one of your house specialty sodas, but I think Margot could use a glass of your Chianti. She's had a trying day so far."

Margot nodded gratefully and smiled at Antonio. "That would be great. Thank you, Antonio." The thought of a glass of wine sounded very appealing to her rattled nerves. Antonio bowed and left them on their own. Margot went right back to her line of questioning. "Well, what do you think? Would something like that push someone like Nancy too far? Far enough for murder?"

Tom scratched his head and gave a little thought before replying. He enjoyed discussing everything with her, including human nature, but he needed to remain objective when it came to police work. Only so much information could he share, and it had to be general and neutral. Nevertheless, he said, "From what I know so far, the Stearns' Academy was to be the most prestigious girls' school on the west coast. In the research we've looked over for the case, their curriculum was planning to meet with the very highest requirements from the toughest college entrance boards. They had brought in some of the finest teachers from around the world to educate these young ladies whose families were being attracted from all over America. This is what the Nancy Lewises of the world live for, especially if she thought it would be free to her and that her girls could possibly be the Santa Lucia elite representatives. Is it possibly a motive for murder? Absolutely. Is it definitely? Absolutely not. We cannot make any accusations until more facts are known." Tom took out his notepad and pen and wrote down, 'Nancy Lewis—Academy?' on a fresh sheet. "Thanks for the tip, it may be a lead worth following up."

Antonio brought out Margot's wine and Tom's soda. "It's so sad about Mrs. Montgomery, no? She was a good person. She was here many times, always very kind to us."

Tom's radar went up. "When was the last time she was here? Was she with Reginald?" Constance was frequently out in one of the many fine restaurants with her society clique, usually discussing the latest fundraising efforts.

Antonio knew right away when it was. He distinctly remembered when, and whose company she was keeping that day. "It was lunchtime, on Monday. No, Mr. Reggie was not here. She was with a young man, a stranger; I didn't know him. Very close, maybe working on big secret? Lots of whispering." Antonio lowered his voice and came close to the table while revealing his news. He tapped the side of his nose—for police ears only. "Could be for the school?"

"Had they been here together before?" Tom picked up his pen and made a few notes, as he'd done with the news about Nancy.

"Um, sure. Once, twice, I don't know. Excuse me." Antonio went to go meet other guests. He left visibly flustered, wondering if he'd said too much. A good restaurateur should keep some discretion.

"Those rumors about an affair are getting more out in the open," remarked Margot. She took a sip of her wine. It was a little sweet and full-bodied, with a nice taste of berries and finished dry.

"That's just malicious gossip and hearsay at this point. That fellow could easily have been working on the school, or some kind of charity event. I'll have my men follow it up. As for her having an affair, it's highly unlikely. It wasn't in her character. She didn't have a history of dalliances; why would she start now?" Tom knew police work and a fair bit about the criminal mind, but he knew nothing about the nature of women.

"I don't know. We don't know what goes on behind closed doors. There's just a lot of chins wagging, that's all." Margot sat back and folded her arms.

Tom looked over his shoulder to see Luigi, Antonio's son and best waiter bringing an *insalata caprese*—a beautiful salad of tomato, mozzarella cheese and basil—for them. It was colorful and tangy, with ripe, sun-warmed tomatoes. They shared the plate and the conversation took a lighter note. Margot and Tom were deciding what they would do on their weekend. They made a plan to drive down the coast a little way, stop and have a picnic. Getting out of town for an afternoon would be great. Tom needed to be in touch with his department, but they could do without him for a few hours. If things remained calm, Margot would end the day with a nice home cooked meal.

The rest of their lunch arrived—two steaming platters of rigatoni and a tomato meat sauce, with bread sticks. It was wonderful and filling, a little spicy, but very rich and homey. Maria, Antonio's wife, was in the kitchen as usual, supervising her staff who helped her prepare all of the sauces and pastas, the same family recipes she grew up with in Italy. They shared a hazelnut gelato, light and creamy, followed by espresso.

Tom and Margot thanked their host and shared more hugs at the door. Antonio believed a man should express his feelings of warmth and generosity to friends. To not reciprocate in the greetings would be offensive to the family. There was always a lot of laughter at Antonio's. They made their way back up the street to the shop. Tom left her at the shop doorstep. "Thank you for the nice lunch. I needed a break." He gave her an embrace. "The information you gave me may give us a lead. Let me know if anything else looks interesting, but by all means, you need to be careful. And above all, don't pry into other peoples' affairs. Leave it to the professionals. We're trained to deal with this sort of thing." He gave her another kiss and a quick squeeze.

Margot rolled her eyes and sighed, "Yes, Detective Malone. And I promise to keep my doors locked at night."

He gave her an 'I'm serious about this' look. "Just be a good girl."

She knew he was only looking out for her. "Will I see you tonight?"

"I would love to see you, but this case will keep me very busy into the night. I'll keep my word for Sunday, though. That's enough time for me to get adequate coverage in the department."

"Okay. See you Sunday, then. I'll make you a special picnic lunch." Margot stepped into the shop and sent Irene and Betty off for their breaks. She found herself alone in the store for the first moment she had on her own since the day began. She looked around for something to do, and straightened out the tissue paper used to wrap purchases. Margot couldn't believe Reginald was a suspect, but his behavior now was awfully mysterious. Surely, he must have been seen by many different people all of the time last night. She shook her head and moved on to restacking the white paper bags with poppies brightly painted on each. But then again, the last thing she'd heard about Reginald before Constance was found, was Daphne saying that he was in a flap and angrily looking for her. Was he mad just because she was late, or was he already angry about something else? If what everyone was saying was true, maybe he knew about an affair. Margot was so lost in her thoughts as she was refreshing the spool of Poppy Cove sealing stamps, she jumped at the sound of footsteps.

Daphne came in, curious to know what Tom could tell Margot about the case. With a glint of excitement in her eye, she eagerly asked, "So what did Tom say? Do they know who did it?"

Margot glanced briefly around the shop floor to make sure they were still alone. Her voice was just above a whisper. "They don't have a confession yet and Charles has been cleared. He was in plain sight the whole evening. However, they have been questioning Reginald since last night. He's still at the station with his lawyer and not answering to anyone."

Daphne began straightening up the jewelry at the sales counter. "That's not like Reginald. He's usually so co-operative. He must be in quite a state."

"I'll say—and it doesn't look good for him. No one can vouch for his whereabouts when the police think Constance was strangled. Loretta and Jake were the last ones to see him when he said he was going to look for her. Then it was as if he disappeared. No one saw him 'til we all saw Constance lying dead in the bushes."

Daphne continued to fiddle with the necklaces. "I just don't see Reginald as a killer, though. He's not like that. I've seen him get flustered and impatient, and even a little angry, but never murderous." Daphne's father had known Reginald since he was a new young man in town.

Margot thought carefully. "But what if he thought his wife was having an affair? Could that push him to murder?"

Daphne shook her head. "Nope. Not even then."

Margot prodded a little further. "But how would Reginald react if he *thought* his wife was conducting an affair in *public*?"

She stopped playing with the chains. "What do you mean?"

"Antonio told Tom and me that Constance had been having lunch in his restaurant and seemed very close with a young man. Now I'm not saying it was an affair—it could have been anything, you know. She was very involved with many charities and the school, of course. They could have been discussing anything, but if the rumors got to Reginald, well…"

Daphne's eyes grew wide. "Was this Constance's lover? Who is he and did he do it? A crime of passion!"

"Somehow Constance and crime of passion doesn't fit well together. Also, it's *supposed* lover, all rumor at this point."

"Perhaps there really was another side to Constance that no one truly knew about." Daphne paused. "You know, she was becoming quite beautiful lately. I mean, she was always a handsome woman, but very sporting, the tweed suits, shapeless sack dresses, the dull make-up and sensible shoes. She downplayed her features and made herself look dowdy. And then, it's like a switch went off. The next thing you know she's getting a permanent wave, buying high heels and ordering chiffon dresses. Sounds like love to me."

Margot shrugged her shoulders. "If there really was another man, I'm sure that the police would want to question him."

Daphne looked down at the appointment book. "Oh yeah, did you mention to Tom about Constance's spat with Nancy that day?"

"Yes. He found that to be very interesting and they're going to follow up on that, too."

At that moment, a stocky, older gentleman walked in the store, carrying a large, bulging suitcase. It was Sam Baker, a salesman for the Textiles Division of Global Industries, Margot's favorite fabric wholesaler from Los Angeles. They carried many beautiful fabrics in cottons, linens, and silks—mainly imported from Europe. Every time Margot looked at the amazing textiles from overseas, she yearned to go and see these places for herself again. Maybe she would, when time and money allowed her to take a break from the shop. Right now, it was a fulltime preoccupation and she loved it.

"Good afternoon, ladies. It's another beautiful one out there today," Sam said as he set down the bulky bag and took out his handkerchief to mop his forehead.

"Always good to see you, Sam," Margot greeted him warmly. "Can I get you a glass of iced tea?" She glanced at the table and noticed that Betty had tidied it up while she and Daphne were gone for lunch and made a fresh pitcher—ice cold and inviting. Betty was like that, a very thoughtful hostess. She treated the store like she was entertaining at home and made the customers happy.

"Ladies, don't mind if I do." Sam gratefully took the glass offered to him. After a long sip, he reached down to the side pocket of his valise. "Margot, I can't wait to show you our new samples. These mod acrylics are coming out so fine and extremely colorfast, too." He handed Margot a stock card of print swatches, made from the newest man-made polyesters and nylons.

Margot sighed as she saw the letterhead on the card. She knew the brand, all right. She gave the swatches a brief glance. These held no interest to her, she was a purist. Nothing could match the rustling of real silk on soft skin. "I don't think these will ever be preferred, Sam. These just don't feel or smell the same. Do you have much call for the artificial fabrics?" She handed the card back to him.

"Every year it's increasing." Sam rocked on his heels and clasped his hands behind his back. "The quality goes up, the price goes down. And to clean?

Washes up and dries like a dream. They're saying that ironing will be the way of the past soon. Drip dry, no wrinkles. You'll see. Martin's just purchased bolts of every style for their homemaker's department." Sam knew his textiles; he was always interested in progress. It just didn't appeal to Margot. Daphne wrinkled her nose at the thought.

"That's all fine and good, Sam. I'm sure Martin's has the market for it. I'm just not interested. Give me wools, silks, cottons, and then I'm happy." Margot smiled and folded her arms. She knew what she wanted.

Sam grabbed the handle of his case. "Then I'll make you a happy lady. I've got the rest of my swatches all in here."

Margot relaxed her stance and motioned to the stairs. "Let's go up to the office and see the real goodies you brought us." She looked past Sam's shoulder. "Daphne, could you see if Marjorie can come up and join us?"

"You bet. I'll send her and follow up myself as soon as Betty or Irene get back."

The two made their way up the wrought iron staircase to the lofty office. The stairs were just behind the sales counter. They led up to Margot and Daphne's shared office above the shop floor. It was a bright and airy space, with a big arched window looking out onto Avila Square. Margot reached for her binder on the bookcase behind her desk.

The binder was the Poppy Cove design book. In it, she had all of the sketches of the designs she'd done for the shop in chronological order, complete with swatches of the fabrics they used and comments on how well they fit and sold. She always referred to her book when she ordered new fabrics.

As she flipped through the pages, Margot marveled over all the hard work her staff had done over the last couple of years. They'd had a few duds, like the brown overcoats they made during Santa Lucia's warmest winter on record, but also some great successes like the fabulous lavender cocktail dresses they made this spring that were all presold after the May fashion show. They never even made it to the sales rack.

"Now, what have you brought us today, Sam?" Marjorie asked as she came up the stairs.

Sam was busy laying out his fabric books on the desk. He looked up and smiled at Marjorie. They'd known each other for a long time, from when she worked at Martin's. "Marjorie, it's always a pleasure to see you. Saw your old crew this morning. They speak very highly of your work here."

"Ah, they're a good group, but being here's much more exciting." She picked up a collection of cotton voile solids and prints that were very delicate, but beautifully woven. They were in a large range of hues, from deep black to sherbety pastels of apricot and mint. Marjorie looked at them carefully. "Margot, these would be perfect for the blouses you were sketching last week. It's a good weave, nice and tight, but still very delicate."

Margot looked closer at the booklet in Marjorie's hands. "I agree. I'll definitely get some of these." She'd been thinking of some spring blouses with a wrapping v-neckline and a wide collar flounce, in pastel shades. There was a beautiful pale raspberry shade, as well as a captivating apricot and an ivory that was so soft, it appeared white in some light and buttery in others. Perfect for early spring sunshine. The fabric draped so nicely, maybe she should even add a peplum. That she could decide later, after she figured out what she would pair them with.

"Those are from France. They still make the best lightweight textiles in the world. The silks are a marvel, too," Sam proudly crowed.

"What about the Indian silks? I thought I've purchased some through you," Margot enquired.

"Yes, yes, you have and they are good. Improving all the time, including their cottons, the weaves are getting tighter and colors are holding faster, too."

Margot and Marjorie spent the next half hour going through the samples, eyes wide like kids in a candy store. Daphne joined them, and the more they looked at all the sumptuous colors, the harder it became to narrow down the choices to just a few.

After spending some time sorting and listening to suggestions from Daphne and Marjorie, Margot decided on a lightweight tropical wool worsted in a pale grey tone that made one of their staple ensembles of the career girl variety and also one in a delicate shade of pink for a fresh addition. She also ordered some silk and linen solids in pastels for early spring. Sam left her a few samples of matching prints in madras plaid, gingham check, modern abstracts and florals for her consideration. She wanted to plan a bit more before purchasing these, but her eyes kept wandering back to a dress weight swatch of cotton, bright white with bunches of red cherries all over it. It would make great summer pieces—a sundress, shorts, and possibly a playsuit. *I'll order this one, most definitely*, she thought. *I'll just mull it over to think how much I'll need.* As the years went by, Margot's experience gave her a sense of what were good impulse purchases, like a good buy on solid classic fabrics, but to hold off on the eye-catching prints to think them over. Many busy prints seemed great at first, but when fifty yards showed up, like with the orange swirled one she got the first season, proved to be tiresome and gaudy very quickly.

The best rule of thumb was to keep the swatches for a few days, look at them and then put them away for a while. If they still had the same draw a day or two later, they usually would be a successful choice.

Sam agreed to leave a couple of his booklets with her, as he had a few copies of them. As he zipped up his case, he said, "Well, Margot, always a pleasure doing business with you. I'll be back in two weeks to pick them up, and I can take your order for anything you'd like to add. I think I'll have some more new pieces and I might even be able to persuade you on the man-made fibers after all!" He gave a friendly wink.

She knew he meant no harm and smiled warmly as she touched his arm. "Oh Sam, try if you must, but I really have enough to choose from with what I see here. Thanks again for leaving these behind," she said as they all went downstairs to the sales floor.

Sam tipped his hat and went through the front door, just as an attractive young lady came through, carrying many handbags. Julia MacKay had arrived for her 2:30 appointment. She was a young woman in her late twenties with auburn hair and a bright smile. Daphne met her at the door to help her with her armload of samples.

"Ooh, here, let me help you!" Daphne quickly scanned the purses as she relieved her. She immediately liked what she saw as she set them down on the counter. "These look great. You must be Julia. I'm Daphne. This is Margot; that's Betty over near the window and this is Irene." She gestured around the room. Irene, as usual, sized up the newcomer as she slinked by, carrying a dress to re-hang from the fitting room.

It didn't faze Miss MacKay in the least. "Yes, I am. I'm pleased to meet you all," she said as she shook hands with Daphne. "I've got a few more items to get from my car. I'll be right back. Please have a look at these while I'm gone."

Irene began pawing through the pile. She picked up a shiny, black patent pocketbook. "I like this one. It is so me!"

"Looks like it was made for you. She's got some great ideas." Daphne's head was abuzz with possibilities.

"That's the last of it." Julia had brought in more purses, as well as a portfolio and sketchbook. Daphne and Irene were busy commenting and admiring her work. The purses were very well made, all finished with satin lining. In her portfolio she had magazine clippings of famous movie stars carrying her purses to lunches, nightclubs and movie premieres. The girls were very impressed. Margot glanced over now and again and was also very happy with what she saw and nodded with approval to Daphne. She left to attend to Mrs. Morgan who had just entered the store.

"Margot dear, where do you have more of that darling navy dress in the window?" Susan Morgan enquired. She was one of the girls' most frequent shoppers. Like clockwork, she came in every two weeks to purchase something with her household allowance.

"Hello, Mrs. Morgan." Margot gave a quick whirl as she looked around the floor. "I think that's the last one. But it's a size 10, just your size and I'm sure that cut would greatly flatter you." She went to the counter and got out their appointment book. "We'll be changing the displays on Wednesday morning. I can put it aside for you."

Mrs. Morgan followed Margot to the counter. "Thank you, I'd like that." She glanced at the handbags strewn across the top. Her eyes lit up as she picked up a navy clutch. "Oh, this is marvelous! It would go very well with my new dress."

Daphne looked at the item in her hand. "I think so, too. Mrs. Morgan, this is Julia MacKay. These are samples of her work. What do you think of her talents?" Daphne liked to get customers' opinions as she decided on new stock. It was her best form of sales research.

"They're very nice. How much is this one?" She still had a firm grip on the purse.

Daphne replied, "Oh, they're not for sale yet. We're just sorting things out right now."

Susan gave a little pout. "You mean I can't buy it next week when I pick up my dress?" she asked, still holding onto the bag.

Daphne smiled at Julia, who happily grinned back. "I'm thinking we might have things worked out by then."

"You should. I'd buy some." She turned her attention back to Margot. "I'll come back later next week for the dress. And if they're available by then, put my name down for this one," she stated as she finally set down the purse. "See you, ladies."

Betty came up to the counter to wrap up a purchase for Mrs. Hillman, whom she had been helping select a pair of cut glass floral earrings for her daughter-in-law's birthday present. She also started sorting through the purses. "You know, Clarissa would love something like this!" She picked up a pink number with hard sides and a metal handle that had a huge fabric flower on one side. "How much is it?"

"They're not for sale yet, Mrs. Hillman. These are the designer's samples. Do you think we should carry these?" Betty eyed Daphne, who was already paying attention to the conversation.

"Absolutely." She was a little disappointed as she set the bag down and reached into her own to pay Betty. "When you have some in stock, please call me."

Daphne decided to take Julia upstairs to work out the details for an order. She particularly liked another black patent leather purse, which had short handles and was squarish, tapering a little to the top, and closed with a clasp. She had bright colors, too, and floral accents, and some clutches shaped like envelopes from a lover. They were pricey, but worth it. Daphne made a deal with her to supply some of her items by October for the Christmas season, and to have a small selection to go with the garments they would feature in next month's fashion show. Part of the conditions of the agreement were that she would not supply to any other store in Santa Lucia, making them exclusive to Poppy Cove. The girls knew that uniqueness kept their business special. Julia also agreed to leave the navy clutch for Mrs. Morgan, which would make her very happy.

Mrs. Jane Peacock arrived for her appointment at 3 p.m. promptly. As her son was marrying a girl from Texas at Christmastime, she was a very excited mother of the groom. The wedding was to take place at the bride's parents' ranch. Mrs. Peacock was in her late forties, with graying hair, plumpish, with a delightful smile and sparkling light blue eyes. This was the first time she had had a dress made for her by a professional. She had always made do buying off the rack or sewing a dress for herself, but Robert was her only child, so she wanted to splurge on this occasion. She didn't know what to expect in Texas—she'd heard they did everything big there and wanted to make her son proud.

Jane stood in the doorway for a moment and surveyed the store. It was the first time she'd set foot in Poppy Cove and was delighted with what she saw. *I'm so glad I took her advice and called for my appointment*, she thought and then a flicker of sadness crossed her face, then a slight butterfly in her stomach. *I hope this is within our budget.* Jane was greeted with a warm smile.

"You must be Mrs. Peacock." Margot walked up to her and gave her a comforting handshake as she introduced herself. "Welcome to Poppy Cove."

"Thank you, but please call me Jane." She glanced at the store once more and exclaimed, "I love your little shop! There's nothing like this back home. This is such a treat for me. Even my Herbert is getting a new suit."

The girls gave her the royal treatment. Betty served her iced tea, while Margot sat down with her in the lounge area, where she had earlier brought out her tools of the trade—a swatch book of different dress weights, a color chart and a sketchbook. With custom clients, Margot always took the time to get better acquainted. It put everyone at greater ease and they could come up with the most flattering dresses together, once they got to know each other. "So tell me about the wedding, Jane. It's for your only son, right?" Margot asked as she began sketching.

Her eyes glittered as she replied, "Yes, and our boy is marrying a Texan. They met at college. Susie's a lovely girl—lively, a real firecracker. Our Robert tends to be a little quiet and reserved. She really brings him out of his shell. She's very welcome in our family."

Jane paused briefly as she took a sip of her cool drink and fanned herself. "I'm not used to this warm weather." Margot smiled as Jane prattled on. "The wedding is in December, on the 28th. Semi-formal at the country club, from what Robert has told me. Susie and her mother have been doing almost all of the planning. It's the bride's day, after all. They've invited 200 people, mostly from their side. We're a small lot."

Jane continued. "We're leaving at the beginning of the holiday season. The engagement party is at their house on Christmas Eve. It's a mansion from what I've heard. They even have a guesthouse on the ranch. That's where my Herbert and I are staying. Ooh, just listen to me carry on. You must have some questions to ask me."

Margot was busily occupied watching Jane talk, her mannerisms and the way she was poised. It helped her come up with design ideas that would suit the customer's comfort. "Actually, you've given me a lot of help. We know how formal the wedding is, the time of year and how long we have to work on the dress. But yes, I do have a few things to ask you. First of all, what time of day is the wedding and also, do you know what the mother of the bride is wearing?"

Jane thought before replying, "The chapel service is at 2 p.m., with the reception to follow at the country club. I believe Susie's mother is wearing pink. I've only talked to her once, you know, when we telephoned them after Robert and Susie gave us the good news. They seem very nice. I've seen pictures. She's around my age, I think, but taller and slimmer than me. Susie says she's wearing pink, in a very simple cut of wool crepe. They say it's cooler in winter, rarely do they have snow, but the nights are cold."

"What about you? What colors do you like to wear?" Margot was busily sketching.

"Oh, me? Well, I don't know, I guess blue. Yes! Blue would be best. Her mother is in pink, so I'll be in blue!"

"Okay, blue it is. A light blue?" Margot commented as she glanced at the lightness of Jane's eyes.

"Yes." Jane was happy and much more self-assured with the dress. "Something smart."

Margot turned as she heard Daphne and Julia coming down the stairs. Both were very jovial, so she knew they had struck a deal that made them both happy. When Julia was gone, Daphne walked over to the lounge area. "Daphne, this is Mrs. Jane Peacock. Jane, this is Daphne Huntington-Smythe, my partner in Poppy Cove. She also purchases the accessories to compliment our ensembles."

Daphne sat down and joined the ladies. "It's a pleasure to meet you, Jane," she spoke as she delicately shook her hand. "How do you like Santa Lucia?"

"Oh, it's very nice. We've only been here since July and everyone is so friendly. The town is beautiful, too. We love it here," Jane replied and then gave a small sigh as her shoulders rounded a little. "I just hope we can stay."

The remark surprised Daphne. "But if you like it so much, why wouldn't you stay?"

Jane sighed again, "We moved here because my Herbert got a job teaching at the new academy. It was a big advancement for him."

"So you were there last night at the ceremony," Irene commented as she walked by after straightening up one of the dressing rooms. Margot glared at her over the top of her sketchpad, somewhat appalled that she had been both listening and bringing up last night.

Jane had no problem replying. "Yes, yes we were. The entire faculty attended. Except, of course, for Headmistress Larsen."

There was a stunned silence. "The Headmistress of the Academy was not in attendance last night?" Daphne questioned.

"No, and I can't say I was surprised. We heard that she and Mrs. Stearns-Montgomery had a huge argument on the phone Wednesday night. She's not the nicest or most social person I have ever met." Jane Peacock sat up straighter and pulled her jacket peplum down with a crisp tug. "And she's still nowhere to be found."

A curious Daphne persisted, but gently, as Irene hovered, straining to hear every word. "Sounds like you and Headmistress Larsen got off on the wrong foot."

"She challenged my Herbert's every method when it came to teaching. If it wasn't for Mrs. Montgomery taking an interest in my husband's background and the success he has had with his pupils, Headmistress Larsen never would have bothered to contact our references and see how he has his own way of giving children reasons to learn. She acted as if her ways of strict discipline and that children should be seen and not heard are the only ways to drill knowledge into them."

"Surely she wasn't the only one who decided which teachers were hired." Margot listened closely as Daphne continued to investigate. Although it was completely unprofessional and she was initially very peeved at Irene for bringing the subject up, Margo had to admit she was intrigued with this new information. Even she wanted to know more.

"No, no, and the interview with the school trustees went very well, but when it came to meeting with the headmistress, that was a different story. She was so mean and severe. Thank goodness Mrs. Montgomery was there to recommend my Herbert. Her influence brought many fair teachers to the school. And it's awful there right now. The police are everywhere and parts of the school are closed off. My Herbert says all of the teachers are concerned about the future of the school. We don't know if it'll go on. There are all kinds of rumors floating around. The entire staff is worried about their jobs." She blushed when she realized how selfish that sounded, compared to the fate of Mrs. Montgomery. "Oh, just listen to me going on.

At least I have my life and we have made it here. Poor Mrs. Montgomery won't see the benefits of all her hard work." She slouched back in her chair and lightly sniffled.

Daphne gave her a little squeeze on the shoulders. "Now Jane, you have every right to be a little concerned for your own. But don't worry. I'm sure Charles Stearns has every intention of carrying on for the family. That is how they built this town. Your husband will have his teaching post. The show must go on, as they say. And," she exclaimed with a twinkle in her eye, "your boy is getting married!"

Jane's smile returned and Margot shared with her the ideas she had for her dress. She suggested an icy blue wool crepe dress with a bolero jacket, smart, but loosely fitted through the waist to help hide Jane's rather thick midriff. It would finish at mid-calf, to accentuate her slim calves and ankles, a flattering area of her figure. Jane was pleased with both the design and the quote, so the girls set out the appointment schedule. Marjorie went into the dressing room with Jane to get her measurements, while Irene made out her receipt for the deposit.

"Thank you so much, girls. See you next week for my first fitting. Oh, it's so glamorous!" she gave a little giggle as she walked out the door.

The girls waved back. She was a sweet lady. It was always nice to help someone kind feel special. But Margot had a funny feeling. "It's very strange that Headmistress Larsen was not at the opening last night."

"That's what I was thinking." Daphne paused for a moment. "You'd think she would be very prominent, wouldn't you?" Daphne was running over all she could remember in her mind about the event. "Most everyone associated with Stearns' Academy was there. I'm sure of it. I talked to almost everybody." Daphne was a social butterfly, always flitting about in all the crowds at parties.

"The opening was an important event for her. I would expect she'd have to be present. It would look very bad for the school if she weren't. Constance wouldn't have put up with that. I'll mention it to Tom on Sunday. He never said anything to me about Headmistress Larsen at lunch. The police must have known she wasn't there. I guess if she's a major suspect, he wouldn't tell me, would he?"

"Maybe she was there, but no one saw her."

Margot shrugged her shoulders. "Well, if she was and no one did see her, what was she up to?"

The girls felt puzzled, and their thoughts were going nowhere on the subject. It was getting near to the end of the long day. Irene was tidying up and the sewing workers were packing up to go home. Just as Margot and Daphne were about to leave, the telephone rang. Daphne picked it up. It was the secretary from Charles' office. Constance Stearns-Montgomery's funeral would be held on Tuesday.

CHAPTER FIVE

Saturdays were always a quick trade day. Besides being a busy shopping day in general, the Avila Square Farmers' Market drew in great crowds on Saturdays and the sales floor at Poppy Cove was always brisk with shoppers, some local and some day-trippers from the city. The back sewing room was closed, so Margot and Daphne were around in the front of the shop, along with Irene and Betty. They didn't do any custom orders or appointments. Those were strictly Tuesday through Friday. Saturdays could be great fun, with a variety of new customers who quickly became regular shoppers. This Saturday, however, was a little dampened by the news of the murder. They were so slow that by eleven o'clock they decided not to have Abigail Browning, their Saturday helper and Dr. Browning's teenage daughter, come in for her weekly afternoon shift. In fact, the whole town seemed quiet. If it weren't for the tourists and out-of-towners, who were largely oblivious to the tragedy, it would have seemed like a ghost town.

As on every Saturday, Lana from the tearoom across the street brought over a plate of fresh muffins—this time they were apple cinnamon—and a pot of coffee. She mentioned that their business was slower than usual today as well. "I've also heard from other businesses on the street that they'll be closing on Tuesday, at the suggestion of Mayor Stinson, in honor of Mrs. Montgomery. We've decided to follow suit. Do you know what you're going to do?"

Daphne and Margot looked at each other. They never really thought about it, but they both were planning on going to the funeral and permitting any staff member the time off to attend. "Yes, I think that would be a good idea. We'll probably all want to attend the funeral and I doubt we'd lose any business by being closed. If anything, it's the least we can do to show our respect to the family."

Margot got out the appointment book and began to reschedule the Tuesday appointments for later in the week. Daphne got to work making a sign to post in the window, informing customers that they would be closed an extra day that week. The rest of the day passed uneventfully and they were glad to leave at the end of it.

As Margot walked home along the tree-lined street, she thought about the conversations she had overheard from some of the regular customers who had come in since the murder. All of the local women seemed to have some opinion about how Constance died and why, ranging from an unrelated accident to Constance having a secret double life to death at the hands of Headmistress Larsen. Margot gave her head a shake and convinced herself to put it all out of her mind. It was a tiring week and she was looking forward to putting her feet up and seeing Cuddles. Often, Saturday nights were spent with Tom, going out for dinner and a movie, or out dancing, but this case had him working around the clock, so she set her mind on the time they would have together. Margot thought she would start on the picnic they would share on Sunday. She could look over her cookbooks and make a special dessert to go along with the menu she'd planned to make. He always appreciated home cooked meals, especially when he was working on a tough case, and this would be one of his toughest yet, because he knew the people involved and they were so well respected in the community. Tom deserved a nice time, with all the nasty trouble he had to deal with.

Margot let herself in the door and gave Cuddles a scratch behind the ears. He was always there to greet her, right at the door, waiting to go out for a stroll himself. Margot let him run out and see his own world. At two years old, he was still a frisky kitten. Quite often, he was out until Margot called him in just before bedtime. She changed his water, gave him fresh food and set about finding herself something to eat. Last week, on a whim, she decided to pick up one of those new TV dinners. It was a different brand than she had seen before. The main course was a Salisbury steak— something she didn't make for herself. Tonight was just the night to give it a try. Maybe she would find a good variety show or a funny play to watch as she put her feet up. While her oven was heating, Margot got out her tattered copy of the *Fannie Farmer Cookbook*, one of the very few possessions she brought with her to California when she arrived three years ago. She found a couple of her favorite recipes that she knew would make Tom happy.

The light went off on her oven, and she put her dinner in, setting the timer for 35 minutes, as recommended on the package. "Wow, this even comes with dessert!" she spoke out loud. "That's a neat idea." Margot's livelihood was all about taking care with others' details, so sometimes it was nice to have someone else think of the little things. She went back to her cookbook and found the fried chicken, potato salad, and brownie recipes and earmarked them for later. She looked over to her timer and saw she still had 25 minutes left. She sighed, not knowing what to do with herself with no work to do for her dinner. She decided to boil the eggs and potatoes for tomorrow's salad. As her hands were busy, her mind turned to fuss over what had happened to Constance and all the things that were coming to the surface in the last two days. Many things did not add up. Once the pots were simmering, she grabbed a pencil and a pad of paper and sat down at her kitchen table.

Sorting her thoughts out on paper always comforted Margot. She started writing out all the comments she'd heard from people since Thursday night about Constance. It was very weird about Headmistress Larsen. If the rumors were true, she still hadn't been seen. If the rumors were false and she really was around, she was keeping a low profile, which in itself was odd for a person of such stature. So, where was she and why? Margot's mind wandered to what if it had something else to do with the school—another disgruntled staff member, a parent or even a student.

It could have been something to do with either the Stearns or Montgomery families, possibly recent or from a long time ago. Spite can harbor in the heart for generations. It's true their families had done a lot of good for the town, but people saw good deeds in different ways, as Tom had pointed out to her.

It seemed that one of the juiciest theories was about the affair. Margot shook her head. That didn't seem too likely, knowing Constance's nature and it probably was just popular because of its salaciousness. But you never know. Tom gave it no weight but Antonio Chelli thought there might be something to it. Then she pondered about Reginald. Had he been cleared or did he have something to do with it? He and Constance seemed to have a healthy, happy marriage, but if he had even thought that she'd *had* an affair—true or not— could it push him to commit a crime of passion?

She looked at the stove. The timer still had another few minutes and the pots were still simmering away nicely. "Maybe we're all over thinking," she muttered. "Maybe it was just an accident. The scarf did look tightly wound around the bush." Margot had a sinking feeling in the pit of her stomach. "What if Constance, who wasn't used to wearing such accessories got tangled up in the bushes and choked herself?" Horrified, she slowed down her thinking and realized that wasn't possible; the scarf was too delicate to leave that kind of bruising on her neck without additional force. The police had already confirmed that. It would be absolutely terrifying to think that she or Poppy Cove had anything to do with the death.

Then on the subject of Poppy Cove, it reminded her of Nancy Lewis again and her strange behavior after finding out about Constance's death. Coupling that with their long time rivalry, Margot wondered if that could lead to murder. "Oh, now this is just ridiculous," she blurted out. "It could be anything or anyone." Then she felt a chill. Are any of us safe?

Margot was deep in thought and jumped sky high when her oven timer dinged. She put her notepad aside, glad for the distraction. She was starving. Margot got up, grabbed her oven mitts out of the drawer, pulled her dinner out of the oven and set it on the stovetop. "Well, it smells okay," she remarked. She drained the potatoes and ran cold water on the eggs, leaving them to cool. As she lifted the foil off the tray, Margot frowned at the sight of peas in her apple cobbler and syrup from the dessert creeping over onto her mashed potatoes. She took out a spoon and scooped out the offending mix-ups and put them on the discarded foil lid. She brought her dinner out to the living room and placed her TV tray in front of her favorite chair. She walked over to her television set and switched it on, sat down and got herself all ready to eat.

Margot was about to take her first bite of the steak when she heard the mewling wail of Cuddles, who was done patrolling the neighborhood and wanted to come in. She got up, let the cat in and settled back down. As she was taking her first bite again, she realized she had already seen the dramatic play that was on the television, so recently she remembered that at the end the husband died and the wife wept uncontrollably. Then she tasted her steak. It was cold in the center and rubbery. The potatoes were pretty much the same with a faint hint of apple cinnamon from the next tray. It wasn't good. She made a sour face and called Cuddles over. When she set the dinner on the floor, he sniffed at it and pushed the tray away with his paw.

Margot got up and turned the television off, deciding that toast and tea would be just fine, an improvement over the tin foil tray. She picked up the ignored dinner and carried it to the kitchen and tossed it straight into the trash. She put the potatoes and eggs in the fridge and went about preparing her simple dinner. Her mind kept wandering back to the murder. Was there anything Constance could have said to her, even in passing at the shop, which could give them some clue into what had happened? By the time she finished eating, nothing had come to mind, other than the fight between Constance and Nancy, Con's change of style and the mysterious headmistress, which were all old news by now.

Feeling restless and going nowhere, Margot got out all the ingredients to make the fried chicken. She was too worked up to do nothing and it always tasted better the second day. It gave her plenty to do, but she wasn't focused on the task at hand. Her mind was racing with all of the new information she was learning about the people whom she had come to know in the last few years. Nancy Lewis could be bullish, but could she really want Constance dead, by her own or someone else's hand? Lost in thought, Margot almost forgot to add the pinch of paprika that made the chicken extra tasty. Maybe there was some truth to the man rumor. Could that be the reason for the girlish new dress, not the school opening? When the chicken was finished, Margot realized that she was still hungry. She took a drumstick and polished it off. And, where was the headmistress that night? She cleaned up the kitchen and tiredness overtook her active imagination. That was enough speculation for one night. She shut off all of the lights, said sweet dreams to Cuddles, locked her doors and got ready for bed.

CHAPTER SIX

Daphne woke up to bright sunshine flooding her second floor bedroom. She yawned and stretched, finally feeling rested after tending to Loretta during the last two evenings. She had gone to check up on her friend right after closing up shop on both Friday and Saturday nights, and was happy to see her feeling more like herself yesterday. They even had a glass of wine and a good chuckle over some of the gossip about their fellow Santa Lucians that proved not to be true over the years. Like the time Nancy Lewis had tried to convince everyone she was related to Danish royalty or that the town's favorite hairdresser, Mr. Anthony, whom everyone suspected favored men over women given his flamboyancy and delicate hand, was actually married to a battle-axe shrew three years his senior. Maybe the same could be said about the rumors swirling around the mysterious death of Constance once the case was solved.

Sunday was a very social day in the Huntington-Smythe household. Church, a lavish lunch at the club followed by a rousing game of golf, tennis or polo, then home for a family dinner. Daphne always enjoyed Sundays, but she was looking forward to this one more than ever, since the recent events had made life so hectic and she hadn't seen much of her family. She sat up in bed, recalling some things in her dreams from last night. They all got mixed up with her preoccupied thoughts. She dreamt she saw Constance being chased by shadowy men lurking in dark places. *And,* she suddenly remembered, *that good looking instructor from the Academy never did come by to see me.* She had truly believed he was interested in her. Maybe with all that was going on at the school, he was too busy to come by. Then she realized that with all the commotion, their picture never made it into the paper's society pages. It would have been very distasteful, but all the same she would have loved to see how they looked together. He was very handsome in a rugged way.

Just then, Eleanor, the maid, knocked on her door and brought in a breakfast tray with a cinnamon pecan roll, orange juice and coffee. "Good morning, Miss Daphne. Did you have a good sleep?" She set it down on the table by the window.

"Yes thanks, Eleanor. Except I kept having strange dreams about Constance and some of the things people were saying. None of it made sense." The details were fading more and more with the daylight, but she still felt off.

"Now, dear, that is to be expected in such times," clucked Eleanor. She'd been with the family for many years and had great affection for all the children. They cared for her, too. She was part of the family. "Is there anything else you need?"

"No, that'll be fine. Is anyone else up right now?" Daphne got up and slipped on her pale yellow silk robe over her matching pajamas. They looked luminescent next to her tanned skin. She walked over to her window seat and caught a glimpse of the blue-sky day. Perfect for the club.

"Your mother is on the sun porch, writing a letter to your grandmother and your father is out walking the grounds with William. I believe everyone else is still asleep."

"Tell mother I'll be down at 9:30. I'll meet her in the foyer." She sat down to her hot breakfast and opened up the copy of *Look Magazine* she'd brought home the other day. Daphne was engrossed in the story of what American life was like for Sophia Loren, when her younger sister Elizabeth bounded through the door. Sixteen and always jealous of her sister's independence, she wanted to know everything of a grown-up girl's life.

"Hey, Sis, is it true that Mrs. Montgomery was bumped off?" Lizzy's eyes were like saucers.

"Wow! Who taught you to speak like that? And what about knocking?" Daphne loved her little sister, but sometimes she was like an unruly puppy, except that dogs were more patient and obedient. "Slow down and quit bouncing on my bed. Give me a minute and I'll tell you what I know." She thought carefully about how to phrase the goings on to her sister. Once the words got out, they'd go to everyone and be twisted as only a teen could do.

The girls were close, even though they were nine years apart. Elizabeth idolized Daphne. Ever since she was old enough to notice she had a big sister, she would imitate her—facial expressions, grooming habits, gestures. It drove Daphne crazy when she was growing up until her mother discussed it with her, explaining that imitation was the sincerest form of flattery. In the last few years, Daphne had taken Lizzie under her wing, giving her clothing, boy and make-up advice. Often on a rainy afternoon, the two could be found huddling over a movie or fashion magazine in Daphne's room, giggling away.

Elizabeth wanted Daphne's freedom. Daphne could come and go as she pleased. Elizabeth had to be home by ten, unless there was a chaperoned event, such as a dance or group outing with another family or sporting club. Then it was eleven. And car dates? Not for another year.

Daphne took a deep breath and replied, "Mrs. Montgomery was found in the bushes at the school grounds. It does look like she was murdered. The police are investigating, and that's it so far." Daphne wanted to keep it low key and calm because of Lizzie's overactive imagination. She didn't want to get it working.

"I heard she had a lover. Can you believe it? An old lady like that?" To Lizzie, thirty was close to death.

"Now that's just malicious gossip!" Daphne retorted, giving her sister a sideways glance.

Lizzie shrugged, "Yeah, but sometimes gossip's true." She picked up Daphne's watch off of her bedside table and started fiddling with it. Lizzie was a commotion unto herself. She was always fidgety. "I'll bet Mr. Montgomery did it."

"What makes you say that?"

"The police think so. They've put him in jail. He's the prime suspect and the motive is clear," Lizzie replied simply and met Daphne's eyes dead on.

Her phrasing bewildered Daphne. "Where did you get that from?"

"Oh, I know things." Lizzie began adjusting the time on Daphne's watch. She puffed up her chest and added, "I've learned lots from *Prime Crime Magazine*. Crimes of passion are common and jealousy is a strong motive."

"Give me that!" Daphne snatched the watch out of her sister's hands. "That's a fine way to talk about your elders and someone we know."

Lizzie simply shrugged again. "I've read about other cases in the magazine and it's almost always the mild-mannered husband. He can snap anytime. In one case, he hacked up his wife to bits!"

"That's terrible! Mrs. Montgomery's murder was nothing like that. And besides, they're only *questioning* Mr. Montgomery. We're not the police and frankly this is none of our business." Daphne began nervously brushing her hair. Lizzie's interest in the crime was getting on her nerves. "Mother would have a fit if she knew you were reading that trash. You've been raised better than that."

"Yeah, I know. But wouldn't it be cool if I figured it out and solved the case before the police did?"

"How? You don't have any of the facts; you weren't even there when it happened; and may I remind you it's none of your concern!" Daphne found the discussion ridiculous. This was where the girls greatly differed. Daphne was drawn to fashion, where Lizzie preferred gruesome fiction.

"Oh, there's lots of clues and similar cases in *Prime Crime Magazine*," she sniffed.

Daphne didn't want to discuss it any further, so she changed the subject. "Are we still on for tennis with James and Robert?" Lizzie's ears perked up at the mention of James' name. They'd grown up together, but something different was happening lately.

"You've got that right, Sister. The match is at 2 o'clock. I've been looking forward to this all week." James and Robert Worth were young men who also frequented the Santa Lucia Yacht Club. James, seventeen, attended Lizzie's school and Robert, twenty-one, was entering into his junior year at the Santa Lucia campus of the University of California, heading toward a law degree. Lizzie and James were always horsing around together, ever since they could walk. This summer however, Daphne could see that James was growing into a strong, strapping young man. And she noticed her sister saw it, too.

"Great. Then go get dressed for church and pack your bag for the club. I'll see you downstairs." Daphne shooed her sister out the door and closed it behind her. She went to her closet to get ready for the day. She took out her tennis whites and sneakers and packed them in her sports bag, along with her racket. She decided to wear her mauve sleeveless blouse with her new pastel plaid pencil skirt, in matching dreamy colors of mauve and mint on a creamy white background. She had a darling little scarf and pumps in perfect light purple. It made a very sweet ensemble. She looked at the time and noticed it was getting late, already fifteen minutes after nine. She quickly gulped down her coffee, washed up, got dressed and with a light application of powder and lipstick, she headed downstairs. At the last minute, she grabbed her light cream cashmere cardigan. The church was often cool in the mornings.

Patricia Huntington-Smythe was waiting in the foyer for the rest of her brood. Her husband and son were outside by the cars, smoking, and she was chatting with Grace, her very pregnant daughter-in-law, who, although glowing, was seeming a little overburdened with the new weight on her tiny frame. They were discussing the topic on everyone's lips in their little town when Daphne came downstairs. Their conversation became hushed and both women turned to greet Daphne as she entered the room.

"Goodness, Daphne, you were there when they found Constance. Were you scared?" The lovely Grace was quite emotional during the last couple of months.

Everything had been happening so fast, Daphne had forgotten to be frightened. Now it was flickering more and more on her mind. After all, there was a murderer on the loose. *Could it have happened to anyone?* she wondered. "Good morning Grace, Mother. You know, it was so strange, like a bad dream. There were so many people around, and, honestly, it didn't seem like a random accident. I have a feeling this was deliberate, by someone who knew her well."

"Darling, that's quite the thing to say about one of our set. After all that family has done for this community, who would even consider such a crime if they knew her?" Patricia was appalled to think that she personally could know a cold-blooded killer.

Grace sat down in a chair. The littlest excitement these days was tiring her more than she would admit. The doctor had told her that most likely her last month would be spent in complete bed rest. "I'm so glad I wasn't there to see it. It must have been just awful." She visibly shuddered at the thought.

"Yes, I'm happy you weren't there either. We want to keep you in tip-top shape. You've got a precious parcel there!" Daphne loved babies, and couldn't wait to be an auntie for the first time. She already had tucked away little presents of rattles and sleepers and a stuffed lion just waiting for the day.

There was a great ruckus as Lizzie came flying down the stairs, hair already loose from her ponytail. "Let's go! What's the hold up?" She was already halfway out the door.

"You, dear. We were waiting for you. And please, Elizabeth, try to be more ladylike. After all those Saturday deportment classes, you should be able to enter a room with a little more care." Patricia had no idea how to rein in her coltish youngster. She wasn't bad, just— well—uncouth. Daphne and her mother helped Grace get up out of her chair and to the door.

The Santa Lucia Community Church was at full capacity this morning. Daphne saw many familiar faces, some who were not regular attendees, but who needed to group together after recent events. There was, however, an unfamiliar new face, a good-looking, swarthy one at the back of the church. Daphne blushed when she realized she was catching his eye too. *Eyes in front, girl,* she thought. *You are in church.* Daphne noticed as she turned her head that someone else saw the new man in town. Nancy Lewis was elbowing her eldest daughter, Barbara, in the ribs, and not so discreetly pointing and whispering about him. Rumor had it that Babs hadn't done very well in her last two years of school, just barely getting her diploma at Lords and was unable to even buy her way into any respectable college or university. Mrs. Lewis was planning to marry her off very quickly. Daphne silently shook her head and focused on today's message.

The sermon led by Pastor Gregory was very timely and poignant. He spoke about communities growing together in times of crisis and uniting instead of turning on each other. The truth will be known in time and we should not to give into mindless gossip and speculation. *He's so right,* Daphne thought. *A murderer may be among us, or maybe it was some kind of strange accident. We must be careful not to judge wrongly, but find out what really happened.*

The Santa Lucia Yacht Club was *the* club in the county. It was situated at the start of Oceanview Drive, just down the hill from the Academy grounds. Tucked away at the end of the bay, it was a safe harbor for the docked luxury boats. The club itself was grand and diverse. Built in 1928, the city elite saw it as a well-deserved playground for all the hard work they had done to remake their town after the quake. There was a dining room, tearoom, ballroom, ladies' and men's lounges, as well as polo grounds, golf course and tennis courts. In addition, there was a heated saltwater pool, sauna, spa and massage facilities. Sunday lunch was a must for the social set, a place to see and be seen. The Huntington-Smythe's table was one of the best in the heart of the Palms Dining Room.

As Daphne's family entered the restaurant, they noticed it was quieter than usual. Many of the regular members were there, but the Stearns-Montgomery table toward the sidewall was vacant. It was covered with tasteful arrangements of roses, lilies and hibiscus. Sunday afternoons were normally lively, but today there was a somber atmosphere in the light and airy room. Their waiter, Michael, greeted the Huntington-Smythe's group at their table and brought the luncheon menus and told them the specials of the day. Daphne decided on the grilled salmon in dill sauce, accompanied with tiny steamed potatoes and French beans, with a glass of chardonnay.

They settled into their own conversations at the table. Grace and her mother-in-law were discussing the upcoming baby, and as usual, Daphne's father and William were having a serious conversation regarding upcoming tax breaks in their most recent land acquisition. Lizzie was across the round table from Daphne and it was difficult to speak with her at a discreet level. Daphne adjusted her scarf and looked around the room. The Palms Dining Room was the epitome of the new Californian elegance. It had gently whitewashed walls, with terra cotta tile flooring, so cool in the hot weather. The large ceiling fans created a slight breeze that gracefully moved the palms planted throughout the room. Daphne got lost in her own thoughts while gazing out through the French doors that opened out to the club's lawn and garden, and further onto the Pacific. A nattering buzz interrupted her moment's peace.

"Anita! Get out of that chair! Let Barbara sit between your father and Mr. Carson." Nancy Lewis was fussing over her family. Daphne looked over her shoulder and saw that Nancy had the new handsome stranger roped into lunch at their table. He looked uncomfortable being forced to sit between the vapid Babs and boring old Andrew. Daphne flashed a quick smile that caught his eye and returned her attention to her own family.

"...And that's what I think." Lizzie was giving her thoughts on the murder of Constance. Daphne just caught the tail end of her theory, something about "crimes of passion" and "jilted lover." *Lizzie has to read better books through the summer,* Daphne thought.

She sipped her wine and changed the subject. "Mother, how was the Lewis garden party on Friday? Did many of the local women attend? We didn't hear much about it. Loretta said they would run a big feature and pictures in Monday's edition." Jake Moore had taken a rookie reporter to get the scoop while Loretta was off duty.

"It really was a lovely party, dear, but a bit somber. You girls did beautiful work on Nancy's ensemble. It was the talk of the party, other than the speculation about the death of Constance and Reginald's involvement. But really, is Reginald capable of such an act? And if it wasn't him, some were feeling if it was one of us, could there be another killing? I shudder to think. Even the out of town guests were curious and forming opinions."

Daphne's father and brother had been at the investors' meeting at the future site of the resort during the garden party. "Yes, the party made a good impression on the wives. Everyone came away happy." Gerald Huntington-Smythe looked past Daphne's shoulder at Mr. Lewis and nodded hello in his direction. Daphne turned and followed his gaze and looked back to her father. "Who is that sitting with the Lewises?"

"Oh, that's Peter Carson. He's from Los Angeles. He was at the meeting, too. Carson's one of our potential investors. Looks like good news if he's sitting at the banker's table."

All through lunch, Daphne could hear the overbearing Mrs. Lewis singing the praises of Barbara to Peter. He couldn't get a word in edgewise, and Barbara sat dumbly as her mother rambled on. Both Anita and Betsy pouted shamelessly at being overlooked for their older sibling by their mother. Mr. Lewis sat quietly and ate his lunch while the circus went on around him, asking Peter some basic questions about himself that he never got to answer as Nancy kept interrupting with all the great reasons Peter should get to know Barbara. Daphne was so glad to be in her family. She could not believe some of the conversation she overheard from the next table.

"Peter, has Barbara mentioned to you that she had special honors from her teacher in her Future Homemakers of America courses? The teacher remarked that she would make an excellent wife for a diplomat or an executive. We were very pleased but not at all surprised. We know she has perfect manners and qualities." The rumors around town were that the school had never seen any girl so inept, she could burn water. The comment was meant for the Lewises to encourage them to make sure she marries into a family that could support a household staff. "Darling, sit up straight for the man." She could hear Nancy hiss at her slouching daughter. "He's interested in you."

Oh brother, Daphne thought, *if she could hear that, couldn't Peter?* Daphne cautiously glanced over and could see that the handsome stranger seemed very out of place. They made eye contact again and she couldn't help but smile. He did, too.

"Hey Sis! Let's go! Court time's in ten minutes." Lizzie was already up and out of her seat. They excused themselves from the table and went to change for their regular match with James and Robert Worth.

At promptly two p.m., the girls were dressed in their fresh tennis whites. The clay courts were warm, but positioned in such a way that they were shaded by large trees from the hot sun and picked up a gentle ocean cross breeze in the summer. The sisters waited for a couple of minutes, warming up by lobbing the ball between them. James arrived at the court with a small crowd in tow.

"Hi, girls, sorry I'm late." James Worth came loping over. "Robert couldn't make it. He has his extra credit course work due next week. I was looking for a last minute partner." Their focus turned to the entourage. Behind his shoulder, to Daphne's pleasant surprise, she saw the same face she'd been smiling at all day. But behind him, she saw Nancy Lewis and Barbara. "Lizzie, Daphne, this is Peter Carson. He'll be taking up Robert's spot if you'll have him."

Peter was sporting a set of tennis whites and Daphne noticed his well-shaped athletic legs. She could feel herself blushing and thanked her lucky stars to finally get to talk to this man. "Fine by me, James. Hello, Peter, it's a pleasure to meet you." Daphne shook hands warmly with Peter and welcomed him to the courts. "Okay with you, Lizzie?"

"Yep. Let's go! I'm ready!" Lizzie was already bouncing around on the court.

"Mother, can we go now?" Peter's newest fans, Barbara and Nancy, were still around. They were hovering outside the chain link fence. Barbara was whining and wilting in the heat. Nancy was incensed that they'd been tossed over for a tennis match. She wasn't giving up on this man. Oh, no. He was good looking, wealthy and knew nothing of her daughter's unfortunate reputation of being more of a burden than a support. "How come father took Betsy and Anita to the pool and I have to stay here with you? It's not fair! It's so hot. I want to go swimming."

"Barbara, we are staying right here. Let Peter play his little game with his new friends. We'll just be patient for the man. We can order lemonade and wait." They sat down at a nearby set of tables. At the courts, they could all hear Barbara's humiliating moan.

James smirked. Peter started to laugh and shook his head. He muttered to the group, "Thank you for rescuing me. I thought I would be stuck with them all day. I'm glad I had my racket and whites in the car."

"No problem. I needed to find another player. So, do you know them?" James asked as they were taking their position opposite the girls on their side of the net.

"I know Mr. Lewis from the bank—a fine man. I ran into him and his family at the church and they invited me for lunch. I guess Mrs. Lewis has taken a shine to me." Peter had a very boyish grin, almost rakish. Daphne wasn't too sure they would win this match—he was throwing her off her game. Lately, it had been Lizzie who'd been a little distracted by James, but this time it was her turn. She found herself thinking more about the lock of dark hair falling across Peter's forehead than the match.

She stood there grinning for a moment until Lizzie said, "Are we going to play or what? The court's only ours till three!"

"Right then. Ladies serve first," James said as he tossed a ball to Lizzie.

Peter turned out to be a great tennis player, well matched to the other three, and the men won only by one good shot that was actually in bounds at the very back of the court that the girls miscalculated. The group met at the net and shook hands and had a good laugh at a game well played. Daphne walked away to the side of the court, hoping to give James and Lizzie a minute or two to themselves to talk privately. More than once in the past couple of months she'd seen them with their heads together talking quietly. A future pairing of those two would make everyone happy. Then she noticed Peter was coming up to her. And just on the other side of the fence, were Nancy and Barbara, craning to see and hear what was going on now.

"Good game, Peter. Thanks for making it interesting." Daphne was so cool on the outside, you'd never know this fellow was making her weak in the knees, but he was.

"You too. I can't thank you all enough for getting me away from those two. Listen, if you're interested, I'd like to take you out for dinner sometime. I don't know many people here and it would be nice to get to know you." Daphne had a flicker of hesitation, but she liked his direct approach. Why not?

"I'd like that too. Dinner here at the club is always very nice." Daphne felt it was a good place for a first date. Social enough to be in public with a virtual stranger, but still a chance to talk privately and maybe get in a little dancing or a walk along the harbor. After all, this was a man she didn't know at all, but if the banker and her father could vouch for his character, maybe it was time for her to date out of her circle. "Are you in town for long?"

"I've been here for about a month and plan to stay for a while, maybe for good if the opportunities present themselves," he coyly said, while gauging her reaction.

"What kind of opportunities are you meaning?" If they could help keep him around, she was all for it.

"Property development. Santa Lucia is ripe for the leisure life." He glanced around the harbor.

"What do you mean?" Daphne found his interest in her town intriguing.

"It's a great town, close to Los Angeles, especially Hollywood and set to be a glamorous playground—deluxe hotels, resorts and all the businesses that go along with it. It's a very nice and quiet little place now, but it could be so much bigger and better." He paused and caught her eye. "Oh, I must be boring you with all this talk."

Daphne actually found it interesting and wondered what sort of implications could it mean for Poppy Cove—new clients, more trade? "No, not at all. You sound like you are very interested in my town. I like it."

He shrugged his shoulders and replied, "About dinner, the beginning of the week is a little hectic for me, but what about Thursday night?"

"That will be just fine, say at 7:30 in the lounge?" she suggested and he nodded. "Great. I'll leave word for you at the front desk so they know you're my guest."

Then he kissed her hand and turned on his heel. "I look forward to learning more about you, Daphne. See you Thursday." He smiled and left the courts with a brisk walk and a nod of farewell to the Lewis women, who were left as breathless as Daphne, as he turned away from everyone.

CHAPTER SEVEN

Monday morning, Daphne and Margot met at Poppy Cove to go over the new week's production schedule. The front of the store was closed to the public on Mondays, but the back was humming. Mondays were active and exciting, full of plans and colors. They started work on the lining of Mrs. Peacock's dress, pressing and putting out more fall stock, including some beautiful rust-colored wool crepe pleated trousers and matching blouses in lightweight wool/cotton Viyella prints. The girls also got Marjorie and her team started on the new garments—cutting the glamorous holiday wear. They had planned dresses, blouses and skirts in jeweled tones of velvet, silk and moiré satin. The vibrant colors would make a great splash at next month's fashion show.

The entire staff was happily immersed with the tasks at hand. "Oh my, that dark turquoise velvet skirt will be just lovely with the blouses you have planned," Marjorie gushed as they looked over their design board, getting ideas for the upcoming season. The skirt in silk velvet was long, down to the floor in a sweeping A-line, leading up to a high, nipped-in waist. The sketches showed the weight of it swirling and falling gracefully. In the first sketch, it was paired with a crisp, white shirt. A second sketch showed a silk, charmeuse blouse, in a lighter shade than the rich skirt.

"Yes, I think so, too. Let's get ten of the skirts done, broken down in the sizes we have listed here. Then we can start on the blouses. The white is a good basic, so I think we could do double that amount. It can be paired with so many of the designs we have planned. Daphne, what would you think if we did the skirt in that ruby red velvet too?" Margot was holding her swatch card in the air, looking at how the light reflected the cut nap of the fabric.

Daphne had her nose buried in a pile of photographs of new necklaces, pins and earrings that had arrived that morning from a Los Angeles costume jewelry designer. They'd sold many of her pieces before and loved the quality. The paste stones were treated in the settings as well as if they were the real and rarest of gems. Many pieces would compliment their holiday line. "Red's a good choice. This earring and necklace set would be just darling with it." Daphne brought a couple of photos over to show Margot. "The green would be smashing with the turquoise as well."

The morning passed very quickly as the girls were absorbed in the colorful designs. By noon, Daphne had her jewelry order ready to be mailed in and Margot was aware that Marjorie had the new garments well under control. They decided to leave their staff to their work and go for lunch at the tearoom.

Daphne popped on her sunglasses as they stood on the front landing. As usual for a Santa Lucia summer day, the morning fog had lifted, revealing a beautiful blue sky. "You had gorgeous weather for your picnic yesterday!"

Margot closed and locked the door behind her. "Yes, it was great. Not even fog in the morning."

"Did you make your famous fried chicken?" Daphne had never so much as boiled an egg, let alone made a meal, but she loved food and thought Margot's cooking was great.

Margot grinned, "Yes, yes, I did. I made it Saturday night. And the potato salad, too."

Daphne laughed and shook her head. "We had such a busy week! Weren't you exhausted? All I was up to was sitting and drinking with Loretta."

The girls walked down the steps and crossed the street. Margot glanced over to the square. Cove Street was bustling with shoppers, visiting Martin's and the other stores that were open on Mondays. The fountain was lively with children playing near its edges, catching drops on their hands and tossing coins in the pool. Margot shrugged. "I couldn't sit still. There was nothing on television, Tom was working on the case and I kept going over everything in my head."

"I know. It's all anyone could talk about. Lizzie had her theories, too," Daphne laughed. "That girl is crazy. She's been reading those nasty detective rags all summer long. They've been firing up her imagination. She must be sneaking them into the house. If mother knew she was reading them, she'd take them away."

The girls reached the tearoom and went up to the counter to order their lunch. "How was Tom? Could he relax or was his mind on the case?" Daphne said as she and Margot sat down at the table in the sunny bay window front of the Poppy Lane Tearoom. In no time at all, Lana had brought their food over.

"It was really nice. Tom had handed the case over to his partner, so he was able to get his mind off the situation. It's hard with Reginald being so closely connected in the community *and* the prime suspect." Margot took a bite of her tuna salad sandwich. "We went down to the state beach and found a great quiet spot to watch the world go by. How was the club?"

"Great. I met someone new—very handsome!" Daphne had a twinkle in her eye and a smile on her lips. "All thanks to Nancy and Babs Lewis."

"What? How would Nancy Lewis help your love life?" Margot had to hear more.

"By boring a fine young man to death! His name is Peter Carson and he was sitting with the Lewises for lunch. He's a potential investor in the new hotel resort going in on the beach. He said hello to Mr. Lewis and Nancy thought he was a catch for Barbara. They hounded the poor man all day. Luckily, we were short a Worth, so he played tennis with us. And, he asked me out for dinner on Thursday." Daphne coyly smiled.

"Why, you little Trixie! How exciting! I'm glad to see you're over your latest heartbreak of Anthony Fielding." Margot was referring to Daphne's most recent former beau.

"That's well over with. What did I ever see in him?" Daphne's romantic attachments were many and fleeting. She was head over heels and as soon as her feet were back on the ground, the romance was over and onto the next.

"Curly lashes." Margot kidded her friend mercilessly about the revolving male suitors. She'd been with Tom and only Tom since she moved into town.

Daphne smirked and looked out the window. "You know, he'll be the first real man I've ever dated."

Margot looked at her sideways. "What do you mean? I've always known you to have had a full social calendar."

"Oh, I've had plenty of dates, but they were all boys. You know, friends of the family, went to school with them, or set up through friends' cousins, that sort of thing. Peter's different. He's from the city, he's seen the world, made his own money. All the rest have been riding on family coattails."

"Some of the 'boys' you went out with were pretty nice men. I've never heard you complain about how you were introduced to them before. I thought you liked getting the scoop on them."

"Well," Daphne sighed, "It's time for a change. I'm twenty-five years old. I want to pick out my own dates."

"I hope you're going somewhere very public." Margot felt a little guarded at Daphne's new view. She was happy her friend was opening up her circle, but Daphne had this way of going off half-cocked, leaping before looking. "What do you know about him?"

"Goodness! You're worse than my mother, and she thinks this is a fine idea. We'll be having dinner at the club. Besides, father knows of him, and he was sitting with Andrew Lewis. He can't be all that bad."

"So, he's still being approved for you. How is this any different?"

Daphne blushed, a little exasperated. "They didn't set this up. I just hunted around a little. They don't know him that well, just enough to vouch for him." She paused and picked at her sandwich. "He's new to all of us and that's exactly what I want."

Loretta was coming out of the flower shop across the lane. Like Poppy Cove and the rest of the Poppy Lane businesses, the florist was closed on Mondays, but was available for private orders during special circumstances. Daphne waved to her to come join them. Loretta grinned and headed their way.

Margot turned when she heard the tinkle of the bell over the frame as the door opened and Loretta came in, ordered a tea and joined them. "Good to see you, 'Retta. You look so much better today."

"Thank you. Those couple of days' rest helped. It really has been a tragic event for our town. I was just over ordering flowers on behalf of the *Times* for the funeral. They do a wonderful job over there, very tasteful." Loretta sniffled a little and dabbed her eyes.

"Oh yes, they'd done a beautiful arrangement on the Stearns-Montgomery table at the club to honor

Constance." Daphne took a sip of her drink. "Say, who is this Michael Weathers? I forgot to tell you that he came by on Friday, saying he was your replacement. What a horrid little man!" She wanted to make sure Loretta knew about his behavior.

"I've had so many complaints about him. He can be a bit brash and tactless. He's this young upstart from New York City and he seems to think he can teach us a thing or two about reporting. He just doesn't get our west coast ways. The social set was so incensed, the boss sent his eighteen-year-old daughter to cover the Lewis' garden party for me instead of him. We met up on Saturday. She did a great job for a young girl. I would rather see her helping me and send Weathers back to the city." Loretta Simpson loved her work. She loved people and making sure that she gave everyone the publicity they wanted made her feel proud. Years ago, she was one of the best gossip columnists in Hollywood, until she left to join Santa Lucia society. "Sorry if he bothered you. He really should be covering business or the police beat more than the socials."

Margot agreed. "I'm sure his style is good for something, but not for us. Have you heard anything new about the case today?"

Many people were coming in and out of the tearoom, getting their lunches on the run. A few tables were occupied, but nothing very close. Lana brought over Loretta's tea, but couldn't stay to chat, as she was busy with the trade. Loretta looked around to make sure no one was paying attention to their conversation and lowered her voice. "I've heard they may let Reginald out this afternoon. They still want to keep a close eye on him; he is the strongest suspect right now, but they don't have enough evidence to keep him. And, it turns out, so many people saw him throughout the entire evening, there really wasn't an unaccounted moment."

"I'm glad about that," Daphne commented. "I don't think it was him. He's too mild mannered."

Loretta simply shrugged. "You never know. I've heard talk of an affair. Could you believe our Con having dalliances? If it was true, how would that send Reginald off?"

Something else came to Margot's mind. "And what about Nancy Lewis? She's been awfully cold and remote about her rival dying. I would have expected better of her."

Loretta nodded. "I know. She's been spewing some crass things around town. If I quoted half of what she's said in public about Con after the murder, it would certainly kill her social footing!"

The girls sat quietly for a moment. Loretta sipped her tea and shuffled in her seat. She was getting more color in her cheeks. The girls knew this sprite woman as their best connection in town and could read her like a book when she had news. She looked around the room again before continuing. "There's a new twist too. Where was the headmistress on that night? Did you know that she knew Constance when they were young girls?" Loretta smiled with glee when she dropped bombshells on captive audiences.

Daphne and Margot looked at each other. This *was* a new twist. There'd been questions all along about the whereabouts of the headmistress, but it wasn't common knowledge that Constance and Miss Larsen knew each other. Daphne prodded, "Come on, Loretta. 'Fess up. Tell us more. You know you're dying to."

Loretta wasted no time. "Apparently, Constance Stearns and Katherine Larsen went to private school together. Creighton, on the east coast, to be exact. They didn't get along." Loretta paused to keep her audience enthralled. "They were always trying to outdo each other, from poetry contests to track and field. Funny that she ends up as headmistress to Con's school, isn't it?"

"Very. Well, maybe she'll have some answers for the police. It's also funny that she wasn't there for the opening reception. Or was she?" The wheels were turning in Daphne's blonde curls.

"From what I know, they were going to question everyone involved with the school, whether or not they were seen that night. This mystery will not go unsolved," Loretta spoke with authority.

"Speaking about the school, do you have the pictures taken of that tasty new horseman? I'd love to see how we look together!" Daphne's eyes glittered as she enquired. Margot quietly laughed and shook her head, but Loretta bristled and didn't reply.

Daphne gasped, "Ooh, were they that bad?"

"Um, fine, they're fine," Loretta vaguely stammered.

"You know something! Something big, and wrong!" Daphne exclaimed and looked directly at Loretta. "What is it?"

Loretta looked nervous. She ran her finger around the neck of her Peter Pan collar blouse. "Nothing," was her short reply.

Daphne didn't buy it. "C'mon. What is it?" She repeated. Then paused. "They have to do with the murder, don't they? Jake got something, didn't he?"

Loretta's eyes scanned the room quickly and she tried to hush Daphne. "No," she hissed. "But all the same, keep your voice down!" The tearoom was quiet and no one seemed to be paying any attention to their table.

"Okay," Daphne whispered, taking another tack. "Then what's the big deal about the snapshots? Why are you being so mysterious?"

"I can't tell you," Loretta sat up straight and stiffened her mouth.

"But you want to," Daphne teased in a singsong voice. "Just here, to us. Get it off your chest. You'll feel better."

"Daf, I really think you should leave this alone," Margot jumped in. Loretta gave a look of relief.

"Okay, if you don't want to tell us, I guess we should go," Daphne shrugged and started to stand up.

"Ooh, all right!" Loretta was bursting. She had news she knew wasn't fit for public consumption yet, but she couldn't keep it to herself. "This is huge. We're working on this for tomorrow's edition and we don't have all our facts yet."

The girls were at full attention again and staring at Loretta. She continued, "I could get into so much trouble telling you this, so please don't mention it again 'til it's out in the paper." Loretta sighed and began her story. "The photos and the negatives have gone missing from the police station. They were checked in on Friday afternoon at the front desk. Some time between Saturday night and Sunday morning, the pictures went missing."

"Oh my God! Tom didn't mention anything!" Margot was shocked.

"I don't think he knew about it until he went in this morning. Apparently, they were circulated around the department on Friday and Saturday, then checked back in the evidence room Saturday night, just before midnight. Then on Sunday morning, when Detective Riley went to sign them out again, they couldn't be found."

"It must be just awful there!" Margot wondered how Tom was doing. Being lead detective would put a lot of heat on him.

Loretta nodded. "It is. Everyone is blaming everyone else and no one has any clue to what happened. Weathers is there, getting the scoop."

"What about the picture on the front page of Friday's paper? Surely, the paper has more shots that the police can have, don't they?" Daphne was recalling the gruesome photo of Constance's body being discovered.

"That's it. That's the only photo we have now. The police only allowed that one copy of the picture to be released from evidence. We don't even have the negative, they kept it. And, apparently, there's nothing in that one that's helpful, just the murder weapon which was visible, but we all know it was the scarf, so nothing's new there." Loretta paused and folded her arms. "I can't say anything more. Really, I'm sworn to secrecy and I've said too much already."

Daphne patted her on the arm. "Oh, 'Retta, you know all of this is safe with us. We won't talk of it again." Margot nodded in agreement.

Relieved, Loretta smirked and looked directly at Daphne, poised to add a new paragraph to her column. "Speaking of mysteries, I've heard that you were seen playing tennis with a dashing young man at the club yesterday. Do tell. Name, rank and serial number."

"For your information only, not to be splashed all over the *Times*," Daphne flatly stated.

Loretta frowned a little and relaxed her reporter stance. "Alright then. Tell me anyway, I'm curious."

"He's an investor involved with the new hotel. He's Peter Carson and if there is anything more to tell you, you'll know shortly."

Loretta tisked, "Is that all you're going to give me?"

Daphne shook her head and sighed, "The Lewises think very highly of him, especially Nancy for Babs. Oh 'Retta, it was just pathetic. The poor girl's being lobbed like a tennis ball on any unsuspecting victim who doesn't know her poor disposition." Loretta rolled her eyes at Daphne's statement. The selling of Babs was all too well known in such a small place.

"Wow! Look at the time. I've got to go, girls. I take a day or two away and my desk is a nightmare. See you tomorrow at the funeral." Loretta was almost cheerful at the prospect. To her, it was more news. A gathering of people always provided a chance for a new story.

Shortly after Loretta left, the girls were joined by another friendly face. Daniel Henshaw came into the Tearoom and headed straight for Daphne. "Good afternoon, ladies. It's good to see you."

Daphne beamed. "Hi there, Daniel. This is Margot Williams. She's my best friend and also my partner in our shop, Poppy Cove." She indicated Margot and properly introduced the pair to each other. "Have you had lunch yet?" Daphne pointed to the chair that Loretta had vacated, inviting him to sit down.

Daniel pulled the chair closer and positioned himself between the girls. "No, I was just going to get a sandwich and stop by your store. I noticed it wasn't open today. And please, call me Dan." He was focused intently on Daphne.

She loved the way his sandy hair fell over his forehead, lightly shadowing his eyes. *I really wish I could've seen those pictures,* Daphne thought. "We aren't open to the public on Mondays. There's so much other work to do. Why were you coming by the store?" she asked as she sipped on her coffee. Margot just sat and watched the way the two of them talked.

Dan laughed. "To see you, of course. Before things went bad at the school, we talked about a riding date. I'm sorry I couldn't see you sooner, but the police kept us busy on Friday."

Daphne looked at Margot; Margot looked at Daphne and held back a smirk. Two dates with two strangers in one week. Daphne regained her composure as she thought sympathetically about what they must be going through at the Academy. "It must be awful up there at the school. Everyone must be so uncomfortable with the police searching and questioning everyone. I guess the future's uncertain about the academy as well."

"One thing that Charles has said is that the school must go on. He says that's what Constance would have wanted." Dan sighed and brushed the lock of hair off of his forehead. "But yes, it is miserable. As soon as we got the okay, I left for my parents' home near Ojai for the weekend."

The group chatted briefly about the weather and the upcoming funeral. Daphne decided that she would go riding with him on Wednesday in the early evening to watch the sunset from the trails on the mountain ridge.

After Dan left, the girls finished their lunch. Margot teased Daphne mercilessly about her new lovers and the two of them returned to the workroom. The girls honored their word and never mentioned Loretta's top-secret information again. The staff had made great progress on the garments, almost completing Mrs. Peacock's dress up to the first fitting. Marjorie had everything under control, so Daphne and Margot left the tasks under her capable supervision and called it a day. Both of them wanted to have some time to themselves before the funeral tomorrow, and part of it involved contemplating the unmentionable new twist.

CHAPTER EIGHT

The fog had rolled in thick and heavy for Tuesday morning, the day of Constance Stearns-Montgomery's funeral. The skies were grey and somber, reflecting the mood of Santa Lucia. Daphne left her family to say hello to Margot and Tom as they were entering the churchyard. Tom looked so handsome in his full dress police uniform, including his hat. Margot was in black, a demure dress with a slim calf length skirt and a short trapeze jacket. She had a matching small hat with a dotted veil. Daphne greeted them with a hug and a peck on the cheek. She was wearing a navy, short-sleeved, linen shirtdress with a tied fabric belt nipping in her waist. She had on a small cloche hat that was worn close to the head which kept her curly hair in check. They talked briefly and greeted fellow townsfolk for a few minutes and then Daphne joined her family, and Margot and Tom made their way into the church.

More people began arriving at the Community Church around ten thirty for the eleven o'clock service. It was filled to capacity. When Reginald arrived, a mixed murmur of rumors, accusations and compassion circulated through the crowd. Reginald had been released from police custody the previous afternoon and no one knew where the investigation stood. He was still the main person of interest, but there was little to support his presumed guilt. The only reason he was still considered a suspect was because he had the most to lose if Constance was indeed having an affair, and the only man visible to question. It was a flimsy case, as he was seen as a very loving and devoted husband with a strong moralistic reputation in the town.

Reginald Montgomery had literally fallen off the turnip truck into Santa Lucia as a young man. Born in 1908, he grew up as an only child in the Salinas Valley in central California, about 200 miles away. His father, Stewart Montgomery, owned one of the most fertile and largest produce farms in the valley. A kind and gentle man, Stewart got along very well with the new Asian immigrant landowners, and they taught him how to diversify his crops that made his farm very lucrative. Stewart was a progressive man and when he saw opportunities, he took them. Reginald remembered when as a young boy, his father took him on a tour of the sugar beet refinery and explained to him how he had a share in the factory. From the age he learned to read and write, he began helping his father with the record keeping of the farm. He studied the farm diaries of the new crops and helped to keep the books of what was a profitable food to grow and sell. Reginald began to see ways to cut down on expenses and increase profits and, in a simple way that children have, shared them with his father who recognized his talent for nurturing business. Stewart told his son to always be open to new ways of making money from what you know. When too many farmers grew beets, he moved on to exotic crops such as strawberries and broccoli. It kept his produce in demand.

It was easy for his father to see that Reginald, his only son, could do much better for himself out in the world than on the farm. He encouraged him to learn and graduate from high school, something he'd never done. When he heard that there was a good university in Santa Lucia opening up, he grew a few risky crops that were very profitable and he saved the money.

Stewart then announced to his eighteen-year-old son
that he would be on the train to Santa Lucia delivering
that week's produce, and remaining there to attend the
newest campus of the University of California, with his
tuition and board paid in full for the year. Young
Reginald was excited about his prospects and new
adventures, but a little fearful of the move. He knew no
one in the town and had never been away from home or
his family.

Santa Lucia was bustling and growing when
Reginald arrived in 1926. Three years after the major
earthquake had leveled the town, the rebuilding was in
full swing. The university was only two years old, but
had a great campus. Reginald was enrolled in the
business courses and lived in a nearby boarding house
that was occupied by young men like him who attended
the university. School was a good challenge for him,
but he wanted to put the theories into action as he had
done on the farm. When he saw an advertisement
looking for a male general office clerk in the Stearns'
building and supply company, he knew the job was for
him and applied within the hour of its posting.

Robert Stearns liked the boy when he met him. He
was quick and not afraid to share his opinion. He
followed his hunches and looked for results. Even
though the company was looking for a full time clerk
who'd already graduated, Robert hired him right away,
declining other prospective employees. Reginald had
convinced Robert that he could do the work of any full
time man in the evening hours and around his studies,
or he would work for no wages. He knew that he could
learn a lot from Stearns and being new in town, he had
no distractions or any close friends yet. He quickly
proved to be an invaluable asset to the company.

The next few years passed very quickly. Reginald
gained his degree in business while the town grew at a

feverish pitch. He worked hard to keep up with the development. By the early thirties, the reconstruction was slowing down, as they had constructed all they dreamed of and the depression was affecting the whole country. With more time on his hands, Reginald began to take an interest in getting to know the people of his town, deciding he would like to stay and put down his own roots. He always went to the Stearns' estate for Sunday dinner and both Robert and Lillian took great pains in introducing him to the elite of Santa Lucia. They thought of him as another son and looked out for his best interests.

One Sunday in the late spring of 1933, just as Reginald was stepping out of his brand new Buick, he noticed young Constance in the garden. At eighteen, she'd just returned from graduating from school in Boston and this was the first time he noticed she had changed from a girl to a lady. She smiled shyly and their courtship began.

Reginald had great plans to provide for his fiancé. To him, love was security and that meant to be a good provider. Over the next two years, he put his plans into action to create a life that Constance would be accustomed to and that Robert would allow his daughter to marry into. He left the employment of the Stearns to combine all of his skills to forge his own business. His plan was to run a gourmet grocery store that catered to the people who wanted only the best. Reginald knew good produce and how to get it and Santa Lucia had a thriving harbor with excellent seafood. The neighboring inland valleys had wonderful grazing land for cattle—both dairy and beef—so Reginald amassed the greatest sources to fill his store with the best cuts of meat, freshest dairy, as well as fruits and vegetables. He laid out his plan to Robert, who said he would introduce him to Andrew Lewis, the manager at the First Bank of Santa Lucia. Robert liked his business idea and was prepared to back him up with 50 percent of the money he needed. With that kind of endorsement, Andrew Lewis granted the loan for the other half and they were in business. Montgomery's Market was born.

It was a dizzying year for the young man. As he travelled all over the area to sign up the farms for their goods, he made a great name for himself among the farmers. Many knew him as Stewart Montgomery's son, which helped him earn their friendship and trust, securing solid, long-term contracts for the cream of their crops. Even before the store was open, there was great excitement in the town to see what the boy could do.

Montgomery's Market opened in the fall of 1935 and was very popular right from the start. The biggest problem was keeping up with demand, but they soon learned to meet the town's needs. Reginald was truly living up to his desire to gain a solid footing in the Santa Lucia community. As things began to fall into place, his mind turned to getting a home built for his bride to be, Constance. He planned a modest home on a lot on the edge of the downtown core. Just a small house, with two bedrooms and a fireplace, but all the same it was theirs.

In the meantime, Constance was being groomed for the roles of wife and mother—learning how to run and manage a household, and being a public support for her husband. She was on his arm for all of the important social occasions and as part of one of the established families, continued her father's role of introducing him into Santa Lucia society. She was there for the store opening and Reginald gave her the honor of cutting the red ribbon. They were engaged by Christmas of that

year and announced it publicly at the Santa Lucia Yacht
Club's New Year's Eve Party.

The beginning of 1936 was a whirlwind blur, with
the business building, a new house for the couple in the
works and a grand June wedding fit for royalty. The
plans included a guest list of 400 people with the
reception being held at the Yacht Club over the course
of three days. Constance and her five attendants all had
their gowns created at Martin's under the direction of
Marjorie Cummings. It was a beautiful affair for a
promising young couple.

Reginald and Constance settled into a comfortable
married life together rather quickly. He was focused on
his market, keeping it steady through the coming years
of war. As the years went by, it became obvious that
the couple couldn't conceive their own children, so
Constance learned to take it in her stride and helped out
with various philanthropic activities to help war
widows and orphans. They weren't a highly romantic
couple, but always stable and became pillars of the
community. Reginald and Constance were there to help
and to be counted upon, becoming reliable members of
society on their own merits.

Great excitement came to the couple in 1946, the
year after World War II ended. There was a renewed
building boom and Reginald opened up his second
market. He also began trying out a new idea that he'd
heard about from the Midwest—ready-made frozen
food. He ran a contest in the stores to have his
customers make their favorite casserole and dessert
recipes. There were pies and cakes, cabbage rolls, meat
pies and chilies galore, and the winners of the
categories would have their recipes featured as frozen
entrees that would be sold at the stores. It caused a
great frenzy that spurred Reginald onto a new business
prospect. He changed the name of the business to

Montgomery's Fine Foods and made plans to ship and sell the new meals to grocery stores around the country. He built a warehouse facility and hired local people to make the food. He helped to create many new jobs for the returning veterans.

As their good fortune continued to increase, Reginald rewarded his wife and himself with a grander home. He purchased ocean view property above the country club where he could have a large estate created and land for Constance to bring her beloved horses from her parents' property to live and graze on her own home land. Reginald built a fine home for Constance and felt that he'd come full circle, giving his wife the life she grew up with and was very well suited to.

But today was a very sad day for Reginald. He was burying his wife of twenty-one years. She'd seen him grow and build his successful empire and helped him create all that he had. Not normally a very emotional man, he was weary and despondent. He'd aged tremendously over the last few days. As he made his way through to the front of the church, he was aware of the eyes on him, and heard the murmurings. He took his place beside Constance's brother Charles. There was a hush as the gossipy snipes in the crowd realized that Charles didn't believe that Reginald could be guilty, affair or no affair.

"Can you believe that Charles is going to let Reginald sit by him? I've heard all along that she was carrying on with another man. That would certainly give Reginald a reason to do away with Constance. It would ruin his reputation for people to think he couldn't keep his wife happy!" Margot turned around to see Nancy Lewis hissing audibly to a woman she didn't recognize sitting in the pew in front of her. She shot Nancy a brief, but glaring, look to let her know her slanderous comment could be heard three rows away.

Nancy grimaced and continued. She had piqued the interest of the woman she was speaking to and Nancy loved an audience. "I think she got just what she deserved. Always parading around town like a peacock, that school was the final straw. I, for one, think she needed to be brought down a notch. To think she had any idea how to raise girls, without any children of her own. Why, I wouldn't let my girls near that place, even before all of this." At that point, Margot stopped listening and just shook her head. That woman had no tact. It was so sad that her true nature was so bitter.

Pastor Gregory began the service about ten minutes late, as it took that long to assemble the large crowd of mourners. There was standing room only in the church. Charles and Reginald spoke lovingly of their wife and sister, while Mayor Stinson gave a heartfelt eulogy about Constance and her impact on the community. Late August was sweltering in Santa Lucia, with the fog trapping in the air and making it even more muggy and oppressive. It was hard to sit still inside the small, airless building. Many of the attendees were fanning themselves with the flyers that Pastor Gregory had placed in the bible racks advertising next Sunday's service, a sermon on the evils of gossip.

By the time the church service was over, there was a cool breeze coming off the ocean. It gently moved the clouds and fog, and became a little brighter. Charles and Reginald leaned on each other as they walked out of the church. Constance's coffin was lifted into the hearse and the mourners were making their way to the cemetery.

As people gathered waiting for the burial ceremony to commence, little pockets of conversation began to form. Loretta, in her perfectly fitting dark brown peplum suit with matching hat and pumps, was making the rounds with her notepad. She wanted quotes about the dearly departed for tomorrow's column.

"Constance will be sorely missed by our community. She helped so many people. Her efforts made such a difference to our hospital." Sarah Browning was very eloquent and well mannered with her thoughts on the deceased, who had helped with the Santa Lucia Hospital Charity Ball. Constance worked tirelessly every year with Sarah to organize the black tie affair that followed the Poppy Cove Fall/Holiday Fashion Show. Their efforts to create a glamorous evening in September at the Yacht Club were memorable and something everyone looked forward to. The previous year's event was talked about all year until only the excitement of a new one coming up could top it. As Loretta walked away, she made a few notes on Sarah's dress, a lovely new chemise style in charcoal grey that was close to the body, but loose fitting. The fine handkerchief linen must have felt quite cool in the warm sun.

"I see the Keystone Cops are in full force. We'd all be safer here if they weren't." Loretta heard the sniper shot coming from the right, just in front of her. Of course, it was Nancy and she wasn't done yet. "They'll bungle this whole thing up. They've lost the picture; who knows what they've done with the rest of the evidence. And look at that! The man in charge is too busy talking up his girl to be catching a killer."

Through the crowd, Loretta couldn't see the face of the woman Nancy was talking at. To her left, at a distance she saw Tom and Margot. Margot was making small talk to some of her customers. Tom, on the other hand, was watching like a hawk. Every now and then, he discreetly motioned to one of the officers in uniform who were standing on guard around the outer edges. Then they'd make a note or two, or move a little closer without alarming anyone. *Bungling, my eye!* Loretta thought. *She knows nothing.* She switched direction to find another, more appropriate remark.

Loretta walked over to Franklin Matthews, one of the school trustees, and also a lifetime resident of Santa Lucia who knew Constance and her family very well. "Mr. Matthews, would you care to give a quote about Mrs. Stearns-Montgomery for tomorrow's paper?" She saw a flicker of discomfort cross his face. "Maybe something about the future of the Academy, perhaps?"

He relaxed a little. "Certainly." He cleared his throat and rocked back on his heels while he thought of what he wanted to say. "Stearns Academy will go on. Constance and her father were dedicated to creating the school in Lillian's name. Charles will see to that continuing. The school is a fine asset to our community that will be here for many generations to come." Matthews nodded and walked away.

One more should do it, Loretta thought. She scanned the sea of faces and spotted the Mayor's wife. "Hi Elaine. I'm making a tribute to Constance in tomorrow's column. Would you like to add something?"

Elaine's soft eyes were misty. "I'd love to. What would you like to know?"

"She did a lot of work for the historical society, didn't she?"

Elaine smiled as she recalled Constance's contributions. "Yes, I don't know where she found the time, but she volunteered many hours to the town archives and museum. She was always willing to share photos and stories from her family's own past. Their presence was so important to our town. I don't know what we're going to do without her." Loretta nodded and made her notes. Pastor Gregory was gathering everyone to the gravesite. She snapped her notepad shut and joined the crowd.

Loretta was discreetly observing the groups of mourners at the gravesite, looking for more quotes when the burial was finished. The faculty, staff and board members of the newly formed Stearns Academy were clumped together, a little awkward and standing to the back. Most of the staff were new to the area and each other, and barely knew the Stearns or Montgomerys beyond their history. Their presence was visibly out of obligation and respect. Someone at the back of the group caught Loretta's attention—a rather tall, slim, middle-aged woman, hunched and hiding behind a pleasant-looking, matronly type and a slightly plump man. She was crying very hard and uncontrollably, her shoulders shaking—standing alone. The graying matron in front of her seemed surprised, but all the same turned to try to offer the other some comfort and friendship. *There's a story there.* Loretta's instincts kicked in and she made a note to herself to find out who these people were. Just as the Pastor's last prayer was given, she noticed out of the corner of her eye, that the tall, weepy figure had turned and left in a big hurry before the rest of the crowd began to move. Loretta also thought she saw a slightly shorter and stockier shadow behind one of the oaks. As she turned to look, the shadow was gone. Midday heat can play funny tricks on the grief stricken.

After the cemetery service, most of the people gathered at the Montgomery estate for refreshments. It was a grand house with a courtyard fountain and a breathtaking view of the ocean and coastal islands. Martinis and punch were flowing. The libations loosened up the crowd and people were mingling a little more socially. Loretta saw an opportunity to learn more about the disappearing mystery crier when she saw Daphne and Margot talking to the older, plump woman who obviously knew her.

"Daphne, Margot, can you introduce me to your friend? Maybe she'd like to say something for the *Times*." Loretta walked over and greeted the source of her curiosity with a handshake and a smile.

"Of course," Daphne replied. "Miss Loretta Simpson, this is Mrs. Jane Peacock. She's moved here recently with her husband, Herbert."

"Welcome to Santa Lucia, Mrs. Peacock. Care to say a few words and get a mention in the local paper? A quote in the *Times* society column is a great way to become known to all the right people in town," Loretta grinned cunningly at Jane, with pen poised, as Mrs. Peacock blushed.

"Oh, I don't know. What would someone like me have to say in the papers?" Jane demurred.

"From my understanding, you're with Stearns Academy, right? So, you could talk about that."

"Well," Jane pondered, "My Herbert is the history teacher at the Academy. We moved here from Portland over the summer."

Loretta gestured to Daphne and Margot. "I see you've already met two of the most important ladies in town."

"Yes. My son is getting married in Texas at Christmastime, and Margot is making my dress for the ceremony," Jane beamed.

"Wow! You must have pulled some strings to get in. Our girl Margot has quite the waiting list, especially for new clients," Loretta commented. Margot rolled her eyes. She was always busy, but loved taking on new customers.

"No. I just called and they made me an appointment." Jane shrugged and then sighed. "I guess mentioning that Mrs. Stearns-Montgomery recommended Poppy Cove to me helped." Tears welled up in her eyes. "She was so kind and helpful to all of us. She really made us feel welcome in the community. I don't know what we're going to do without her."

Loretta made a few notes. "Yes, she surely affected everyone." She paused and gauged Jane's face while she made the next remark. "I noticed one woman in particular seemed very distraught."

Jane's jaw became tight. "That was Headmistress Larsen."

"I thought that's who it was. Is she always so weepy?" Loretta enquired.

Jane shook her head. "No, she's normally such a cold fish and always having words with everyone associated with the school, including rows with Mrs. Stearns-Montgomery. We don't have more to do with her than we have to, my Herbert and I."

Loretta felt she was making great progress on her news angle. "So, they didn't get along very well." It was more of a statement than a question. Loretta thought about the two women's history.

"No, they were always at odds with each other. They were on opposite sides of everything, sometimes just for the sake of arguing, I think. I first met them when my Herbert was being interviewed for his post. Mrs. Stearns-Montgomery was very nice and stood up for hiring him, but Miss Larsen was indifferent, if not downright rude," Jane huffed.

Loretta glanced around and moved in closer. "I don't see her here at the house."

"No, she's not here," Jane stated. "Headmistress Larsen isn't very social." There was an ominous pause.

Daphne and Margot stood and sipped their drinks, watching the intriguing conversation. Loretta pressed on further. "Yes, I've heard she wasn't seen at the opening ceremony either. That's pretty odd, don't you think?"

"Suspicious, if you ask me," Jane conspired. "It was expected of all of us to be there, especially her."

"Rumor has it that she hasn't been around at all. Including that the police have been looking for her. I'm surprised she even showed up for the funeral."

Jane thought for a moment before she spoke cautiously. "I guess she felt she had to."

Loretta shook her head, "Obligation didn't seem to bother her before."

"I think the death affected her more personally," Jane alluded.

Loretta's eyebrow went up. "In what way?" As she asked, Jane's face became red. "She was so upset. Did she say something to you?"

Jane was flustered and stammered. "I'm sorry. I can't say anything more; I promised. I've said too much already. Miss Simpson, you must promise me that none of what I've said here gets out to anyone, especially in the paper. It could cost us my husband's job and we just love it here." Jane folded her arms and took one step back, pleading with her eyes, but firm in her stance all the same.

"Please don't worry, Jane." Margot put her hand on one of Jane's folded arms and reassured her. "Loretta may be a bulldog at times, but she also has a great deal of discretion and wouldn't put half truths or hearsay in her column, would you, Loretta?"

Loretta shook her head and put down her pen. If she got a lead from this conversation, she would have to dig a little deeper to substantiate the details. Jane Peacock could not be her 'source,' reliable or not. "There now, nothing to worry about, you're among friends." With Loretta's words, Jane became a little more at ease.

Margot faced Jane and looked directly into her eyes. "But Jane, if you have any information that could be important to the case, for Constance's sake, you need to tell the police and soon, before you forget the details."

Jane met her gaze and nodded. The women's conversation became brighter and more pleasant as they talked about more lighthearted matters, such as the move from Portland and the upcoming Texas nuptials. Over Jane's shoulder, Daphne caught a glimpse of Dan Henshaw. He smiled and made his way over to the group. She caught herself smiling back at him, admiring how well his athletic body filled out his slim black suit.

"Sorry to interrupt, ladies. May I have a word with you, Daphne?" Dan acknowledged the group, but only had eyes for her.

"Yes, of course." She glanced around and saw that there was a seat in a bay windowed alcove. They walked over and he motioned for her to sit down.

"Are we still on for tomorrow? I thought we could meet up at the school stables around six," he suggested as he sat down closely beside her. "If you don't mind, there are a couple of horses that belong to the Academy that haven't been ridden much lately, with all that's been going on. I thought that maybe you wouldn't mind riding one of them and tell me what you think. I could use a female perspective on their behavior, seeing as how they're going to be ridden by young girls." He took a sip of his drink. "As long as you don't mind riding a horse other than your own."

She was flattered. "No, that sounds great, but seven is better for me. I can take you on some trails up above the school grounds. It's beautiful up there and close by."

He agreed and they parted. Dan went back to the group of other male Academy employees and Daphne strolled back over to Margot, Loretta and Jane. Their conversation came to a halt as they all looked at her. "What?" she chirped. The three smirked and giggled. Loretta was thinking of a romance scoop, Jane was thinking of a wedding match and Margot was just pleased that Daphne was happy.

"Are you ready to go?" Tom asked as he placed a hand on Margot's shoulder.

"Almost." Margot introduced Jane to Tom. "She might have some information about the case for you."

"Well, yes," Jane hesitated. "But I don't want to talk about it here."

Tom fished out of his jacket pocket a business card and gave it to her. "Why don't you come by the station tomorrow morning?"

Jane took his card and nodded. With that, the group dispersed. Jane went to find her Herbert, Daphne met up with her family and Loretta went fishing for more bites. After Tom and Margot said good-bye to their friends, they went up to both Charles and Reginald. As Tom shook Reginald's hand, he assured him that they would solve the case and make sure justice was served. Margot was happy to get out of there. It was claustrophobic with grief, even with the ocean breezes and summer sun.

Tom and Margot went back to her house and sat on her front porch swing, drinking lemonade. They laughed and relaxed, and talked about nothing for a while, but the murder of Constance still weighed heavily on their minds. Before long, Margot brought up Headmistress Larsen. "I wonder what Jane will tell you about the headmistress tomorrow? The two of them talked about something at the funeral. Jane commented to me that the crying jag was completely out of character for her." Margot sat up and looked at Tom. "Did you know that Constance and Katherine

Larsen went to school together?" She was hoping that she might actually have one up on him this time. He was always more in the know than she was about the people in the town, given the nature of his career.

"Yes, we have complete background reports on all of the staff at the Academy." Tom was careful with how much he would discuss about the case. Only common knowledge could be shared. A breach of confidence could cause problems and all Tom wanted to do was find out the true killer's identity. Katherine Larsen was a hard one to pin down. As she was leaving the cemetery in a rush, Tom had a couple of undercover men follow her and bring her into the station for questioning.

Margot recalled snippets of conversations she'd heard earlier in the day. Katherine Larsen wasn't visible at the opening, hadn't been staying at the school and no one had heard from her. The general reaction was surprise to see her at the funeral. Margot's wheels were turning. "It doesn't look good for her, does it? The secretive behavior appears bad to begin with, then she can't be reached, she doesn't show up for one of the most important days of the school and she's acting out of character at the funeral from what people are saying." Margot was listing off points on her fingertips. "And, she and Con had a long time rivalry. Maybe her disappearance was all about avoiding the police. Sounds like she's the guilty one, the more I think about it." Margot was somewhat relieved when she realized they might have caught the killer.

"There's a lot to consider," Tom sighed as he scratched his head. When it came to work, Tom saw everything in black and white, fact and fiction. "But it's all just speculation at this point. We need to stick to the facts and hear what she has to say. If she has anything to be guilty about, we'll get it out of her."

"There are so many rumors swirling around." She paused before asking, "Is it true that the photos have gone missing?"

"Yeah," he admitted. "They turned the station upside down on Sunday. Jenkins returned them to the evidence room Saturday night—he personally signed them in. Then on Sunday morning when Riley went to sign them out again they couldn't be found."

"Could someone else have checked them out overnight and left them on their desk?"

Tom shook his head. "No, that was considered, but the case was put to bed for the night. Two rookies worked the night shift and it was quiet," Tom stated, replaying the facts he'd already gone over many times at the station.

Margot played with the water condensing on the outside of her glass. "So that means it was someone from outside the department." Her eyes grew wide and she looked at Tom as she jumped to her conclusion, "Could the mysterious Katherine Larsen be both a murderer and a thief?"

Tom sputtered, choking on his lemonade. "Anything else at this point is confidential. I can't discuss it further." He was surprised at her focus and involvement in the murder case. "Besides, you usually don't want to hear anything about my work. Since when have you been more interested in crime than fashion?"

"I don't know," she shrugged. "Maybe it's because it's the first time in my life that something so violent has happened to someone I know. Constance was one of my best customers and I also liked her. I want to see the killer caught and all of us safe, I guess," Margot sighed.

Tom drew her close and kissed the top of her head. "Don't worry, darling. We'll get to the bottom of this, I promise you." He finished his lemonade and set his glass down. "I really should be getting back to the station. There's a lot more work to do. Now stay safe and lock your doors when you go to sleep. I'll call you tomorrow at the shop and try not to think too much about this. You've got a career to run, my girl," he smiled, gave her a kiss good-bye and went back to work.

CHAPTER NINE

Daphne was the first to enter Poppy Cove on Wednesday morning. She got in bright and early around seven thirty with coffee and a Danish. It was her turn to merchandise the shop's front window. The girls took turns on the last Wednesday of each month. Although the murder of Constance hadn't been solved yet, Daphne felt the desire to move on, to bring a fresh light to the sad town. Doing the window would be wonderful for her today. She sat in one of the chairs in the shop, sipping her coffee, and looking around at the colorful racks of clothing, thinking about what would look grand and new for the fall season. She thought about what autumn meant to her. Although the climate was very mild and moderate, it was visible in the surrounding hills that the trees were changing. With the autumn harvest crops of apples and grapes, it was the richest time of the year. The light was different, too. Crisper days, lots of reds and oranges, golds and greens turning to brown. And the start of school. *What will happen with Stearns' Academy?* she thought. *Will they open? Will it be later? And what really happened up there?* She shook her head and brought herself back to the store. It's for our boys in blue to handle, not me. *I have a shop to help run and a new family member on the way. And,* she blushed, *two new men as well!* As excited as she was at the prospect of romance in her life, she wanted to make sure she played it low key with her friends and family. They teased her mercilessly over her boyfriends. *I can't help it,* she thought, *I love*

love. I love the prospect of love. She sighed and got back to the task at hand.

Daphne closed the curtains and began taking out the current display in the window. They always closed the drapery when they changed displays.   Naked mannequins were distasteful and the act of mystery behind the curtains always created drama and attracted attention to the change of scene. She put the madras plaid, turquoise and peach, sleeveless blouse that tied in the front with the matching, lively, turquoise, shantung clam diggers and headscarf aside for Mrs. Marshall, who had been in every week since seeing the ensemble in the window and pleaded with the girls to hold the display outfit for her which was exactly her size. They would call her later today so she could purchase it and take it home. Mrs. Marshall couldn't wait to wear it at her family's Labor Day picnic.   It seemed that everything they put in the window lately generated great interest and brought people into the shop. That was the last of that outfit. The rest had sold out two weeks ago. The other mannequin was wearing a dress that looked like it could attend a barbeque too. It was a gaily printed sundress, with a low cut, square neckline, and an open back with straps and a wide mid-calf skirt and cinched-in waist in navy cotton. The reason why it was particularly appealing was the summery all-over apple print that made it so fun. They had done it in a seashell pattern in July that sold out in days. This copy was the last one left and had been requested by Mrs. Morgan, who tried it on the day before it went in the window, and decided to purchase it two days later and, happily, waited until the display was taken down. Daphne placed the dress on a hanger beside Mrs. Marshall's outfit.

As the fall always made Daphne think of going back to school, she figured out a smart look that would be great for both teachers and secretaries. It was a flannel suit made of a light, tropical wool in dusty gray with cuffed, three-quarter sleeves. The rounded neck had a pointed collar and buttoned up the front (but looked great left open), with a narrow waist and short peplum and was a little longer and rounded in the back. The matching slim pencil skirt went down past the knee and had princess seaming in the front and back with small, kick pleats from the knees down. It was very well shaped, but not constricting or immodest. It was practical, but feminine. She paired it with a red blouse that had a sweetheart neckline and slightly puffed sleeves that still fit under the jacket well. She grabbed a hat from the back—a new, grey felt one done in a feminine version of a fedora with a slightly, turned down brim that gave it a mischievous look. For the other model, she continued on with the grey and red theme. She took the slim-legged, ankle-length trouser with a flat front, side zipper and faced waistband in the same grey flannel and matched it with a beautiful, paisley-print, silk charmeuse blouse. The shirt was in autumnal reds, golds, oranges and greens with long, narrow sleeves. The bodice was constructed in a surplice style with a wide sash that knotted and trailed down the side. She complemented the outfit with a smart, red, leather clutch purse and red, spectator pumps that really tied it together. She got out a garland of paper leaves in fall colors and hung it up behind the mannequins and strew some individual ones on the floor of the window. Finally, she pulled open the drapes and stepped outside to critique her work just as Margot arrived at the store.

"That looks great, Daf," Margot commented. "The oranges and reds really brighten up the grey flannel. Good colors for the fall. It almost makes you feel like there is a chill in the air." It was at least eighty degrees already this morning and the hot sun was shining down out of the late summer sky.

"Thanks. I like a change of seasons. We get to put something new in the window." Daphne brushed a curl off of her forehead. "How was your night? Did you tell Tom that Headmistress Larsen and Constance had a past?" The girls couldn't stay off the topic for very long.

They ventured back into the store and started opening up for the day. "Briefly. He already knew about that. They took Katherine Larsen in for questioning after the funeral. He was talking with her last night."

"I would've liked to have been a fly on the wall for that meeting," Daphne remarked as she adjusted the tilt of the mannequin's fedora. "I'm dying to know what went on there. Given what's been said about her nature, her behavior was really odd. I wonder where she's been all this time. And, if she's not guilty, why has she been hiding?" Her face looked like a huge question mark

"I know. I'm curious, too. Tom gave me heck last night for getting too involved in the case, but I can't help it." Margot turned the door sign from *Closed* to *Open*. "It's hard not to jump to conclusions with all the gossip in this town. When Tom calls later, I'll ask him if he can tell me anything."

"Why would you ask him? The police are always the last to know," Irene demurred as she slipped in from the back.

The comment stopped Daphne in her tracks. "What do you mean by that?"

Irene strolled nonchalantly over to the counter and set her purse down behind it. "Well, if you want to know anything, the word's on the street. The cops, they get it later." As she spoke, she challenged Margot with her eyes.

The comment didn't phase Margot. She was used to Irene's catty remarks. She just kept on making up her schedule for the day. She went to the back and greeted Marjorie and the girls. They were discussing the funeral and the gossip surrounding the death. Margot understood their need to express their feelings, but they had a full day's work ahead of them. She discreetly glanced over to Marjorie, who caught on and helped her refocus the group. It was hard, knowing that a friend and good customer was gone, but they were still there and had paid their respects. Even though the murder hadn't been solved, they had plenty of work to do for the upcoming fall/holiday line and fashion show. It was time to move on.

And that was exactly what Nancy Lewis apparently wanted to do. She came in early, just after opening to purchase hats, gloves and purses for Betsy and Anita to take with them to Boston. They were leaving for Lord's on Friday on their very first flight. The girls needed some good basics to get them through the fall social season at school. Daphne showed Nancy some leather clutch purses in grey, navy, black and red patents, and three different hats—a soft cloche that came in navy and red, a sweet little beret in black, as well as the new grey fedora in the window. She picked out a couple of necklace and earring sets as well. Nancy decided to purchase duplicates in all of them, so the twins wouldn't have to share. She was in a very brisk but happy mood, getting all her errands done.

"It's about time this town forgot Constance. Other Santa Lucians are important, too. I, for one, am happy to see her dead." Nancy looked at her list and was checking off the items as Irene was packaging up her accessories. She glared at Nancy for the remark. It was callous even by Irene's sharp-tongued standards. Nancy looked up at Irene. "What?"

Surprisingly, it was Daphne who spoke up first. Usually she let others' thoughtless remarks pass by her without a ruffle, but this was even too much for her to let go. "Nancy, that's a pretty cruel comment even for you to make. Constance isn't even cold in her grave yet and the killer's still on the loose. Don't you have any compassion, if not for Constance herself, then at least for her family?" Nancy's tasteless behavior was becoming embarrassing to be around. The girls were having a hard time respecting her, even though she was one of their best clients and well-known in town.

"I don't have time to discuss this. The girls need to get to Lord's." Nancy realized she'd gone too far and became flustered. "Besides, I'm just being honest. That's how I feel," she shrugged. "Now, may I have my package?" Irene handed it over, and just like that, Nancy started to run out the door. She was in such a hurry that she bumped into Jane Peacock coming in and almost knocked her over. "Watch where you're going, you inconsiderate oaf!"

Jane looked at the frantic woman and stepped out of her way. She was speechless and turned to stare at the retreating figure.

Daphne walked over to Jane. "Are you all right?" she said, taking her by the arm and leading her to the salon.

"Yes, I'm fine, I think. No broken bones or bruises," but Jane did seem a bit rattled. "Who was that? I'm sure I've seen her before." Nancy's frequently brusque manner affected people. It got her noticed.

"That's Nancy Lewis, the banker's wife, and long-time resident of Santa Lucia. She was at the funeral

yesterday. Her behavior can be memorable." Daphne
settled Jane down with a cup of tea.

"I did see her yesterday, but I've seen her
somewhere else. She looked different. I can't place
her." Jane still looked perplexed.

"She's very well known around town. Maybe you
saw her at the Yacht Club, or her picture in the society
pages?"   Daphne sensed that the recognition was
important to Jane and kept on the topic.

Jane thought carefully for a moment. "No, we don't
belong to the club and I haven't looked at a paper since
we've moved here. We've been so busy, I've hardly
left the school grounds since arriving," she sighed and
her face relaxed. "Well, maybe I'm just mistaken. She
just looks familiar to me, you know how that is."

Margot brought the lining of Jane's dress into the
showroom, followed by Marjorie carrying pins,
notebook, and measuring tape around her neck.
Marjorie's blonde hair mixed with grey was swept up in
a bun with a couple of loose curls framing her face.
She pushed up her glasses from the end of her nose and
smiled at Jane. "Here you are, Mrs. Peacock—the first
fitting of your new dress!"

Margot led Jane into the largest fitting room, the one
that was a room to itself. It had three-way mirrors, a
chair for a companion, and space for the women to
work in privacy. Margot took the garment out of its
protective cover. "This is just the lining of your dress.
It's the closest fitting piece of your ensemble, so we
make this first and check the fit. That way, if we need
to make any adjustments, they'll be corrected here
before we cut into the more costly fabric. It helps it
look much better, too." The lining was in an intense
French blue. The dress shell had no sleeves and was
cut on the bias, draping beautifully from the bodice
below the bust in a gentle A-line silhouette to just

below the knee. The jacket lining had complete sleeves and fit well, but they decided to let it out a half inch at the back of the underarm seams for comfort. Mrs. Peacock was very pleased. It was different from anything she'd ever owned, but suited her to a T.

"Oh, girls, this is just wonderful. You've made me look so glamorous. I'm going to outshine the bride!" Jane did a girlish twirl. Her eyes shone when Margot showed her the rhinestone buttons for the jacket. Margot and Marjorie were very happy.

Daphne came into the room with a matching small hat, clutch purse and gloves "Margot, you and Marjorie have done it again. Jane, you'll look so beautiful."

"Glasses!" chimed Jane.

"No, I don't think they would be a good accessory piece, too much clutter at the face. You don't wear them, do you?" Daphne was making notes of the pieces to set aside for the outfit.

"No, not me. I don't wear glasses, but that's what was different with that Lewis woman. She was wearing horn-rimmed glasses and a floppy hat at the opening ceremony." Jane was very relieved that she'd figured it out.

The group was silent for a moment. Then Margot shook her head. "Oh, that couldn't have been her. She wouldn't have set foot on the school grounds. She was adamantly against the Academy bearing the Stearns' name. Besides, her girls won't be attending the school. There was a mix-up with the registration and she was very miffed about it." Margot was dismissing the notion with sound, logical points. But as Daphne listened, she watched Jane's reaction and wasn't too sure. "And, she doesn't wear glasses and I don't think I've ever seen her in a floppy hat."

"Oh, yes, I know it was her." Jane's chin was firm as she nodded. "It's her hair. She had a couple of red curls peeking out from under the brim that she kept trying to tuck under." Jane was becoming more confident as she remembered more. "She was in a dark green, almost black, suit and ballerina flats. She looked so out of place on that hot evening."

"I don't remember anyone like that in the crowd." Margot was still skeptical. In the two and a half years that she'd known Nancy, she'd never seen her out of heels or in a floppy hat.

Jane was insistent. "She wasn't in the crowd. When my Herbert and I were walking from our residence on the school grounds to the main building, we saw her lurking around the back near the bushes. We commented to each other that the people around here seem to act a little strange." She blushed. "Present company excluded, of course, but we did find that odd. She didn't seem to notice us. We just kept walking to the front of the school, where everyone else was."

"Have you mentioned this to anyone?" Daphne had a sneaking suspicion that this might have some meaning to the case.

"I forgot all about it until I saw her now. I've had so much on my mind with all that has been going on—our move, the new school year, the funeral, our son's wedding. Say, you don't think... ." Her eyes widened.

Time stood still as the women pondered the situation. Could Nancy be so heartless as to murder Constance? Margot spoke first. "Have you spoken with Tom yet this morning?" she questioned as she recalled their conversation at the funeral.

"No," said Jane. "I was planning to go to the station right after I left here. Ooh, I wish I had remembered this sooner. It might have helped the case." Jane fretted.

"Now, now Mrs. Peacock, it's just good that you recalled it now," Marjorie soothed. She turned her gently by the shoulders, back towards the mirrors. "Don't you look lovely?"

Jane started to beam again and the ladies turned a little more critical of the work. They made a few more minor adjustments, a couple of small darts in the jacket to fit the back of the neck better, and a quarter inch taken up in the dress between the neckline and armhole on the right side to allow for Jane's slightly sloping shoulder. Once everyone was satisfied with the look, Jane got changed and the girls set up her next appointment. As soon as she left, Margot called Tom, letting him know that Jane Peacock was on her way to the station and had some new details concerning the case. They also made a date for dinner the next evening.

The girls got on with their day, making slower than usual progress, as once again all of them were pre-occupied with the murder case. The thought of Nancy or someone who appeared to look like Nancy lurking around just before the murder was unnerving. Everywhere one looked there seemed to be a possible murderer. A mysterious man, a mysterious woman and where was Katherine Larsen in all of this?

CHAPTER TEN

Daphne arrived at the school grounds just after seven. Everything was new—the tender shrubs that hadn't yet formed a full hedge surrounded the black asphalt and white painted lines in the parking lot. After she gave herself a quick once over in the rear view mirror, she raked a couple of errant curls back into place, and was satisfied that her hair was not the worse for wear from her ride down in her convertible. All she needed was a little dab of lipstick. She did so and got out of the car.

There were a couple of other cars around which surprised Daphne. She figured that the grounds would be deserted, but that was not the case. She could see a few people milling about, mainly on the paths by the gardens and the cliff on her left. From a distance, she didn't recognize anyone. She figured that they must be people associated with the school. Looking at the Academy buildings gave her a chill. The police tape and any evidence of the crime that had occurred had been removed and left the buildings looking formal and austere, ready for classes to begin. She shook her head to clear her thoughts and reminded herself of why she was there.

The crunch of the gravel path that cut between the academic buildings and sports lawns under her riding boots brought her thoughts of happiness back. It was still beautiful, although more tamed than the rugged fields of grasses and wildflowers that used to grow there. Further to her right, she looked beyond the manicured playing fields and saw the living quarters and dormitories for the faculty and students. The dorms looked empty, but there were many people whom she figured must have been teachers and such, sitting outside their houses, mingling and visiting with each other. Daphne thought about how tragedy can bring people together. 'It'll make them a tight knit group, good for the school. Constance would've liked that.'

Almost straight ahead, Daphne saw the stables and other equestrian outbuildings. And Dan Henshaw walking around with a couple of saddled horses. He looked very attractive in his riding boots, jeans and a lighter denim shirt. He was fit and tanned, with his blonde hair falling casually into place. She looked down at her own clothes—also a pair of jeans, well fitted to her slim but feminine figure, and a red and white gingham blouse with the sleeves rolled up and knotted at the waist. Daphne smiled and was glad that she'd worn what she did, even if her mother did scold her for leaving the house in jeans to meet a man. She had suggested a sundress and shawl. "Inappropriate for horse riding, Mother," she'd replied as an easy dismissal of the notion. Daphne didn't even know if this was a real date, or just a friendly ride in the hills. Her mother was a bit old fashioned for her and didn't even consider that grown men and women could be friends.

"Hi, there! Beautiful evening for a ride, isn't it?" Dan said as Daphne approached him.

"Yes, it's perfect!" There was a light breeze and the sun was still high in the summer sky, giving plenty of time to hit the trails. She walked closer and patted the neck of one of the horses, a pretty light brown one that nickered softly as she touched it. "They're lovely animals."

He handed the mare's reins over to her. "This is Shadow. She's a four year old, quarter horse and very gentle." Daphne approved and so did Shadow. As Daphne took the reins, the horse gently nuzzled her way. "She likes you."

"Nice choice. Who do you have here?" she asked, referring to the horse Dan kept, a beautiful, black gelding just slightly bigger than Shadow.

"Licorice. He's six and a little more rambunctious. He's for a more experienced rider, a good horse for the older girls," he commented.

Daphne peered over his shoulder and caught a glimpse into the stable, seeing the other horses. "How many does the school have?"

"Ten, but we also have extra room for some of the students to board their own horses, especially if they're competitive riders. The ones that the Academy owns are all quarter horses. They're usually the most even-tempered, with still some spirit." Licorice snorted and stamped his front hoof. Dan gently pulled on the bridle.

She looked around the grounds. "It's a nice set up around here." There were three buildings, attractively designed and landscaped in a ranch style. They were at the foothill of the easy, sloping trail range that led up from the ocean, further into the hills.

"Yeah, it's sort of on its own," Dan replied as he was making sure the straps on Licorice's saddlebags were secure.

"Do you live on the grounds with the rest of the staff?"

"In a way." He motioned to the stand-alone cabin near the stable building. It was a small rancher, neat and compact with a front porch and flowers blooming in planters along the railing. "That's my cabin. I have to be near the horses."

A Hispanic man passed by. He tipped his hat in Daphne's direction as he walked into the stables. "You don't take care of all of these horses on your own, do you?"

"No, I'm the only one who lives up here, but I have three workers to help out. All are local boys and they're good guys, not afraid of a little hard work." Dan looked up in the sky. "We should hit the trails if we want to get some riding in before sundown."

"Good point." Daphne mounted her horse with ease. She'd been around them all her life. "Have you been up on the trails yet?"

"No, it's been so busy getting everything settled in here. I've heard they're nice. Easy riding, well trodden paths with great views. Do you know them well?"

"Yes, before the school was here, it was just vacant land and everyone would ride their horses all over the ridge." She pointed up over the incline ahead as they started to climb. "My place is just on the other side of here."

They were riding up the grade, directly behind the stables, following the dirt trail that was well traversed. The view was breathtaking. Towards the west and south was the Pacific, to the east was the downtown core and to the north they could see the top of the gentle mountain range. All around them the sky was starting to turn golden from blue, as the sun was descending.

As they loped along the grasses and low-lying shrub, Dan carried on the conversation. "So you have your own horse?"

"Yes, a chestnut mare called Misty. I've had her about eight years, but I've been so busy lately I haven't ridden her much, I'm afraid. Lizzy, my sister, has been taking her out more than I have. What about you? Is Licorice your own horse?"

"No, but I helped pick him out for the school. My own horse, Pete, is at my parents' ranch." They were at the top of the range and stopped to admire the panorama. He asked her if she was hungry. He dismounted off of his horse and opened up a saddlebag. "I brought a picnic, if you hadn't had dinner."

Daphne was pleasantly surprised at his thoughtfulness. *I guess this is a real date,* she thought. She hadn't had time to eat before she left home and, being unsure of the details of the evening's plans, she thought she'd just grab a plate of leftovers when she got home. There was always something in the fridge. "Wow! That's great. Actually, I'm starved. I haven't eaten since lunch." She got off her horse as well.

"Good. Reach into your saddlebag, the left one," Dan said.

As she did, she smiled. There was a blanket folded up neatly inside. She took it out and unfurled it onto a level and clear patch of ground. "What else do you have tucked away?"

"Oh, just a few things." He pulled out a bottle of wine, corkscrew and mugs, and set them down on the blanket as Daphne laughed. He went back to the other side of the horse and took out a couple of wrapped sandwiches and a container of macaroni salad. "I went by the deli on Cove Street today and picked these up. Not too presumptuous, I hope?" He looked pleased with himself as he read Daphne's expression.

"No, not at all." Daphne set up the meal on the blanket while Dan tended to the horses, giving them a drink from a nearby stream and feeding each of them an apple from Daphne's other saddlebag.

They sat down together, facing the ocean view and ate quietly for a few minutes. "So," she began, "Did you grow up in Ojai?"

"Yeah, my family has a horse farm there," Dan said as he reached over to the salad container and helped himself to a forkful of macaroni and passed it to Daphne.

She did the same. "Oh, so the horses came from your family's ranch?"

He shook his head. "No. They breed and sell Arabians, mainly for dressage, show and jumping. Beautiful creatures, but the Academy needed calmer and more adaptable horses. They're expected to handle students with abilities ranging from beginner to expert all day long. Quarter horses are better suited to different terrains as well."

"I guess you've been around horses all your life," she stated.

"Pretty much. My parents wanted me to stay on with my older brother and take over for them when they didn't want to run the business anymore," he replied with a slight trepidation, having given the explanation numerous times to people. Everyone always questioned his choice for leaving the family's successful endeavor. "It felt so cut and dry to me. It was more about money and people than about the horses."

"And it wasn't yours," Daphne nodded. She understood and that surprised him a little. "That's why I love Poppy Cove. I'm not married yet and I wanted my own business in something that had nothing to do with my father or brother."

It was his turn to nod and smile. "That's it in a nutshell. I may not want to work at a school stable for the rest of my life, but living out here with the horses gives me a chance to sort it all out and plan my own future."

They sat in companionable silence for a couple of minutes watching the sun continue to descend. Dan's shoulders rounded slightly as he sighed. "I just hope now that Con is gone, we can live up to what she expected for the Academy."

The casual reference from an employee regarding Constance Stearns-Montgomery caught Daphne off-guard. "Um, did you know Mrs. Stearns-Montgomery very well?"

He shrugged. "She knew my parents from when she got her first horse years ago. I'd see her from time to time when I was growing up. We got to know each other a little better at the spa in Ojai."

Spa? Since when did Constance frequent spas? She silently wondered. He made it sound so innocent, but it seemed strange to her that he would be meeting Constance at a place like that. "Oh," was all she could manage for a reply.

Dan continued on. "She talked me into coming to the Academy. I got to hire the helpers, set up the stables and pick out the horses. It was a great opportunity."

Daphne felt numb. She wanted to get away. This information was a little boggling and confused her. She decided to play it cool on the outside and carefully got up, brushed the crumbs from her lap. "We should get going. We've got to get back before dark."

Dan agreed. He got up and helped gather the remains of their meal. As they got ready to go, Dan went to Daphne's side to assist her into the saddle. Their eyes met. "Thank you for showing me the trails. And for being so welcoming." Then he sighed. "The only person I knew around here was Con, and it was seeming a little lonely with, well, what happened. I almost thought of leaving, but I remember how much this place meant to her. The horses, too."

She melted a little. He seemed sincere. No, he couldn't be.... For heaven's sake, she'd known him since he was a boy. "Of course. You really should stay, Dan." She looked down the gentle slope to where the stables and other buildings were. "I think you've done a beautiful job."

With that, they set off down the hill, making it back just before dark. They handed the horses off to one of the stable hands to walk off and curry. Dan escorted Daphne back to her car. They talked of light things, of her and her family, and he mentioned that he planned to go see his own on Friday for the weekend. Daphne felt more at ease. She decided he was too nice to be a killer. And too young to be a lover of Constance, she hoped. So much so that when he asked her for another riding date next week, she said yes without hesitation.

CHAPTER ELEVEN

Daphne arrived at the store late on Thursday morning. She had a rough night again with a lot on her mind. Her thoughts of Dan and the evening were conflicting. She truly liked him. His picnic was a very thoughtful touch, but the revelation that he knew Constance so well, intimately, it seemed, really unsettled her. He was so casual about them being at a spa together and then Constance moving him to Santa Lucia. He seemed so innocent. Maybe she was just jumping to conclusions, but it certainly would make it convenient for them to carry on an affair.

"Well, well, well. Nice of you to show up," Irene said slyly as she looked up from the appointment book. "Good thing you own the joint. You'd never let me get away with it."

It was just after ten. Irene's cattiness ticked her off, but she chose to ignore the comment. "Good morning. Where's Margot?"

"In the office," Irene buried her nose back in the book.

Daphne made her way up the stairs, feeling leaden. The same questions kept running around in her head. Since when did Constance start going to spas? Her mother, who frequently did, never mentioned that she saw Constance where she went and personally Daphne never knew Constance to go in for much pampering. Did she go because *he* was there? And if she had known him all of his life, would they have had romantic feelings for each other? She shook out her thoughts as she reached the top of the stairs. He just didn't seem like the type to go after an older woman.

"Morning. Sorry I'm so late." Daphne plopped down in her desk chair as she greeted Margot.

"Wow! Was the riding date that bad?" Margot looked up from her desk, surprised at Daphne's weary appearance. Daphne's bright blue eyes had lost some luster and her curls were limp and flatter than usual.

Daphne shook her head. "No, it was really nice. He was thoughtful, even set up a picnic for us. Just confusing, that's all."

"Oh?" Margot didn't look up again. The loft was a busy little hive. It was where most of the creative decisions were made. As always, there were many things on the go. She was involved in finances, working out the fabric budget for the spring season. To her right was the adding machine, tape flowing over the top and down the front of her desk. Directly opposite were the swatches that Sam had left with her. She had the custom client's list on the far, right-hand corner of her desk, which she had to go over with Marjorie that morning. Behind her right shoulder on the bulletin board were the sketches of the fall/holiday line of garments that were in process or had to be done over the next few weeks. The date for the upcoming fashion show was looming, and they still had to decide which garments to feature.

Daphne placed her purse in her desk drawer and began shuffling through her own workload. "Yeah, Dan told me that he'd known Constance since he was young." She too had piles of tasks set out that needed her attention. Over her left shoulder on the bulletin board were torn out magazine photos of models carrying purses, wearing jewelry and shoes that she was interested in finding for the store. She had a half dozen samples that Julia had left for her to peruse and choose from in a variety of colors. "They got reacquainted while Constance was away."

"Away? Constance and Reginald haven't been on a vacation in years," Margot's head was still in the figures and wasn't paying much attention to Daphne's news.

"Come to think of it, he never once mentioned Reginald. It sounded like Constance was alone. He said that after spending some time together at a spa, Constance offered Dan the job at the Academy stables."

Now Margot not only glanced in her friend's direction, but also physically sat up straighter. "Were Con and Dan on holiday together?"

Daphne walked over to the percolator and felt it was still warm. She poured herself a cup of coffee and sat down in the soft chair by the big window overlooking the square. "No." She shook her head. "I don't think so. He said that they'd seen each other there."

"She never mentioned anything about spas or vacations. As far as I know, she was never out of town for very long." Margot was just as puzzled by the new information.

"It was at a spa in Ojai, just over the hill," Daphne explained as she thought it out. "So, she could've gone for a couple of days or even on day trips without many people being aware of it. Who knows how often she did that?"

"Huh, I never pegged our Con as part of the spa set." Margot got up and turned the radio off. They usually had it on while they were working. If she was sketching, it was jazz from an L.A. station. When they were working on business matters, the local classical station. Right then a particularly strong Wagnerian piece was blaring out unnerving dramatics, adding to the exploding thoughts the girls were working out of Con's possible double life. "It sounds like Dan and

Reginald didn't know each other at all. What do you think he makes of all this? Would an affair turn him into a killer?"

"I don't know. I mean, did Reginald even know anything about this before Con died? Who knows what their marriage was like, but as far as I know, the rumors didn't surface until after the murder."

"So other than this, you never heard any talk about Constance and other men through the years?" Margot was already in an analytical mood, but her thoughts moved full on from math to gossip.

"No, it's just recently that she'd been acting differently," Daphne shrugged. "The *change*? Would that spur her on to getting involved with a younger lover?"

Margot was skeptical. "But would Dan be that man? He doesn't strike me as the lothario type, unless he said something to you on your date. What was he like? How did he behave?"

"That's the thing. He was nice, even talked about his family. He paid attention to me, but cared about the horses, too. He made sure they had food and water. He was very thoughtful." Daphne softened a little as she thought back to his behavior.

"Was he fresh with you?" Margot asked frankly.

"No, not at all. He was, well, a gentleman. He was affectionate enough, but he didn't try to paw me over, with his hands *or* his eyes." Daphne drifted off as she tried to remember every detail of the evening, for both pleasure and clues to Constance's murder. "He did talk about Constance a bit."

Margot continued fishing. "How did he talk about her? Overly emotional, angry, dismissive? Did it seem out of line?"

"He seemed a little lost without her there, sad. He wasn't even sure if he would stay on now that she's gone." She picked at a nonexistent piece of fluff on the arm of the chair and sighed. "Even so, the thought of him being romantically involved with Constance just doesn't add up."

"What about for you?" Margot eyed Daphne, watching her response.

"Me with Dan? It's early to tell, but definitely not if he's a gigolo! I must be willing to find out, because I've accepted another riding date for next week," she chuckled. "The more I think about it, the crazier it seems. Maybe Con was just there for the horses. They've got some great trails up in Ojai."

Margot nodded. "Yes, and it would definitely put her in line with spending time with Dan. How exactly did he say they knew each other?"

"His parents breed horses and Constance had purchased hers through them," she recalled. "And then he mentioned seeing her at the spa."

Margot put the radio back on and settled in her chair. "See, there's a perfectly logical explanation to it all. She knew his family, trusted them, so she trusted him. Maybe she just ran into him in Ojai?" Margot picked up the price list she was looking at when Daphne had come in. "I'll even bet that he was the mystery man everyone claimed to be her lover. I'm sure their relationship was platonic and professional." She relaxed her shoulders and grinned at Daphne. "Besides, you've got another man on your mind too. He's a bit of a mystery as well."

"Yes! I'm quite intrigued by him," Daphne replied. She drained the last of her coffee, set the cup on the serving table and went back to her desk. She had every intention to sort through the piles of tasks, but her mind went back to men. She was looking forward to getting to know Peter. He was a little older, she guessed, by the way his eyes slightly crinkled in the corners when he smiled. He also looked at you when he talked to you—very attentive—and seemed to actually be a part of the conversation. He was certainly more sophisticated than Anthony, who did little more than play polo and spend his father's money. At least Peter seemed to be creating his own way in the world. And, he met with approval already from the male members of her family. Her father's opinion meant a lot to her. He was a good judge of character.

She liked being in the dating scene. It had been just over a month and a half since her last date with Anthony, who had an obnoxious habit of forgetting his girl. They would be out on a date and he would walk paces in front of her, letting the door almost hit her and flirt shamelessly with other women. They saw each other for about three months, and she would bring this up to him, subtly at first, but the final straw was the July 4th celebration at the town square when he brought a drink to a young lady from out of state visiting her relatives whom they did not know and forgot one for her. She left him talking with the woman about Santa Lucian hospitality and never returned his telephone calls.

Fatigue was settling in and she couldn't focus. She felt rumpled on the inside and that would never do for a date. Daphne needed professional help. "Are you good if I nip out around two to Mr. Anthony's? If they have time, I'll get my hair and nails done."

Margot, lost in thought, nodded and mumbled an approval. Daphne made her appointment and settled in on the samples. The girls worked quietly over the next hour before returning to the sales floor.

Daphne came back around four with Cherry Bomb Red fingers and toes and the bounce in her hair restored. "I need to figure out something fun and cute to wear tonight."

Loretta came bounding through the door. "Girls, I have news. All the staff has been working on the big story all day. Seems like the police have cleared Katherine Larsen of any wrongdoing. She was at her relatives' up near Solvang. They have a dairy farm." Loretta was flushed and breathless. "I had to wait until it had gone to press before telling anyone anything. I hate when I've got a good scoop and can't say a word." She then lowered her voice. "And, the latest is that Nancy's been called into question! Can you believe it?" Loretta started browsing through the racks.

Margot wondered how much they should say to Loretta about what Jane had said about Nancy yesterday. She decided to say nothing and see what Loretta would tell them. "So Headmistress Larsen was out of town the whole time? What about the school opening? Why wasn't she there?"

"Apparently, she and Constance had a big disagreement about that. Katherine Larsen felt that all the pomp and circumstance was taking over from the purpose of the school. She doesn't go in for all the social protocol and is awkward about such things. She bowed out at the last minute, called Constance at home from her Uncle's place up in the hills and said she wouldn't come down until Monday. Maria, Constance's housekeeper, overheard the call. And, the police checked out the farm and many of the hands had seen her the whole weekend, right up until late Monday morning."

Loretta's information filled in a lot of blanks. "Say, I like this!" She held up one of the new olive-colored, cotton blouses to herself. "I need something new." Loretta always needed something new, as she attended every social event in town and rarely wore the same garment twice. It just wasn't the thing to do.

Daphne was also busy shopping. "Girls, help me find something that goes with my smashing new nail color for tonight. Something still summery." The girls continued their conversation while flipping though the racks. "So why was Katherine so distraught at the funeral? I'd heard she was pretty unemotional. The faculty seemed to think it was quite out of the norm for her." She came across a striped cotton sundress and showed it to Margot and Loretta. "What do you think?"

"Did you ever try that one on? I always thought it would suit you." It was sleeveless and very sporty. The sundress had white, black and turquoise vertical stripes with a small collar and buttoned down the front. It nipped in at the waist and widened to a swirling hem. It looked especially fetching when the top two and bottom two buttons were left undone. Margot also handed Daphne a navy, linen number that was slim with a square neckline and a double-breasted, button closure that was just put out on the floor that week. It was part of the fall line, but would still work well for now. Margot turned to Loretta. "Yes, Katherine's behavior seemed to go against everything that we've heard about her. How well did she know Constance? I know you said that they had gone to school together, but Constance never mentioned her before."

"I've been asking around and found out plenty. The two of them were always big rivals at school, competing for everything, but they were such opposites. They never kept in touch with each other. Katherine became a real career girl. She never left school. After she graduated, she stayed on the east coast and got her teaching degree. Education became her life. She never married, just poured everything into teaching. Eventually, she went back to Creighton and became the headmistress there. Her success was tracked by the Creighton alumni newsletter; she was always being featured as she became more prominent in the school systems, much to her dismay. She really is a private one, that woman. She strongly dislikes any attention. Anyway, she was easy for Constance to find, since Constance always received the newsletter. When they started planning the Academy, Constance knew she wanted her for the headmistress. Despite their differences, Constance knew she would be the most dedicated and finest woman for the job." Loretta picked up one of the new paisley, silk, surplice blouses. "I like this! What's new for the holidays? Will I get a peek at the line before the fall fashion show? From what Sarah Browning told me, the Hospital Charity Ball will go on. Constance would have wanted it that way."

Poppy Cove had three fashion shows a year and they were always gay affairs. They were great charity events and busy times for the girls. All throughout the year, the shows were always on the staff's minds. It was their main form of advertising, and it reached a lot of their customers for the rest of the year. The fall fashion show featured the latest in daytime casual sportswear and evening glamour for the upcoming holiday season. The September show was held at the Tropical Ballroom of the Yacht Club, on the night of the Santa Lucia General Hospital Charity Ball after dinner, before dancing. The men would retire to cigars and brandy, while the women sipped liqueurs and nibbled on cakes as they watched the current year's Miss Santa Lucia and other local college girls model Margot's latest creations with Daphne's accessories. Margot was very pleased with how the new collections were coming along. "We're putting a few, new, casual, sportswear ensembles on the floor—that blouse being one of them, but you'll have to wait for the holiday wear. I promise you, we have some gorgeous ideas shaping up.   Could you do a feature on the new garments in the paper?"

"What do you have in mind?" Loretta glittered.

"What if you came to the last fitting of the models here at the store the evening before the show?   We could go through the details and it would give you more time to describe the garments better.   But you have to promise me that you won't print anything until the day after the show.   You can't give anything away." Margot looked Loretta right in the eye.   Daphne grinned. She thought it was a great idea.

"Then we could take the pictures at the show. That's super!   And, I get to be the first person in Santa Lucia to see the new items. I love it! The *Times* will be so happy with me. What's the date of the show?" Loretta got out her date book and pen.

"Saturday, September 28th.   Would seven on the Friday be a good time for you?"

"For this, I will make time. I can't wait. There, I've written it down in my calendar.   We can have the feature, including the pictures from the ball, in the paper on Monday morning."

As on the mark as ever, Irene dutifully wrote down the date in the store's appointment book at the cash register.   With that being settled, she brought the conversation back to the town's biggest topic. "So, if all that Katherine Larsen had in common with Constance was the school, why was she so upset at her funeral? It doesn't fit."

Loretta had a captive audience. She put the blouse down. "Well, over the last couple of months, the two got to know each other better. They still went about education in different ways, but they could find ways to compromise. About a month or so ago, Miss Larsen was really acting like a bear, wouldn't agree to anything, arguing just for the sake of picking a fight.

Finally, Constance put her foot down and said either you tell me what is wrong or I am selecting another headmistress. Katherine then broke down, and told her that she was worried about her Uncle's situation. He had a long-term contract with Stewart's Supermarket chain and they decided to get all their dairy products from farms closer to Los Angeles where their main offices are, which left the Larsen's in the lurch. Most of their sales were through this one company. Katherine's uncle had just invested in new milking machines and a new barn; they were financially in deep and could lose the farm. He's had it since '35 and it would be quite a blow. Katherine is closer to this side of her family, even more so than her parents. They never gave her any grief for her choice of school over marriage.

"Constance told her that Reginald dealt with many farms up in that region, and she was sure that it wouldn't be a problem for him to go see them, maybe they could work something out. So Reginald went up and saw their farm and tasted some of their milk and cheese and thought they had a fine product. It was easy for Montgomery's Fine Foods to take on their goods and it saved the Larsen's. Katherine was so grateful that she and Constance began getting along much better. That is, until the day before the opening."

"What happened then?" Daphne's voice came from over a dressing room curtain. She had taken a few items in to try on.

"That's when they had a huge fight. Katherine had left Santa Lucia Wednesday night after the last staff meeting before the opening ceremony. She called Constance from the ranch on Thursday morning and said that she wouldn't be attending the ceremony and they could meet on Monday afternoon to continue the opening procedures for the school year. Constance was furious. She needed her headmistress there. She told Katherine on the phone that it was imperative that she be there. Parents and the press would expect to meet her. Katherine said that they could do that on the first day of classes and that was her job. Constance threatened to fire her and Katherine said that she would do no such thing; she was the one who really ran the school. It got ugly and that's the last the two women spoke to each other."

"You would think she could put aside her feelings for just one night. I can understand it would be awkward to be there in front of all those people, but for the sake of the school it's just something a person has to do." Margot could be a little shy at public events. She always enjoyed putting the fashion shows and clothing together, but she really disliked having the spotlight on her instead of her work. She appeared at the shows, talked to a few people, but faded out from the crowds very quickly. "The headmistress could just give a quick speech and talk to a few parents and bow out. It's the least she could have done for the school and to show her personal gratitude to Constance."

"That's not how she saw it. She told the police she felt that the ceremony had nothing to do with the school. To her, it was just a big society event and took away from the seriousness of the studies. She couldn't abide the thought of being on display. She felt that if the parents wanted to meet her, they could do so on school hours, in her office, by appointment. That was how it was done at Creighton and everywhere else she'd taught. She didn't see the importance of this night; she'd never been at the opening of a new school and felt that the classes were far more important than how the grounds looked to society."

Loretta continued on. "After Katherine hung up the phone, she realized how upset Constance was. She didn't think she would be; she truly thought Constance would prefer to have all the attention on herself and her family's history rather than how the school was to be run. And then, it was too late for her to get there on time to make a decent appearance at the event, so she thought that somehow on Monday they could make amends and she'd concede to some kind of appearance before the first day of classes, a tour with the parents or something. She thought they could discuss it when she got back. Katherine was personally touched by Constance and Reginald's generosity for her Aunt and Uncle and she wanted to do something that would make Constance happy. And of course, she didn't get the chance."

The room fell silent for a moment or two. "So that's why she was beside herself at the funeral. For as much as they disagreed, the two women were finally getting to know each other better, and she really let Constance down. She told the police last night that she felt very guilty for not being there to help. Had she been there to oversee the events, Constance might not have been around the back of the school, checking things over. She might not have been killed. Also, Katherine's concerned about the upcoming school year—if there will be a delay, or maybe no classes at all. But now that she has been cleared; Reginald and Charles have put her in complete control of the Academy and have asked her to help keep it on track—opening on as close to the original date and speaking personally with the parents to assure them that the grounds are safe for their girls," Loretta sighed.

"Huh. So what about Nancy stalking the school?" Even as Irene said it, she could see Margot shooting daggers with her eyes at her, telling her to proceed with caution. The girls didn't know what Loretta knew about what Jane had seen. If they leaked out more information than the police gave Loretta, they could be in big trouble, possibly messing up the investigation.

Loretta looked amused. "That's still coming down the wire. Michael Weathers is at the station getting the story. I don't have any details; can't comment, but it would be something, wouldn't it? And say what you want about that Weathers kid, but he's really a top-notch reporter. He's been the one digging up the facts on this one." Daphne came out of the dressing room wearing the striped sundress. Loretta turned to look at Daphne. "I like that on you. Very becoming."

The stripes looked bold and accentuated her figure nicely. "Thanks. I thought those new turquoise sandals I bought last week would go well. What about the little black scarf around my neck?" Margot handed it to her and she tied it in a knot to the side. "There! I like it too. Sold! Irene, write it in the book. I'll take it."

Loretta tried on the paisley blouse and trousers. The pants were a little looser than the slacks that had been so popular, wider through the legs and hip area. Margot always liked to give variety to the styles. "These are so comfortable. I could really work in these. I'm always in a skirt. I'm going to get these for a change. I love the rust color too. Makes me think of autumn back home." Loretta grew up in Vermont, but spent most of her adult life in California. "Do you have any more blouses to go with them?"

"Yes. In the next week or two, we'll have some cream charmeuse blouses done as well as another print that will go. I'll put one of each aside for you."

"You're a doll." Loretta looked at her watch. "Wow, I can't believe the time—almost five already. Make up my bill and pack up my new clothes, girls. I've got to dash." She flew into the dressing room and handed the blouse and trousers to Margot who packaged the clothes while Irene prepared the bill.

Loretta came out and wrote a check for the amount. Over her shoulder as she left out the door she said, "Oh, and lover girl, have a good time and don't do anything I wouldn't do. At least not that I would admit to!"

Daphne crinkled up her nose and laughed. "See you 'Retta. I guess I should be going, too. I wanted to go home and freshen up before my date. Do you need a hand closing up today?" Daphne offered, but really hoped she could leave early.

Margot just looked at her. "Go on, get out of here. Irene and I will finish up. Just tell me all the details tomorrow."

"Thanks, you're swell. What time are you meeting Tom tonight?"

"He's picking me up at the shop around six-thirty if he can make it. I'm dying to find out if Jane went to see him. I'll do some sketching while I wait for him. And you, have a great time and forget all about this for a little while."

"It'll be good to talk to someone who's not from here and all caught up in the murder," Daphne sighed as she grabbed her purse to go out the door. She left the new dress on. "See you tomorrow!"

After Irene finished up the books and the store was tidy, Margot locked up the doors and turned off the lights. She went upstairs to the office. At the corner window above the front door, Margot sat down at her drawing board. It was a pretty little view of the downtown street, now quiet at the end of the day, and if you looked far off in the distance—a glimpse of the ocean. She sat there lost in thought with not much getting sketched, because the idea of Nancy as a murderer kept coming up in her mind. Before she knew it, Tom was ringing the front door chime. She flew down the stairs.

"Hello, Darling. How was your day?" She greeted him with an embrace and let him in the store. He locked the door behind him.

"Hectic. Reginald and Charles are still pretty steamed that the photos disappeared and are putting pressure on the department to find answers. They want the case solved, not only to put Constance to rest, but also they're concerned about the reputation of the school and the investment property. Their secretaries are fielding all kinds of questions so not only is it affecting them all personally, but their businesses as well."

Margot stroked his back and murmured gently, "Poor dear. Are you at least getting closer to solving the case?"

Tom sighed. "Well, we've cleared Katherine Larsen, so that allows us to focus in on a couple of other suspects we've been looking at."

Margot wondered briefly if Daniel was one of them, but decided to ask about another candidate. "I have heard that Nancy Lewis was taken in for questioning." She paused. "Did Jane come to see you? When she was here for her fitting, she remembered that she thought she saw Nancy or someone similar to her skulking around that evening before the ceremony."

Tom nodded. "Yes, Jane did see me. I took a statement from her." He rubbed his furrowed brow. "And really, that's all I can tell you." Tom just wanted a break from the case and a few minutes with his girl. He turned to face her and placed his hands on her shoulders. He looked into her eyes and they both softened a little. "Now then, I only have about an hour and then I need to get back to the station. Can I get a real kiss and then some dinner?"

She grinned and gave him a nice, big kiss, melting into his arms. That was much better. She got her bag and they left the store, determined not to talk about the case over dinner.

CHAPTER TWELVE

Daphne hummed to herself as she showered and toweled off. After she carefully removed her shower cap so as not to ruffle her freshly revived curls, she lightly dabbed *Youth Dew* perfume behind her ears. She put on her little diamond, stud earrings that were a present from her parents on her last birthday. Lizzie came in while she was getting dressed. Lately, Lizzie loved to watch her big sister get ready for dates.

"So what are you and Peter going to do tonight?" Lizzie sprawled across Daphne's bed, chin in her hands, legs bent up and swinging.

"We're just having dinner at the club and getting to know each other. Careful, you'll wrinkle my new dress!" Daphne moved it off her bed, away from her hurricane of a sister.

"It's cute. I like it. It's not frilly. I could wear that," Lizzie commented as she looked at it draped over window seat.

Daphne looked at her tomboy sister. "You, wanting to wear a dress? Since when?"

Lizzie shrugged, "I dunno, maybe now."

Daphne stopped getting ready and looked at her. "Are you serious?" The thought of Lizzie actually becoming feminine would bowl her mother over. "What's gotten into you?"

"Nothing." She blushed. Daphne decided not to push it. Maybe she really was becoming interested in James. Lizzie would let them know in her own time. "Are you going to let him kiss you?"

Daphne stopped again, mid lipstick. "That's none of your business, young lady. What's with all the questions? I feel like I'm being given the third degree. Isn't there something else you can do?"

"Nope." Lizzie wasn't budging. "Dinner's not ready. Mother's talking boring baby stuff with Grace and I've finished reading my book. Besides, this is fun, right?"

"Yeah, you're right. I just need to get ready, okay?"

"Okay. Hey, guess what I've heard? Mrs. Lewis is in big trouble. They've got her in jail." The statement moved the conversation from out of the frying pan and into the fire.

"I don't think they have her in jail exactly. I *have* heard something about her being questioned by the police at the station, but not arrested. Where did you hear that from?"

"Sally Baker told me. She and her mom were driving by the station today and they saw Mrs. Lewis going in between two policemen. Her mom said that she hated Mrs. Montgomery," Lizzie reported with an air of authority.

"Hate's an awfully strong word to use. They had their differences, but for Mrs. Lewis to be capable of murder? I honestly don't think so." Daphne had to get Lizzie off of the topic. "Besides, this really isn't your concern."

"It's more believable than that old lady having a boyfriend." Lizzie's face registered true disgust.

Daphne rolled her eyes, but then gave her hair one last primp in the mirror. She was ready to go. "What do you think? Do I look first date glamorous?"

"Yeah, you look great. Can you maybe one day show me how to do that?"

"Do what?"

"You know, get the make-up on right. Maybe I could wear it now and then."

"Sure. Let's talk about it tomorrow. I have to get going now."

Daphne drove up to the Yacht Club valet at seven thirty-five precisely. She took a detour around the harbor to make sure she was just that little bit late to keep him waiting, but not worrying. She walked into the lounge and saw Peter sitting in a club chair, his back to the door, sipping on a tall, cool drink. He turned and stood up when he heard the click of her heels on the tile floor. He was wearing a light, grey suit and a white shirt with a wing collar, open at the neck. On him, it was very sophisticated, European. He wasn't wearing a tie and Daphne liked the casual approach. He still looked very well groomed and his easy manner was appealing. When he smiled, his white teeth contrasted nicely with his olive complexion and dark hair. Daphne felt her heart skip a small beat.

"Good evening, Daphne. You look beautiful. Is that one of the creations from your shop?" He reached out and took her hand. He brought it up to his lips for a very light kiss.

"Yes, yes it is." She felt flattered, but even so, in the back of her head, she didn't remember telling him about her business. "How do you know about Poppy Cove?"

They sat down in the lounge chairs. "Andrew Lewis told me. I asked him all about you. Forgive me, I hope you don't mind." His smile was disarming.

She wasn't sure that she liked someone asking others about her, especially a virtual stranger. But then she realized that she'd done the exact same thing. "No, that's fine, I think. What did he tell you about me?"

"Not much, just a bit about your store that you share with another young lady, very successfully." He took a sip of his drink. "And that your father was a good man to know around town. I've already met him and your brother at the investors' meeting for the resort."

"Oh, of course." The waiter came by and Daphne ordered a martini. She began to relax. "So tell me, how do you like Santa Lucia?"

"It's very nice, a charming town. It's so beautifully built and a perfect place for the resort," Peter affirmed.

"Wow, sounds like you're sold on it. What about the other investors?"

"From what I've heard, most are very much in favor of the project. Unfortunately, it's been a little slow getting the meetings together. It seems that all of the locals are caught up in this murder case." He waved his hand airily, dismissing its importance.

Daphne sensed his annoyance and felt a little defensive. "It's a shocking thing for us." Daphne paused and took a sip of her drink, considering how to phrase her feelings without causing an argument. "Constance was a prominent member of society and things like that just don't happen here every day."

"No, you're right. I'm just eager to get the project going. Tell me something about this Constance. I understand that the new school on the hill was named for her family." Peter eased back into his chair, ready to listen to Daphne.

"Yes. The Stearns go way back in Santa Lucia. They were some of the first townsfolk and also helped to rebuild after our big quake in '22. Even in her own way, Constance made an impact on the community. She did all kinds of charity work and her death left Reginald Montgomery a widower. You must have met him, or at least heard of him. He owns Montgomery's Fine Foods. Are you familiar with their brand?"

He nodded. "It seems to be everywhere. They say she was killed on the school grounds during some kind of event."

Daphne confirmed his information. "It was the opening ceremony. I was there and it was just awful. No one could find Constance and then the next moment she turned up dead, strangled in the rose bushes."

"And no one saw anything? You would think with a party going on that someone would have seen something."

"No, that's just the thing. There's a lot of rumors going around about the case and Constance herself," Daphne revealed.

"You mean that she was having an affair?"

"See? Even you've heard your share. I don't believe that one. Constance wasn't the type. She loved her husband and that just wasn't her." Daphne was surprised. She was actually pleased to run over the details in her mind with someone new; maybe she could get a fresh understanding of Constance.

"Sounds like you knew her well." Peter touched her arm in sympathy.

"Our families attended many of the same functions. Plus, Constance was becoming a regular customer at Poppy Cove. She was a long time acquaintance. It's just sad to think that she was taken in her prime, with so many things going well for her."

"Have you heard if the police have any strong suspects?"

"No, they've cleared a few people, such as Reginald and Charles, her brother. The headmistress came into question too, but she was out of town and it was an honest alibi." Daphne remembered back to Nancy Lewis and decided not to mention that bit of information to him. He knew the Lewises and she didn't want it getting back to Nancy that she was talking about her in such a way or to deter Peter from dealing with Andrew, who was a good man regardless of any of Nancy's behaviors. *Besides, that was enough of that conversation,* she thought. "Why don't you tell me about yourself, Peter? I've heard that you're from Los Angeles." She realized that maybe doing a little homework on someone was a good thing.

The conversation took on a more pleasant tone as Peter informed Daphne about himself—how he grew up in the Los Angeles area, the only child of an attorney and a loving housewife. They raised their son to graduate from UCLA Business School and he began investing in real estate ventures right out of university. During the last six years, he'd travelled all over the globe, sourcing out ventures. He had a few losses, but many successes, especially in the hotel and resort market.

As they moved from drinks to dinner, they realized they had a lot in common. In addition to playing a mean game of tennis, they both enjoyed golfing and yachting. They had seen a lot of the same movies, both loved to go dancing, and best of all, he listened to her, which made him far more attentive than Anthony ever was. They were shaping up to be a very good match.

It was getting late in the Palms Dining Room, just after eleven. Daphne had an early day the following day and as much fun as she was having, she knew when a girl had to call it a night. Peter walked her to the front entrance and waited with her while her car was brought around.

"Thank you, Daphne, for an enchanting evening." He moved in closer and kissed her hand again.

She let him. "It was very nice."

"I would enjoy getting to know you more intimately." She blushed and wondered how he meant that. He paused as he held her hand and looked into her eyes. "I'm not sure of my plans with the meetings and I may need to attend to matters in the city. When I have a better idea of my time, I would enjoy the pleasure of you company again. I've heard of this great little Italian restaurant in town that I'd like to try."

"I'll bet that's Antonio's. Their food is wonderful and they are such nice people. Sure. I'd like that." Daphne smiled.

Peter gently let go of her hand and gave her a kiss on the cheek. "Good." She gave him her phone number that he wrote on the inside of a Palms Dining Room matchbook.

When her car arrived, Peter tipped the attendant for her and handed him his set of keys. He watched as she was escorted into her car. She gave him a wave and a smile as she drove off, her foot a little heavy on the gas, making the car skitter abruptly. *I think he has me flustered,* she thought.

CHAPTER THIRTEEN

As soon as Margot flipped the sign in the window to *Open* on Friday morning, Nancy Lewis flew in the door in a rampage. "Are you the one responsible for ruining my life?" She hissed and glared at Margot as she threw the morning copy of the *Times* on the counter. On the front page was the headline 'Prominent Socialite Under Suspicion' with a picture of Nancy being escorted into the police station by two uniformed men. Margot stepped back from Nancy. Her irrational behavior was unnerving. "What have you been telling people about me?"

She took a deep breath before responding. "Good morning, Nancy. I haven't said anything about you. There's nothing to tell. Besides, you know we're more discreet than that." Poppy Cove, like a beauty salon, was privy to many confidences and they were kept quiet.

"You must have said something to your high and mighty boyfriend to make him suspect me, of all people. And I mean, really, the idea of me killing anyone! Even Constance. And you must have said something to Loretta that made me look bad. How else would she get such a picture, taken from my worst view?" Margot looked at the picture, which was taken by Michael Weathers, who also broke the story and wrote the article. Loretta's name was not involved in the story. Nancy was right about one thing, though. The picture prominently featured her backside, not her best attribute.

"Look for yourself, Nancy. Loretta's name is not associated with the story. And I repeat, I have said nothing at all to incriminate you to Tom or the paper of all things. I personally know of nothing that would cast any shadow of suspicion over you. I can assure you that neither Daphne, my staff nor myself would do that to you."

"It was so insulting," Nancy sighed and slumped against the counter. "Being escorted down to the station like a common criminal. Someone put the idea into Tom's head that I couldn't be trusted." Behind Nancy's angry face, Margot could see how frightened she was.

As Margot was getting Nancy to sit down, she was thinking about what Jane had said. There was definitely some truth to what she'd seen. A woman in disguise with Nancy's build was sneaking around the school grounds, but Margot didn't feel it was her place to mention it to Nancy. It could harm the case and also cause hardship for Jane if she had mistakenly described Nancy. It could have been someone else. Besides, if Nancy wasn't there and hadn't done anything wrong, it shouldn't matter if she was questioned. Margot tried to calm Nancy down with another approach. "Nancy, if it was all a misunderstanding about your presence at the school that night and you weren't there, it'll be proven and you'll be cleared. It'll all blow over very shortly when the case is solved."

"Easy for you to say. I *was* at the school that night." She avoided Margot's eyes, defiant as she sheepishly confessed.

Margot's heart sank. "You were? I didn't see you. If you were so against the school, why were you there?" Could she really have been the figure lurking about?

Nancy bristled up again. "I had every right to be there. I was around the back, just looking around. I was curious. I wanted to see the grounds. Lords is much better, by the way. I swear I never saw Constance. I left long before most of the crowd got there, but obviously someone saw me. When I find out who that was, their standing will be destroyed in this town! The way they told the police what they saw must have made me look bad. How dare they!"

The conversation was very troubling to Margot. She felt that Nancy was telling the truth, but it did look bad. She chose her words carefully. "I'm sure you meant no harm, but, Nancy, think about how that must have looked, considering Constance was murdered that night. And, the two of you were not the best of friends, especially lately. Whoever brought it to the attention of the police must have felt they were doing the right thing."

"Do-gooders need to learn to keep to themselves. They need to get their facts straight before telling the whole world." As Nancy spoke the comment, Irene breezed in and shot a glance her way. Pot calling the kettle black—she was the biggest gossip in town.

"I don't think the witness meant to tell the world. It went to the police and the newspaper just did their job, and unfortunately for you, it doesn't look good—sneaking around—even if it was innocent." Diplomatic as ever, Margot tried to help Nancy see reason. It wasn't working.

Nancy stood up and pulled down the peplum of her jacket. "I must be going. I need to get out of here. I can't be seen until this blows over. After all, I have a reputation to maintain. I'm leaving by your back door."

Daphne came in through the front. Nancy glared, "And you, you heartbreaker! How could you do that to my Barbara? You know we were arranging for her to get to know Peter Carson better, yet you threw yourself at him. My girl was beside herself after finding out you demanded that he take you out for dinner last night."

"Hello to you too, Nancy. Boy, news travels fast around here. And for your information, he will be taking me out again. He never mentioned that he was dating anyone else in town." Nancy's indignation made Daphne feel a bit smug.

"I said they were just getting to know each other. A proper young lady takes her time and allows nature to take its course, not hound a man down. I know your sort." Nancy had so much venom in her, it was coming out in all directions. "What did you tell him about us?"

"As a matter of fact, Nancy, we never spoke of you or your girls. And thank you, we had a very pleasant evening." Her eyes twinkled as she looked Margot's way.

"What are you thanking me for?"

"I guess it's really your husband I should be thanking. When Peter asked him about me, he put in a good word for me and encouraged him to ask me out."

The color rose in Nancy's face. "Ooh, that man! What has gotten into him? He's recommending suitors away from my daughters and wouldn't help me defend myself."

"What do you mean by that? Defending you?" Out of the corner of Daphne's eye she saw the headline and Nancy's backside on the paper. "What's this about?" She picked up the paper and quickly scanned the article.

"Andrew said he didn't know where I was that evening. He took the girls to his mother's for dinner that night and didn't get home until after eleven. I was home by the time Constance was killed and no one was there to prove that. He could have said he was home earlier to see me there—no one would know the difference—but he already told the police when he got home, and that he couldn't say where I was precisely when Constance was murdered."

Things were not looking good for Nancy. Without knowing all the facts, it looked very incriminating for her. "I've got to go. There are so many things I need to get ready. Because of all this nonsense, I can't leave town now and Andrew has to take the girls to Boston. The airline tickets must be changed, and Andrew knows nothing about looking after the girls, getting them settled in and socially connected with the other students. It'll be a disaster. Damn that Constance! She's turned my life upside down again!"

She turned on her heels and walked out the workroom door. Margot and Daphne just looked at each other for a moment. At first, they didn't know whether to laugh or cry. Underneath it all, they both privately wondered about Nancy's explosive anger and if she really could have caused harm or even death to Constance in one of her fits.

Irene broke the ice. As usual, she had a knack for voicing the most malevolent of thoughts. "The apple doesn't fall far from the tree."

Margot turned to watch Irene sorting out scarves at the front counter. "What do you mean by that?"

Daphne filled Margot in on the history of Nancy's family. Nancy was the only child of Richard and Stephanie Harrison, long time residents of Santa Lucia. They were a very prideful couple. Nancy's father worked at the bank, under the supervision of Andrew Lewis, who was slightly younger than him. He was an investment clerk, advising bank customers to put their money into various industries. He was quite risky and at the end of the 1920's had made a few people very rich on paper in a short time. Unfortunately, after the crash in '29, most margins were called in and many of the town's richest citizens suffered heavy, financial losses, including Andrew Lewis, and also affecting the bank's assets.   Andrew had to let go of many of the employees and Richard was one of them.   He took it very hard.   He couldn't find work; there wasn't much in town unless you could swing a hammer and help with construction.   Richard couldn't bring himself to do manual labor or move to find employment elsewhere. So, they sat.   Eventually, Stephanie got work at Martin's cosmetic counter, which angered Richard, to have his wife bringing in money, when it was the man's job.   People would see him wandering around town.   He was drinking and becoming an embarrassment to Stephanie.

By the early thirties, things were picking up. Richard went to Andrew to get his job back, but by then Richard's mental state and appearance had really gone downhill.   Andrew felt terrible, but he couldn't have someone so unstable representing the bank or its clientele.   Richard went into a terrible rage and the police had to come and take him away.   Poor Stephanie couldn't take Richard anymore and was advised to commit him to a mental hospital an hour's drive away.

Through it all, their daughter Nancy was kept on the east coast.   Her mother Stephanie worked as many hours as she could to keep up with the school fees and during the holidays Nancy was sent to her mother's sister's family on Nantucket.   She didn't know of what was happening in Santa Lucia.   Nancy enjoyed her time, but missed her parents and did her best not to show it.

Nancy's father Richard continued to deteriorate— throwing angry fits, and then going into silent depressions.   At end of 1933, during one of his routine electroshock therapy treatments, he died of a heart attack from a power surge.   The hospital paid out a large settlement to Stephanie, enough that she could terminate her position at Martin's and set up a trust fund for Nancy. She sent word to Nancy that she could come home at the end of her graduation from Lords. Nancy was overjoyed. She couldn't wait to see her home and family.

Nancy was given a rude awakening when she arrived home. Their little house and yard were well kept as she remembered it, but so much had changed. Her mother didn't tell her of her father's illness or death all the time she was away. It hurt Nancy deeply as her mother told her the facts of her father's death and the hospital settlement. She realized she'd never see her father again. The whole time she was away, she had written letters to him, and her mother would dutifully reply for the both of them, never letting on to the troubles befalling the household. Nancy learned the details of the whole story over the course of years from petty gossip. Until her mother's death of cancer in 1945, Stephanie always maintained a stiff upper lip and felt she'd always done the right thing by never revealing all the painful truth to her daughter.

It made Nancy a real fighter. She knew her social standing was everything in this town. She made up her mind to prove that all Harrisons were not cut from the same cloth—she still had that fiery pride. She set out to get herself a well-respected husband and create a good life for herself. At eighteen, she was a stunner, with a slim figure and auburn hair. Stephanie's expert skills with a makeup brush had made her girl turn heads. Her mother encouraged her plan, and in an odd way, the women got along. They would spend every morning pouring over the society pages, making plans on where Nancy should be that evening to be seen by the right people. With the settlement money, they bought their way into the best clubs and events in Santa Lucia.

Most of Santa Lucia society knew the story of the Harrisons and did not take well to the intrusion of Nancy. She made sure the eligible bachelors in town knew she was available. The respectable ones, such as Charles Stearns and Reginald Montgomery, showed no real interest. Constance's younger brother, Charles, was the first man Nancy went after. Constance could see right through her flirtations to her motives of securing herself into the Stearns' hard-earned wealth. Charles was flattered by her direct approach, but Constance stepped in and put a stop to it. Not easily thwarted, Nancy turned her attentions to Constance's new fiancé, Reginald. Reginald was smitten with his new love and had no time for Nancy, but Constance was not amused. The girls barely knew each other, but began crossing paths, all in the public eyes of Santa Lucia.

Some newcomers thought Nancy was a fetching young woman, but found her to be too forward. One day in early January, when she was sitting rather dejectedly by a fountain in the yacht club gardens, Andrew Lewis took a good, hard, long look at the young lady. He'd been seeing her around town and felt some sympathy for her. He had watched her throw herself at men and understood how difficult it must have been for her to come home to such hardship. Underneath the façade, he felt there was a girl worth knowing.

Andrew Lewis was almost old enough to be Nancy's father. He'd spent his early years establishing the bank and rebuilding the town. He never found the time or the interest in pursuing a family life for himself. Still living at home with his mother, he looked at Nancy and decided he could help this girl. When he sat down to talk to her, she straightened up and batted her lashes at him. It was time for Andrew to have his own family.

Once the decision was made, they got married quickly. The short courtship lasted about eight weeks and they were married in a small ceremony in March of '36. They did, however, have a lavish honeymoon, spending two months in Europe. They came back just in time for Nancy to gloat over her triumph at Constance and Reginald's wedding.

The years passed quickly as Nancy and Andrew started their married life. Nancy found happiness in the birth of her three daughters and setting up a home. The town came around to Nancy, with the general consensus that if she was good enough for the banker, she was good enough for them.

But Nancy was still Nancy. She had the Harrison pride and felt that the town owed her. She used her position as the banker's wife to become ensconced in all the social whirls and cliques in town. Although she was brash, Nancy was also the consummate hostess. She connected herself to all the right people and, more importantly, had them connecting with each other. Her social skills pleased her husband, as at many of their gatherings, important deals and decisions were reached among the guests, such as the most recent garden party for hotel investors. The one person who did not become won over by Nancy was Constance Stearns-Montgomery.

There was always one thing or another that the women would disagree upon. Whether it was the suggestion of where or when an event was to be held, or which charity it should benefit, there was constant friction between the two women. At best, the two could be at the same event at the same time and respectfully nod at each other, but usually, there would be at least one terse word uttered directly to the other before the evening was over. Santa Lucia's social set was a small group and both women felt they had a place in it and over time agreed to disagree.

Things had been quiet over the last few months. Both women had been busy with their own and their husbands' projects, so there hadn't been many public blowouts lately. However, the last one that had taken place just prior to the school opening, where Nancy had taken for granted her girls' place at the Academy, was a doozy.

"I always thought their spats were just silly. I guess she really meant all those nasty things she said about Constance after her death. And to think she was prowling around the school in a disguise that night, to me that's just crazy. She's really unhinged." Irene hastily slammed shut the scarf display case drawer while passing down her judgment.

"Irene, I would appreciate it if you'd keep this morning's conversation to yourself. Simple gossip is one thing, but something like this could ruin people's lives if it's not handled with discretion. There will be plenty of time to talk about what really happened when the case is solved. I agree it seems odd, but it's not our place to be judge and jury. If there is anything to be made out of the situation, the police will sort it out." The revelation of Nancy's history gave Margot cause to wonder, but she didn't want to stand around and idly chatter any further. "Besides, we have lots of work to do. We have clients coming in today, a fashion show to plan for next month, and I have a date to get all the details on!" She linked Daphne by the arm. "So tell me, have you stolen Babs' boyfriend?"

Daphne laughed as the girls walked up the stairs to their office. "We had a nice time and, yes, I plan to see him again. He seems very nice, a good head on his shoulders, plus easy on the eyes. We'll see. Honestly,

I don't think he's Babs' type.   He likes to hold a conversation."

"Poor thing. I guess like mother, like daughter. So, what do you think of these?" When they got into the office, Margot held up to Daphne a swatch card that had arrived in the afternoon mail yesterday. It was a selection of wool suiting plaids, small hound's-tooth and checks in a wide variety of tones. "The letter says we can get the fabric in as little as eight weeks. Might be something we could work on for the spring."

"I like this one." She pointed to a pale gray-green with a fine, silver line every few inches.

Margot had been looking at that earlier. It was the first one that had caught her attention.   "Yes, that's interesting. It's refreshing. Maybe a day suit, or even a car coat."

"I've come across some great new necklaces that would work with those stripes."   Daphne rummaged through the piles of pictures and catalogues on her desk and pulled out a blue booklet. She quickly ran through the pages 'til she found what she was looking for. She curled the magazine open to the featured picture she wanted Margot to see and handed it over to her. "Here."

Margot looked at the photograph. It was a necklace of long, thin, silver chains, so many of them that it flowed like a river. It was mid-length and closed at the back of the neck. The piece was very different from most of the bold baubles that were so popular. It was still very glittery and glamorous, so it could hold up to the current styles. She placed the swatch next to the photo and was pleased. "Look how it would pick up on the threads! I love it." She reached over and grabbed the swatch card of charmeuses she kept on hand. She fingered the pale pink and the silver samples. "I was thinking of basing an outfit on this." She gestured to the worsted wool, the solid version of the striped fabric. "We could do a couple of day suits in this, two jackets and two skirts, one in each of the wools, with matching blouses in the pink and silver and, of course, a white cotton blouse." Every season had a basic white blouse, always varied from collection to collection, but always present. It was a signature piece. They made double the number that they usually made of that item. It went with almost everything they made.

"That sounds great. Any idea what the blouse will be like this time?" Daphne asked.

"Nope." Margot grinned. "Not yet. It'll come to me." Often it was the last item she designed in the season. It summarized her theme. She set aside her samples and looked at the list she made for the day. "How are you doing with the accessories for the holiday collection? Will we have everything in time for the show next month?"

"I think so." Daphne rummaged through the piles on her desk. She came across the show list. The jewelry for the show was bright and colorful. Big, bold gems in large cut pieces of ruby, emerald, amethyst and diamond-like, clear glass in impossibly large, stone facets that rivaled the beauty of the velvets and satins of Margot's Holiday Soiree Designs. "I'd like to use black patent shoes, purses and belts for the eveningwear. It'll make everything pop. Do you like that?"

Margot affirmed. "That'll be great. It'll offset all the colors. What about the accessories for Autumn Splendor?"

Autumn Splendor was the name of the fall collection, mainly consisting of daywear suits, dresses, pants and blouses. The fall in Santa Lucia was a busy time for the society ladies. The Charity Ball and Fashion Show were the big draws for the fund raising, but there were lunches throughout the season for the continued building and restoration of the town. The historical society had a big place in the town's heart, since many of the population was raised from it.

Daphne found her list and scanned the details. Being that the fall garments were more daytime oriented, she paired up items such as clutch purses and matching pumps. In keeping with the social occasions, she chose small jewelry, such as pearls and simple studs in one-piece settings. She nodded and said, "Almost everything is here, and we're just waiting for a couple of odds and ends to arrive. I'm going to use some of Julia's more colorful purses, too. I've selected some possibly matching shoes. I'll pick them up from Wright's just before the show." Wright's on Cove Street was the best family shoe store in town. They always carried the latest styles and the girls had a standing account with them for all the shows. It was good business for them and they gave a discount to any customer who mentioned they saw them in the show. "Are you ready to get the models? Do you know what looks you need?"

Every year, as soon as the university started in the fall, the girls posted ads for students to model. Often they would get the same girls, but as students graduated and/or got married, they would need new faces. "I'm hoping Cathy Whitman will be back. It would be her third show and she carries herself so well. The flyers are ready to be posted next week in the dorms. We'll need the usual eight girls, and I figure we'll have three or four repeat models, including Nora Burbank, this year's Miss Santa Lucia. Once we know who we have, I'll confirm the hair and make-up appointments at Mr. Anthony's."

The girls settled down to concentrating on the rest of the work for the day. Shortly after eleven, the office buzzer rang, alerting the girls that they were busy downstairs on the sales floor and needed their help. After the relative calm of the upstairs office, the girls noticed how distracted the staff and customers had been by Nancy's disruptions around town that morning. It felt awful to think that Nancy may be going mad or worse yet, a murderer. Somehow, in both Margot and Daphne's hearts, they believed that no matter how mad Nancy could get, she couldn't take a life. Or maybe, that's what they wanted to believe. The comments that were flying around were strong enough to encourage the swaying of opinions.

"She came up to me this morning and accused me of tattling on her to the police. I didn't even know she was there that night," Mrs. Cooke announced to Mrs. Johnson.

Mrs. Johnson replied, "I've heard she was skulking around the school in a drab gray suit just before the opening, acting crazy."

"Like her father," stated Mrs. Cooke, with a flourish as she flipped through dresses on the rack. "I'm telling you, she did it. She's always had it in for Constance."

"She's had it in for everyone at one time or another," Mrs. Johnson snarkily remarked. "She's always been a jealous sort."

Mrs. Cooke laughed ruefully, "We'd better watch our backs until the police arrest her or Andrew finally learns to reign her in."

The two women hushed up when Margot flashed them a stern look. She didn't like to pass judgments in general, but she felt the loud comments between the two women about another customer were highly inappropriate for the shop floor.

The buzz continued all day and it seemed that everyone had something unkind to say about Nancy and her behavior, including Betty, who usually stayed out of such gossip.

"The last time I saw the two of them together in the store, there were daggers flying," Betty whispered to Mrs. Hillman, who had dropped in to see if she could pick up the purse for her daughter-in-law.

"That's no surprise to me, dear. They were like that everywhere."

Betty was insistent. "No, this time it was different. She actually threatened her and when Mrs. Lewis came in the day after Mrs. Stearns-Montgomery was killed, she seemed glad that it had happened."

Margot stepped in as Mrs. Hillman contemplated the remark. She interrupted with, "Now, Mrs. Hillman, we told you it would be a few weeks before the new purses would arrive. We don't have any for sale yet." As she spoke to the client, she looked sharply at Betty, who got the hint and walked away.

"Oh, I know. I just thought I'd check." Mrs. Hillman was a good customer, but was very persistent when she wanted something. The girls knew she'd be in at least once a week to enquire about it, but she'd purchase something on almost every visit. Today it was one of the last cotton lawn skirts on the summer clearance rack.

After she left, Margot took Betty aside and said, "I'm surprised at you. You know we don't talk about personal details from one customer to another, murder or no murder. It's not nice and bad for business." Irene sniggered as she walked by. She was usually the one who got in trouble for her remarks.

Betty blushed. "I know and I'm sorry," she sighed. "It's just, well, I've never known anyone who's been murdered. I guess I got caught up in what all the customers were saying today."

Margot gently touched her arm. She could see Betty was sincerely remorseful. "I understand; let's just not let it happen again, okay?" That was enough on the subject. Betty nodded and all was put behind them.

The girls kept hearing more truths and half-truths about Nancy all day long. It was very draining and exhausting, as they tried to remain neutral, but naturally formed their own theories and opinions privately. While the girls were tidying up the shop after closing, there was a rap at the door. Margot looked up from the rack she was straightening and saw Tom. She smiled when she saw him and let him in.

"Hi, darling, how was your day?" Margot gave him a heartfelt embrace and brushed his hair from his eyes. "Your day must have been awful. Nancy's been railing around town all day."

He gave her a little kiss and nodded hello to both Daphne and Irene. "I wish I could say that this was a social call, but I have some official questions for you, ladies." The girls noticed that Officer Davis had also come in with Tom, signaling that there was some trouble.

Margot led them to the sales counter, while Daphne and Irene gathered around. "What kinds of questions?"

"We've found something at the murder scene. Can any of you identify this ring and who you've seen wearing it?" Tom took out of his pocket a plastic evidence bag containing a signet ring.

Daphne turned on the desk lamp that sat on the counter. The room fell silent as the girls looked at the initials on the ring. It was a scripted *NH.* Irene audibly gulped. No one answered.

Tom continued. "It was found on the ground, near where the tail of Constance's scarf was tangled in the bushes. Our crew found it this morning, on the last sweep of the site." Tom paused to read the women's faces. He nodded to his assistant to make a note of their reactions.

Daphne spoke first. "I don't like to say it, but 'NH' are Nancy Lewis' initials," referring to her maiden name of Harrison.

Tom stated, "That's true, but have you ever seen her wear this ring? Think carefully." It was funny. It seemed a little large to fit Nancy's slender fingers, especially the pinky, which was the proper way to wear such rings. And, it was very understated for Nancy's showy tastes.

Margot replied. "I don't think I've ever seen that on her hands. It's too simple for her liking. She likes gemstones and diamonds. That's just not her style and not familiar." No one was feeling any more relieved. Margot couldn't think of any other NH at the moment and Nancy did admit to being at the school grounds that night, seen behind that very same building.

"Nope, to be honest, I cannot say I've seen that ring on her finger and I've fitted her for gloves and they always had to compensate for some pretty spectacular rocks." Daphne was adamant. Irene just shrugged, shook her head and walked away. For the first time in her history at the shop, she was speechless.

"You're not the first people to be perplexed by the ring." Tom sighed. "In Andrew's most recent statement, he doesn't remember ever seeing it on Nancy's finger or the ring being around the house."

The girls took one more look at the ring. It didn't look like a possession of Nancy's. However, she was in disguise with the drab suit, hat and flat shoes, all of which were out of character for the Nancy they knew. Perhaps there was a darker side to Mrs. Lewis. Could the ring have been a part of that disguise?

Tom put the evidence bag away in his pocket. "Does anyone have any more information pertaining to the case that they need to report?"

Margot shrugged, "I don't know if it makes any difference, but when Nancy stormed in here this morning, she freely admitted to being at the school that night. From the sound of it, she was making the rounds, accusing everyone of going to the police about her. She told Irene and me that whoever told the police that they saw her that night was going to be sorry. She threatened that she'd ruin their reputation. She was so mad she was spitting nails."

"We've been tracking her movements around town, so we knew she'd come here. She's under surveillance and was told not to leave town. Did she say anything about that?" Tom nodded again towards Davis, who was continually making notes.

"Only that she wasn't able to go to Boston and that Andrew would have to take the time to get the girls settled in." Margot paused. "Tom, do you honestly think Nancy could do such a thing?"

"Margot, that's what we're trying to figure out. We can't say anything until we have checked our theories, and positively identify the owner of this ring. One thing I know is that everyone who was present and unaccounted for at the school that night is considered to be a suspect."

"That leaves me out. If you don't need me, Policeman Tom, I'm on my way." He gestured for her to leave and Irene grabbed her purse from behind the desk. "See you tomorrow, girls," and out the door she went.

"We'll be on our way too. There's lots of work to go through tonight." Tom's broad shoulders slumped. He was looking very tired as his eyes met Margot's. Daphne, sensing the interrogation was finished, took off upstairs, giving Tom and Margot some privacy. Davis awkwardly milled around the front door.

"Are we on for a dinner and movie date tomorrow? It's Saturday night and you need a break." She touched his arm, concerned about making sure he got enough rest.

"Absolutely," he brightened. "We've got things under control. After the photos went missing, we've had extra staff on, so it's tight as a drum at the station. My men can work without me for a few hours."

"Good. I hear the new Ava Gardner movie is playing at the Majestic, seven o'clock. I think it's called *The Sun Also Rises*. We can go for dinner after."

"That's the Hemingway story, right? Sounds like just what I need." Tom gave Margot a peck on the cheek. "Davis and I must get back to the station. I'll call you tomorrow if there's any change in plans. Otherwise, I'll meet you at your house at 6:30. We can walk to the theatre and dinner. I could use the fresh air."

"I'm looking forward to it. To be honest, I'm looking forward to this case being finished. I hate the idea of Nancy being thought of as a killer. I mean, I know of the mental instability of her father and her animosity towards Constance, but really, I find it very hard to believe that she'd actually hurt someone."

Tom looked skeptical. "The story of her father is inaccurate. There was never any proof he was mentally incompetent. He was sent to the hospital because his wife couldn't handle his drinking problem. They didn't know what to do and there's a possibility that he had absolutely no mental condition. The electroshock therapy weakened his heart and killed him."

The more Margot was finding out, the less she wanted to know. It was a tiring day. A tiring week. "I'll let you get back to work. Officer Davis is eager to go." Margot saw him with his hand on the door, ready to leave.

"Um, yes. See you tomorrow." Tom shouted up the stairs, "Bye, Daphne. Have a good night, too!"

"See you, Tom." Daphne replied as she bounded down the stairs. She turned to Margot after they left. "What are you doing tonight? It's Friday night, so don't tell me you're going to stay here and work."

"No, but I don't have any plans." Margot started flipping through the appointment book. "What about you? No hot date?"

"Nope. I have no plans and don't feel like going home." Daphne covered the book with her hands. "Let's do something together. It's been a while since we've had any fun outside of here. Why don't we go down to the wharf and get fish and chips? It's a nice warm night and we haven't been down there all summer."

Margot lit up. "That's a great idea. We could just walk around, people watch. We haven't done that in ages. Let's go."

CHAPTER FOURTEEN

The girls took Daphne's car down to the end of Cove Street and parked near the entrance of the Santa Lucia Fisherman's Wharf. The Wharf was a long wooden pier that jutted out into the harbor from the wide coved beach. Years ago, it had been a working pier for commercial fishermen, but as the town grew and industries changed, it became a great spot for people to eat and wander. It was always lively with busking musicians and artists selling their wares, as well as benches to sit on where people could take in the breathtaking views of both land and water. There were amusements such as restaurants and shops, including a penny arcade that attracted the teenagers. It was a great place to lose your troubles.

The sun was still high in the sky on a brilliant summer evening, with just a hint of breeze off the Pacific. There were many people milling about along the promenade, both tourists and locals. The girls nodded hello to those they knew, moving pleasantly through the crowds. At the very end of the wharf, they got fish and chips and lemonade from the take-out window of the Sand Dollar. They sat down at a bench facing the water. They laughed and talked about nothing, like they used to, before things had changed. After the shop had gotten up to full steam, Margot had started seriously dating Tom, and the two girls rarely spent any time together that didn't mean business.

"This is really nice. Why don't we do this more often?" Margot asked Daphne.

"It is, isn't it? I don't know," Daphne shrugged. "I guess we've gotten really busy with the store—which is great—but it seems so crazy right now with what's happened." She brightened and affirmed, "We should make a point of doing something every month, no matter what."

Margot smiled. "I agree. Not work, not murder. Just fun." There was a long, companionable silence as the girls ate, but eventually she just had to ask. "Daphne, do you really think Nancy is capable of murder?"

Daphne gave it some real thought. "I don't think so, but I'm not sure. What do you make of the ring?"

"The style of it is out of character for Nancy and she is very particular of the image she portrays," Margot stated and took a sip of her drink. "But really, this whole scene is out of line for everyone involved." She started listing facts and perspectives on her fingertips. "We've got Constance all flirty and girlish, Nancy running around the school in a disguise, evidence stolen from the police department, and now this ring that points toward Nancy by maiden name only. And this is just what we know, never mind all the other rumors floating around and information that the police have."

"It's spooky with the ring." Daphne poked around at the rest of her fries. "I know she'd never purchase it for herself, but if it had been given to her at a young age, say by her father, wouldn't she keep it close to her at all times, even hidden? And, it doesn't help that she was there that night. We know that's true; she's admitted it."

"That surprised me, too. Nancy strikes me as the kind of person who doesn't admit to anything. She seemed scared, vulnerable, and maybe even guilty. Again, not the Nancy I know." Margot shook her head.

"The only consistent thing is that the two of them fought on a regular basis."

"She was always really nasty about Constance, but I think she truly respected her and, in a funny way, misses her," Daphne sighed. "They were sparing partners. Nancy may be a vindictive social climber, but I've known her a long time and can't see her killing Con. What is upsetting is that all of the evidence points to her."

"So, if it's not her, who else could the evidence point to?" Margot was going through her mind thinking of other possible logical suspects.

"Good question. Well, they've eliminated Reginald and Charles, also Headmistress Larsen." Daphne paused as she chewed on her last French fry. "There was the rumor about Constance having an affair, but no one's mentioning that anymore, now that Nancy's the main suspect. We don't know anything more about that."

"So that takes us back to square one. I do hope we get to the bottom of this before long. It's creepy thinking there's a cold-blooded killer walking the streets. For all we know, they could be right here on the wharf with us," Margot shuddered.

Daphne laughed. "Ugh. You've been watching too many episodes of *Mystery Theater*. My guess is that it *was* someone who personally wanted to do Constance in. Nothing else has happened to anyone before or since then."

"Do you think it was for money?" Daphne shook her head at Margot's question. "No, I don't think so either. The whole crowd of suspects is moneyed." Then there was a glaring fact that Margot had to express. "She was acting so differently lately. The dress she requested for the school opening was stunning, but hardly her style either. She was so vivacious in the last couple of weeks. I've never seen her like that. Have you?"

They were back to the topic of Constance's behavior over the last month or so. "No." Daphne mulled over her thoughts. "At first, I chalked it up to the excitement over the school opening, and you know what they say about middle age, but she seemed giddy, like newly in love, but she never mentioned Reginald at all, did she?"

"Come to think of it, no. She really wasn't mentioning much of anything. She didn't bring up details of how the school was coming along, the business, any charity events, nothing. She was secretive, coy." When fitting customers, they often gave away intimate personal details to the girls. There was something about standing around in your unmentionables that made even the most private women open up. It was second nature for Daphne and Margot who'd heard it all from the Santa Lucia society, but kept it confidential. Constance was no exception. "She even hinted to me about needing some new pretty undergarments, more lacy than that girdle she was always in."

"I remember that. It almost made me laugh. Constance was always so practical. And the dress you made, at her suggestion! It was very pretty and made her look so beautiful, but it really was such a change from her usual. I don't think I'd ever seen her in pastels or a lighter fabric than tweed."

Margot recalled her regular orders. "We've done overcoats, two piece suits, a couple of cocktail dresses in wool crepe that covered her up quite severely, even for teas and parties. She was always dressed more like Reginald's business partner than wife. Steady, reliable and smart rather than seductive. That dress, it was definitely cut to draw attention and did you notice that she put on perfume before she left the store that day?"

"You know, you're right—she never wore perfume. I don't remember ever smelling any scent around her, other than horses. And she left the shop wearing the dress. She still had hours to go before the school opening on that day." A light bulb appeared over Daphne's head. "The more I think about it, it seems odd for her to have worn the dress right out of the store. She was so excited about her new look, I got all caught up in her mood, but see, that too was not one of Constance's traits."

As the girls exhausted all the possibilities, the sun was lowering into a golden pink glow over the water, still warm. Margot wadded up her wrappings from dinner and stood up. "What do you say to an ice cream cone, my treat?"

"I'd say hello, double strawberry vanilla!" Daphne laughed. "It's been ages since I've had a cone."

The girls made their way back from the end of the wharf to The Milky Way Ice Cream Shop and Soda Parlor, nearer to where the deck narrowed down to the pier. The shop was a town favorite, as they made all of their own ice creams, sundaes and malteds. True to everywhere else on the wharf, it was very busy on the warm Friday night.

As Daphne and Margot left the shop, they ran smack dab into a familiar face. "Daniel!" Daphne exclaimed. "Hi!"

Dan smiled, "Hi, yourself. Those look good," he said, indicating the cones. Accompanying him was Rick, one of the stable hands from the Academy. He introduced him to the girls.

"I'm surprised to see you here tonight. I thought you were going to your parents' this weekend," Daphne remarked.

"Oh, there's been a change of plans. One of the horses had a bad run and could have a sprain or even a fracture, and we need to keep an eye on it, so I'm staying around after all. He seems to be managing okay right now, so we thought we'd come down and grab dinner and a beer. I've heard how great the scene was down here on the Wharf. Rick mentioned that the fish and chips at the Sand Dollar are delicious. Do you want to join us?"

Daphne held up her cone. "Oh, that's too bad. We were just there. Another time, I guess. The food is really good."

Dan looked down at himself. They were still in their work clothes—jeans and denim shirts. They were dusty from the trails and he felt awkward. "If I'd thought we'd run into you here, I would've dressed up a little."

"Yeah, well, that's okay," Daphne stammered. Secretly, she thought he looked just fine, all ruffled and rugged. Margot stepped back a little, amused that her friend was a little stymied.

"I know, why don't we make it a date for tomorrow? We can get dressed up and go somewhere really nice. What do you say?"

Daphne had no idea that Dan would be interested at all in fancy dinners and nights on the town. It pleased her, as that was an aspect of her social life she loved. "Sure! Do you know Antonio's?"

"The Italian place on Cove?"

"Yes, that's it."

"Sounds good to me. Would you like me to make reservations for seven tomorrow night?" She nodded happily, licking her cone that was now dripping down her hand. "Great. Let's meet there."

"Daniel? I thought that was you!" A woman, slight, in her mid-forties came up from behind and tapped him on his elbow.

He turned around. "Mrs. Wrightman, hi. How are you?"

"Oh, we're fine," she turned back to indicate the man just behind her. "David and I were just speaking about your family."

Dan introduced Daphne, Margot and Rick to David and Christine Wrightman, a couple from Ventura who'd purchased horses from his parents' stables. "How are the Arabians?"

"They're doing just fine, such beautiful animals. Actually, we might have something of interest for your family," Christine replied.

"Oh?" Dan was listening, but keeping his eye contact on Daphne, who was equally enamored, as her ice cream started dripping down her cone again.

"Yes, my boy, a business proposition!" David Wrightman looped his arm through Dan's, ready to enthusiastically relay his pitch. "Let me buy you a beer and tell you all about it!"

Dan and Rick exchanged looks. Rick seemed to be compliant to go along for the ride. David Wrightman didn't leave them much choice as he started leading them down the pier. Dan waved goodbye to the girls as they were being escorted away. Wrightman's excited voice remained audible. "Now then, let me tell you what I have in mind and you can share it with your old man. How is good old Nicholas Henshaw, anyway?"

The words made Margot freeze. "Did you catch that?"

Daphne was still gazing off in Daniel's direction, giving a little wave as he looked back. "What?"

"The name!"

"What name?"

"Dan's father's. Daniel Henshaw! His father is *Nicholas Henshaw*!"

Daphne was busy mopping up with a napkin as she finally noticed that the ice cream had dripped down onto her hand. "So?"

"Henshaw—Nicholas Henshaw. $\mathcal{NH}$! The ring?" Margot exclaimed.

Daphne's eyes grew wide, "No! That can't be!"

"It could be! The ring might have been his father's. Maybe Dan was wearing it." Although shocked, Margot kept leaping forward.

Daphne kept up the pace. "Which means Dan still might be…"

"…the lover. And or murderer," Margot finished what Daphne could not. "I'll call Tom as soon as I get back."

"Oh, great! I've made a date with a murderer," Daphne muttered, half joking but not sure about anything any more.

"We don't know for sure." Margot paused. She was equally puzzled at the idea that they were onto something or just jumping to false conclusions. "Just stay in public places with him, okay?"

"And ask him lots of questions!" Daphne affirmed. "Let's go. I'll give you a ride home." The girls walked very quickly, almost running to the beach.

There must have been a party on her block, because as Daphne drove up Margot's street, there was nowhere to park. She circled the block and Margot got out of the car at the stop sign on the corner. Daphne crept the vehicle along the street, keeping at Margot's walking pace. Two cars caught up with Daphne and started honking behind her, wanting her to speed up. Daphne was insistent on keeping a close watch on her friend, but Margot was finding it embarrassing. Margot flagged her off and Daphne finally sped up when Margot wouldn't budge until she did.

It wasn't very far to her house—about half a block— but she still walked very quickly. All of a sudden, she heard a twig snap and the clicking of heels. A chill rose up the back of her neck. She caught her breath and momentarily panicked. Was she being followed? Was it Nancy? She stopped, gulped and turned around.

"So sorry dear, I didn't mean to frighten you." Mrs. O'Leary, Margot's neighbor, was out walking her little white terrier, Sparky. She looked concerned at Margot. "Should you be out so late on your own? Well, never mind. We should be safe right now. They've caught the murderer. That Nancy Lewis always was a bad apple." Sharon O'Leary might have been older and frail, but her judgments were firm.

Margot really wanted to get in and call Tom, but she knew if she didn't acknowledge Sparky she'd hear about it. She reached down to pat him. "Out for your evening walk, huh, pal? Beautiful night, isn't it?"

"Oh yes, especially now that we're all safe again," Sharon repeated. "You knew her, didn't you? The whole town knew of her, but you actually knew her from the store, didn't you?" She was eager to talk.

Margot could tolerate Sharon O'Leary from a neighborly distance, but she could be a busy body, especially about people she didn't personally know. "It's all still under investigation, Mrs. O'Leary. The police have their suspects, but the case isn't closed yet."

"And you should know. You're in well with the police, your Tom and all. Ooh, he must tell you about all kinds of goings on!" The gleam in her eye was annoying.

"Actually, we don't talk about open cases. Tom is very dedicated to his work and wouldn't jeopardize situations." Margot could feel herself getting suckered into another friendly spar with Sharon O'Leary. It was time to end it. "Good night, Mrs. O'Leary. Busy day tomorrow!"

"Your Tom coming by tonight? I see he's been spending a lot of time at your place lately, hasn't he?"

Sharon called after her as Margot walked closer to her own walkway.

She decided not to answer as she smiled and politely waved. *Has she been keeping tabs on me?* she wondered. *No matter. I guess the widow needs her activities.* As she approached her front porch, Mr. Cuddles was seated on the chair by the door waiting to come in. She picked him up and they went in. Margot made a quick call to Tom at the station to reveal to him their findings and then settled in for the night.

CHAPTER FIFTEEN

Margot woke up at six thirty feeling more refreshed than she had in days. After phoning Tom at the station last night and telling him what they'd found out about another NH, her shoulders relaxed and her mind cleared. The information was now in the right hands. He thanked her and without telling her too much about the case, he assured her that he had it under control and his command of the situation made her feel at ease. She got ready for work in half an hour. She skipped breakfast, as Lana would be bringing her usual muffins and coffee from the café. On Saturdays, the office and back room were closed. Margot spent the day on the sales floor, so she dressed more casually. She slipped on a pair of paprika cotton capris with a cute, sleeveless blouse that had a wing collar in a cream color with tiny, rusty, red flowers. A quick touch of lipstick and eyeliner, and she was good to go. She saw the morning newspaper neatly folded and tossed on her stoop and threw it in her front door, narrowly missing Mr. Cuddles as he shot out of the house.

As she walked briskly along Laurel Avenue to the town center, she could hear the familiar sounds of the Saturday market—people milling about, a mariachi band tuning up to play by the fountain at Avila Square. The market was so much fun that it always put her in a good mood. Last week had been the exception. It had been a ghost town—just two days after Constance had been murdered. Now it was getting back to normal. She could see the usual temporary barricades just past

Bay Street to keep the cars out of the way and let people wander about safely around the stands. Being that it was a long-standing event, it was lively but orderly and attracted townsfolk and tourists alike.

Margot liked to get to the market early and watch the vendors set up. There were pick-up trucks parked along the main streets from the nearby farms within the cordoned-off area. They were able to come in early and set up from the crack of dawn to greet the eager shoppers for the first pick of the crops. It was already abuzz with activity as the farmers and their families were displaying their goods. There were fresh, golden, red peaches piled gently into wooden crates, crisp, early apples the shade of tender, green, grass shoots and lemons, limes and oranges colorfully arranged in pyramids. The smells were heavenly. She made her way to Hector Avila's stall, the grandson of the square's namesake, still farming the family's original land.

"Hector, your tomatoes are to die for. Look at the size of them!"

Hector beamed with pride as he held up a tomato the size of a grapefruit. "Good morning, Miss Margot. Come see my corn. Fresh picked this morning. First crop of the year! The silk is so fine, you could sew with it!" he joked with her as he led her to the other end of his booth, where his wife Carmella was arranging the corn, squash and zucchinis. She demurely smiled and nodded her head in Margot's direction. "You pick out what you like and I'll have my boy bring it to your shop later." This was the usual arrangement for them.

She nodded and smiled back to Carmella. "Thank you, Hector. I'll take you up on that. I think today I'll get a couple of tomatoes, three cucumbers, some of your leaf lettuce, a bunch of carrots, a basket of raspberries and of course, some corn—a half dozen ears. I'll cook some for Tom, too. Now then, who else's fruit looks good this week?" The Avila's mainstay was ground crops, but he knew everyone at the market.

"Victor's plums are perfect, just right, but I would go over to Samuel's to get my peaches and apples."

They squared away the bill as Carmella packaged up Margot's food. The market didn't officially open until 8:00; however, merchants around the square were allowed to purchase their goods before they opened their own doors.

Margot's eyes lit up as she saw the gladioli at one of the flower stands. Every Saturday, the girls took turns buying big, beautiful bouquets for the shop from the vendors. This week was Daphne's turn. Margot hoped she would get armloads full. The brilliantly, blooming stalks of orange, fuchsia, pink, white, yellow and red got her creative wheels visibly spinning.

She continued on over to Samuel Francisco's stall where he met her with a warm smile and showed her all the fresh, tree fruits picked from his orchard an hour south of Santa Lucia. She purchased the first apples of the season and the last of the summer peaches for the year. "I think some fresh lemons and limes are in order too. If this warm weather continues like this, I'll be making a lot more lemonade." She picked up a lime and inhaled the aroma of the zest. She arranged for the Avila's boy to pick up the fruit later to deliver with the rest of her produce.

She made one more quick stop at Victor Rodrigues' stand where she bought a few purple plums to complete her shopping. She took those with her and headed to the store. *It'll be a busy one at the square today,* she thought. *Back to business for everyone.*

Margot walked up the stairs to the Poppy Cove front door around 8:30. She started gathering the vases from the window displays. Daphne came in a few minutes later, struggling with bundles of gladioli in every color imaginable. She barely made it to the front counter without splaying them in all directions. Breathlessly, she greeted Margot with, "Did you call Tom last night? What did he say?" Daphne had dark circles under her sleepless eyes and the concern over their latest discovery continued to show in her curls, which were more frazzled than bouncy. However, her clothing reflected her naturally, adorable self as she was dressed in white capris with thin blue, black and gold stripes, black ballerina flats and a royal blue sleeveless shirt tied at the waist.

"Let me help you with that." Margot helped gather up the stray flowers before they hit the floor. She smiled, pleased there were so many. "He said they would check it out."

"That's it? That's all he said?" Daphne, stunned by the mild reaction, kept dropping the bundles she was attempting to straighten and shoved the vases over so firmly, they clattered.

Margot moved past her, taking the vessels to the lunchroom. "About the case, yes. He never tells me about the details of his work. He can't. You know that."

Daphne followed behind her and set her batch of bouquets in the kitchen sink. "Yeah, I know, but I thought he might say something, even small about it. Like, not even surprise, or that they know something else about Dan, or that it was irrelevant."

Margot raised her eyebrows at the last comment as she looked at her friend. Obviously, Daphne wanted to believe Dan was in the clear. "Nope, nothing. Look, you know Tom—he'll get it right. The whole NH thing with Dan may be just a co-incidence. They're his father's initials, not his, after all." The girls went back out to get the rest of the items. "The easiest thing would be to just ask him about it. Does he wear any jewelry?"

"Come to think of it, not that I've noticed, no chains, no other rings, nothing. Well, other than a watch," Daphne seriously considered.

"Then ask him in a roundabout way tonight. Bring up jewelry in general, or think up something, like maybe getting his opinion on a men's line or something, or even just ask him about his father. You can think of something," Margot replied.

Lana was knocking at the front door, carrying her usual Saturday offerings of coffee and muffins. Margot unlocked the door and let her in. "Morning, girls! Have you heard the news?"

Margot glanced quickly at Daphne who paled and froze in her tracks. She turned her attention back to Lana. "No, what news?"

"Reginald's house got broken into last night!" Lana continued on to the kitchen, where they regularly had their Saturday morning breakfast. Behind her back, Margot and Daphne exchanged looks as they scrambled up the last of the flowers and vases, indicating to each other that they decided to not reveal their own news, but scope out Lana's instead. They followed behind her silently.

Lana set the tray down on the table. "It's all anyone at the tea room was talking about. It was on the cover of this morning's paper. Didn't you see the story?"

Margot spoke first. "No, I left early this morning and just tossed the paper in the door." She turned from the counter and asked, "Was Reginald hurt?"

Lana shook her head as she arranged the table for the three of them. "No, I don't think so."

"No one said anything at the square," Margot commented, thinking about what they had pieced together so far.

Lana shrugged and replied, "Busy morning for the farmers. I doubt they had time to read the news today, or really care that much. It's a different world from theirs. Anyhow, it does make the murder even more mysterious. Apparently someone broke in through a window in Reginald's office on the ground floor around midnight."

Daphne finally piped up as she was trying to get a rather full and drooping stalk of orange blooms to co-operate with the rest of the stems in a vase. "Did they catch the person?"

"No. The maid's quarters were right off the den and she heard a commotion and ran into the room. The place had been ransacked and she shrieked when she opened the door. Whoever it was fled out the window by the time Reginald came downstairs. The police won't say if the break-in was connected to Con's murder, but it must be. They say things were only rifled through and nothing was taken. No jewelry, money, nothing." Lana motioned for the girls to sit down.

Preoccupied, Margot continued fussing with the mixed bouquet she was working on and stated, "So, she must have gotten a good look at who it was." She eyed Daphne, who she could tell by her shallow breathing was dreading the answer, but needing to know all the same.

Lana shook her head. "It all happened so fast. All she could see was that it was a slight person, not very tall and they were dressed in all black." She broke off a piece of muffin. "Girls, come eat—they're fresh from the oven, still warm."

The girls passed glances quickly, with Daphne looking a little relieved, as it could not have been Dan, or even his co-worker, as Dan was tall and Rick, although shorter, was stocky and could not be considered slight by any means. With that conclusion reached and the floral arrangement ready for the displays, they joined Lana at the table.

Lana turned and held up a muffin to Daphne. "Try these. They're new—strawberry almond."

Daphne's eyes lit up for the first time that morning. "Oh, that looks divine. Thank you!" She took the muffin from Lana. "Say, these are good," she said as she broke off a piece.

"If you ask me," Lana said between bites, "it all sounds fishy. Someone slight? That could be Nancy Lewis. That would be just like her, to go through someone else's things, snooping around. She claims that's all she was doing that day at the school. Who's to say she wouldn't do that at Constance's home? And what could she have been looking for?"

They really needed to stick to the facts, or it could become a McCarthy trial, a witch-hunt that made everyone suspicious of everyone else. "No one said that it was Nancy." However, even as she said it, Margot had to admit that the description fit Nancy to a T.

"Well no," Lana thoughtfully acquiesced as she picked at her muffin. "The paper didn't say Nancy or even mention her in the article, but it does seem that someone was really out to get Constance and not a random murder. Maybe the Montgomerys were involved in something darker than any of us realize." The girls stopped talking for a moment as a chill entered their thoughts. Lana shook off the feeling and got ready to leave. "I'll be back around eleven to get the tray. Be sure to get your share away from Daphne before she devours them all!"

"See you later, Lana!" Margot poured herself a second cup of coffee and grabbed another muffin. "She's right; these are great."

Daphne paused and thought while she ate her breakfast. She couldn't get her mind off the break-in. "Well, if it was a slight figure, that counts out Dan," she sighed with relief. "I don't want to say it, but it sure sounds like it could be Nancy."

"They never said it was Nancy," Margot impatiently reiterated. She didn't want to give in that she thought it, too. She really hated to pass judgment on someone without full proof.

"I know, but it's a logical guess. Who else could it be?"

"Exactly. Who else could it be?" Margot brightened at the prospect of a new suspect, maybe someone they didn't know.

"Lana said something interesting. Maybe Reginald was in on something crooked and Con got in the way. I know he's been cleared, but what if he hired someone to do it?" Daphne's blue eyes grew wilder with excitement. "What if he hired someone to do it all? You know, kill Constance?"

Margot glared at Daphne.

"It could be. It happens. It's always the quiet ones," Daphne confirmed. "Maybe I should mention this to Tom."

"Maybe not," Margot frowned. "Come on, do your really think that Reginald could do such a thing? He's got too much established here, and too much class to pull something like that off."

"Yeah, I guess you're right about Reggie. He's not the type, at least not that we've seen." Although

210 *Strangled by Silk*

Daphne was content to think better of Reginald, she was disappointed to still be at square one.

Margot nibbled at breakfast and sipped her coffee. "It does look like Constance had ruffled someone's feathers. Maybe she came across something about one of the students' parents?"

"Good point. I've never thought of that. Could it be some kind of blackmail or cover up?" Daphne mused. Coffee, food and the prospect of all three of the people they knew—Dan, Reginald and Nancy—being innocent, perked her up immensely.

Margot paused before replying. Daphne had a point, but she didn't want to encourage her overactive imagination. "Yes, there may be something there, but we don't know anything about it. Tom's lead about the man having lunch with Constance at Antonio's is still under question. They were in a dark corner of the restaurant and no one got a really good look at him. For all we know it could have been business about the school."

Daphne nodded emphatically. "Which we don't know if it was good or bad. I think he had something to do with it. Maybe he did it, or knows about it. They need to figure out who it was and talk to him to decide if it's relatable to the case."

Margot thoughtfully considered what Antonio had told Tom. "He was a stranger to Antonio, so to me that means he's either an out-of-towner or new to Santa Lucia." With all that was recently happening in town lately, it left the field of suspects wide open again, including the suspicion of the new resident, Dan, who clearly knew where Antonio's was, according to last night's conversation. But come to think of it, Peter was another new man around town, and obviously liked to be out in the scene. The situation was getting more confusing, not less. Margot wanted to shake that off and think more clearly. "Other than that, she wasn't seen around town very much lately. Con had been secretive, but also it could have been construed as her just being really busy and out of sight, working."

"You're right, but there was some reason for Con being murdered and Reginald's break-in." The girls' reverie was broken by the jingle of the front door bell. Daphne looked at her watch. "Oh my goodness! It's nine! We're open!"

The girls gave themselves a quick once over in the lunchroom's hanging mirror and each grabbed a vase to take to the front, prepared to greet the first customer of the day. It actually turned out to be Irene, coming in for her shift. She looked as sultry as ever, in a royal blue sheath dress, with a pencil skirt ending just below the knee and had a low square neckline, tight bodice and little cap sleeves. It buttoned down the back, and although it was very snug, it stayed on the respectable side of vulgar. The confident women, who were the main kind of Santa Lucia females, would want to emulate it. The insecure ones, well, Irene didn't care and—quite frankly—were not the store's biggest spenders.

Irene straightened out the front and got the cash desk ready. Margot went back to the lunchroom to clear away the breakfast dishes while Daphne arranged the floral displays. They all worked quietly. Irene most likely was still working off last night, and Daphne and Margot didn't feel like discussing the current situation with her, as her acerbic comments would feel a little more offensive and personal than usual.

Just before ten, Betty started work. Margot was pleased to see Betty in one of her favorite dresses from the shop. It was from last summer—a white cotton sundress with cap sleeves, a sweetheart neckline with a fitted bodice and a wide, full skirt. Around the hem

were large, tall-stemmed, reddish-orange, full-bloomed
poppies that Margot had hand painted which rose
halfway up the skirt. It was finished with a slim green
leather belt, the same color as the flower stems. Betty
took such great care of it that it looked as fresh and new
as it did on the hanger. The lively style suited her so
well. She was a young married woman, happy in her
life, pretty and with the world at her feet. Although she
and Irene were very different from each other and
sometimes had personality rows, the contrast worked
beautifully in the store as they appealed to a wide scope
of clients. Each in their own way gave customers a
vision of the people they liked or wanted to be in
themselves.

With the front door propped open, there was plenty
of sunshine and fresh ocean air as usual, but the
Saturday market made it even more idyllic. The sounds
of the mariachi band and the aromas of the flowers and
food drifted in all morning long. Poppy Cove's inviting
corner entrance and pretty windows attracted regulars
and visitors alike, giving them a steady stream of
customers.

As the morning progressed, Daphne relaxed. Sure,
there was lots of speculation about the break-in, the
customers were abuzz about it, but there was no
mention about the ring or the initials NH. Even Irene,
who usually loved to spread half-truths and watch
people grapple with them, never mentioned a thing
about it.

Not everyone was happy with the uneventful
morning. Loretta came in around eleven, looking
forlorn and lost at sea. She entered the store with a
heavy sigh, made her way to the sales desk and started
fiddling with the necklaces. Irene, who'd been
updating the appointment book, glared at Loretta, not
interested in her mood. She closed the book, put it

away in the drawer and left to do anything else. Loretta continued playing with the baubles and chains, letting out loud sighs as often as she physically could, while glancing around the shop, trying to get anyone's attention.

Margot came from the back, carrying an armload of new gray flannel skirts from the workroom. She quickly surveyed the situation. To her immediate right, was the mopey, petulant Loretta, customers scattered around the store, and Daphne in a far right corner, adjusting a display. Daphne eyed Margot with a smirk, who subtly rolled her eyes and took the approach to console the listless, gossip columnist. "Loretta, take a look at these!" She draped all but one of the skirts on the counter and held up the remainder for Loretta to ogle.

Loretta sighed again and glanced over, "Umm," was all she said and continued to play with the necklaces.

Margot was undeterred. She began to point out the beautiful garment's attributes. The skirt was made of a light-weight, gray flannel, a full circle with gored seaming for shape and fit, with a slim waistband and finished with a narrow black patent leather belt. It was made of the same cloth as the other new suiting to match perfectly. With the new white and red blouses, they would make stunning daytime ensembles. Also, she knew Loretta loved to see the new pieces first before anyone else. Quite often, they ended up in her column, which was a great business move for the store. She enthusiastically pointed out the features and displayed the drape of the skirt like the best games show hostess would, but Loretta was unfazed. Finally, she gave up and asked, "What's wrong, Loretta?"

Loretta took a deep breath and sighed again. "Well, nothing really, but that's the problem. There's nothing for me to write about. Because of the funeral, no one's scheduled any parties or luncheons this weekend. The school opening has been postponed indefinitely. No one other than Nancy as been publicly misbehaving and I'm drawing blanks on how to make something up. And I have a deadline!"

Betty came to a sudden stop as she was flouncing back from the fitting rooms. "Ooh, you should go up to Smart's Oldsmobile! They're having a big sale today. I helped Dwight blow up balloons since the crack of dawn this morning. There's hot dogs and lemonade, and a marching band! You just never know who's going to buy a car today!"

There was a pause as Loretta glanced at Betty's perky face and turned back to Margot. "See what I mean?" she muttered.

Betty just shrugged and bounced off. "I think it's exciting."

Margot smiled. "You never know. There might be something there."

"Hmmuh," was Loretta's reply.

Margot, flagging but still persevering, said, "Well, what about a social angle on someone else's story? What are the other reporters working on?" Daphne paid more attention, wondering if Margot was leading Loretta into giving them the scoop on the crime beat, and if their new friends were involved.

Loretta shook her head. "There's no news. Everyone's out of the office, snooping around. The police are tight-lipped. They won't tell us anything about Nancy, the investigation, or the break-in."

Hearing that, Daphne sauntered over, relieved. "Maybe there's nothing new to tell."

Loretta shook her head. "No, I think there's something big brewing, they just won't tell us. Weathers is stalking them like the bloodhound he is."

She slumped back down. "Not that it makes any difference to my column." She gave up futzing with the accessories. "Ooh, you've got to have something for me. What about something for the fashion show? Please tell me you're still having it!"

"Yes, we are."

"What can you give me?" Loretta poised with pen and notepad at the ready.

Margot pursed her lips. She thought about what she already had shared with Loretta about the new season's colors and styles. They'd covered a lot of the details and Margot still wanted to leave some air of mystery for the big night. "Sorry, but I don't want to give too much away before the show."

"Oh come on, something. Anything."

Daphne lit up and rescued the situation. "I've got some new handbags coming. I've got the samples upstairs. I'll go get them."

Pawing over the handbags kept Loretta occupied while the girls could assist their clients on what was becoming a busy day. After she was done *oohing* and *aahing* over the gorgeous items, she said, "Thanks, this is great! I'll do a full write up on these." She snapped her notebook shut and dropped it in her purse. "Well, time for lunch. See you in the funny papers!"

As she was leaving, Betty called after her, "Don't forget the car sale at Smart's!" Loretta waved her off and went to the Tearoom to sort out her notes and have lunch.

CHAPTER SIXTEEN

The morning had passed by like a blur and, other than the gossip about the break-in and speculation, it was slowly beginning to feel like before, except if you counted that Constance would never come in the door or that Nancy under house arrest could not be by to rant and complain, but still buy something. Before they knew it, it was noon and Abigail Browning was coming in for her Saturday afternoon shift. She was a great girl, always ready and willing to help. She had such grace and poise for someone so young, and looked adorable in her blue gingham blouse with white collar and cuffs on the short sleeves and freshly pressed white cotton circle skirt. She straightened out the clothing and re-hung the tried-on garments with great care. She was well spoken and often telephoned customers to remind them of their appointments and items on hold or layaway, as well as for upcoming events like the fashion shows. Originally, the girls had considered Daphne's younger sister for the position and although Lizzy was very energetic, Abigail had maturity beyond her years.

As all the girls were each busy helping customers, a murmur of interest wound through the store. Santa Lucia, being close to Hollywood, attracted its fair share of weekending movie stars. Today was no exception. Standing by the rack of the newest daytime dresses was Joyce Jones, a beautiful young starlet. Accompanying her was a rather stern looking woman, briskly flipping through the garments, constantly commenting and critiquing items as she went along. Every so often, she would hold one out to Joyce and either nod and drape it over her arm, or frown and put it back. Margot smiled and nodded in their direction and was pleased to have caught Joyce's eye, who returned the gesture. By the time Miss Jones' companion was demanding assistance, Betty had finished packaging up Mrs. Falconer's latest purchase and was ready to help them.

"Oh, Miss Jones, my name is Betty and I just love your movies!" she gushed as she rushed up to the pair. "Especially *Moon Over My Heart*! It was *so* romantic!"

Joyce Jones, used to the adulation, turned her head to make eye contact with Betty. She smiled dazzlingly, accepted the compliment with grace and simply said, "Thank you."

"Here, take these." The brusque woman, shorter and plainer than both Miss Jones and Betty in her rather masculine gray pantsuit and frizzy short dark hair, shoved the garments in Betty's direction. She resumed flipping through the clothes. "We're on a schedule," she spoke to Betty, but aimed her comment at her charge.

"These dresses are just darling! I could use a few," Miss Jones said as the woman pulled out a slim-fitting, red number and held it up to the star. Her dark brown curls and fair complexion set it off beautifully.

"Oh, that suits you! I'll set up a dressing room for you, Miss Jones," Betty offered, as the stranger handed more garments off to her.

"These too, please!" Miss Jones exclaimed as she quickly took another three off the rack herself. "Oh, and call me Joyce." She motioned in the direction of her companion. "This is my manager, Frances Keating."

"Yes, Frances Keating," the woman stated, handing Betty the armload of garments and extending her hand for a firm shake.

Betty juggled the clothes awkwardly, shook her hand and winced under the squeeze's pressure. Frances immediately dropped her hand and reached into her jacket pocket and took out a small notepad and pen and began checking off items while looking at her watch. She paused and looked up and said, "Well, what are you waiting for, Betty?"

Joyce rolled her eyes and shrugged sympathetically at her while flashing her another charming smile. Betty happily nodded back and scampered off, pleased as punch to be conversing with someone so glamorous. Joyce continued to shop, moving around from display to display, with Frances chattering and picking up the occasional garment or trinket, oblivious to the other customers, as they tried to discreetly watch the pair and comment among themselves, clucking like hens.

Daphne had just finished up outfitting Dorothy McGillis with a new black patent clutch purse and hot pink sheath dress and brought her to the sales counter. Irene was there to assist her by ringing up the sale while she continued to converse with Dorothy as she wrapped up her purchases.

"Oh my goodness! Imagine a big star like Joyce Jones shopping in our town," Dorothy exclaimed, fluttery and breathless. "Oh, I think she just picked out the dress I just bought!"

"Mrs. McGillis, the total's wrong. You've got a five written here instead of a nine," Irene flatly stated as she handed the check back to her.

"Oh yes. Sorry, it's just so exciting." She turned her head back over her shoulder to watch the scene, ripping the second check as she moved. "Oh dear!"

Irene responded with a glare and exasperated sigh, but Daphne just smiled and reached her hand to pat Dorothy's. "That's okay. Just write us another one. Third time lucky!"

And so it was. Daphne finished wrapping the package. It looked lovely with the tissue and Poppy Cove sticker concealing the purchases. Irene put the correct check in the till for safekeeping. After they were finished, Dorothy still lingered at the counter, watching Joyce Jones' every move. Daphne said goodbye to her and smiled at Irene, indicating for her to be nice, and left the two women, after noticing a commotion from the corner of her eye. Suppressing a smirk, she walked up to Margot who'd been straightening up a stalk of orange gladiolus that was leaning against a skirt hem on a mannequin in the front window and quietly tapped her on the shoulder.

Margot stood up and turned around. Daphne motioned silently in the direction from where she'd just been and they watched one patron in particular with extreme interest. Over in the back corner, just under the stairwell, Loretta had snuck back in and was furiously taking notes, her little birdlike eyes darting up and down through her rhinestone, cat-eye glasses, following Joyce's every move. From her crouched position, she suddenly reached up to the nearby cash desk, blindly fumbling and pawing at the surface.

Irene glanced over from the ledger and watched the hand for a moment. She looked at Dorothy, still standing at the desk, clutching her purchase, agog at the movie star and looked back at the hand, following the line of sight down to Loretta. She hotly sighed and questioned in disdain, "What are you doing?"

"Pass me the phone," Loretta hissed from the corner.

"What?"

"Pass me the phone!" she repeated. "I've got to call Jake. We need pictures of Joyce Jones. I've got my scoop!"

Dorothy absentmindedly turned her attention briefly to Loretta. "Yes, he needs to get a picture of Joyce Jones in my new dress," and promptly turned back to watch the action.

"Oh brother." Irene put the phone, base and all, on top of Loretta's hand and grabbed her purse. "I'm going for lunch," she grumbled and left the store.

"Oof." Loretta scrambled to stand up as the phone fell off her hand and clattered to the wood floor, bell clanging as it landed. She looked around as she picked up the phone. No one had noticed the noise.

She righted herself and stood behind the desk, dialing Jake's home number. "Come on, come on, be there," she impatiently muttered as she let the phone ring fifteen times. She hung up and immediately called the newsroom bullpen, hoping that he might be at work. Someone answered on the fourth ring. "Newsroom, Chuck speaking."

"Chuck? Loretta here. Is Jake around?"

"Yeah, he's in the dark room, came in about half an hour ago. Said he had a bunch of pictures."

"I've got a big scoop and I need him. Go in and get him out for me."

"No way," Chuck stated flatly. "Last time I went in there for you, I bleached out the front page photos. Nearly lost my job."

"Oh, for heaven's sake," Loretta blustered. "Just knock on the door and tell him to get down to Poppy Cove as soon as he can. And to bring his camera and flash, too."

"Yeah, yeah," Chuck said as he hung up on Loretta.

In the meantime, the starlet and her manager carried on, moving from rack to rack, handing Betty more clothing.

"Do you know who that is?" Loretta hissed. She had raced over to Daphne and Margot, who were surveying the scene at a distance.

"Yes, isn't it wonderful?" Daphne was thrilled. "She's so pretty!"

"What a great little figure, too." Loretta nudged Margot. "She'll look darling in the clothing."

Margot quietly beamed, as she'd already been thinking just that. She'd been watching what Joyce was selecting for herself and was pleased that she'd chosen the most flattering garments for her trim, yet hourglass figure. There was no need for her to step in with suggestions.

"Ooh, this'll make my column sing! I have to get a quote from her!" Loretta made a scramble towards Joyce and her manager.

"Hold on!" Margot clasped Loretta's arm, halting her. She was adamant not to let Loretta disturb any one of their customers. "Let her finish up and then go slow. I don't want to have any of our clientele feel uncomfortable."

"Oh, pooh, I'm a professional. I know how to handle this." She relented slightly and relaxed under Margot's grip. "No one will know I'm here."

Loretta went on the move. As soon as Joyce was out of her sight, she repositioned herself to a nearby hiding place—behind another rack, a potted plant, anything she could get a surreptitious view from. Twice she knocked into other customers, namely Mrs. White and Miss Parker, to be exact, both who yelped in surprise.

The girls watched her antics for a few minutes. Loretta continued to fumble along in the store, writing notes and keeping an eye on the star. Although she didn't do any permanent damage, she left a wake of ruffled customers and askewed merchandise. She was becoming a nuisance. Just as Margot and Daphne made a motion to step in, Loretta made her presence known.

"What are you doing?" Frances barked at the face peering guiltily through the clothing rack. Loretta had maneuvered herself in a crouching position, notebook and pen furiously scribbling away, behind the stand that Frances and Joyce had reached.

"Umm, Loretta Simpson, Society Editor, *Santa Lucia Times*," she stammered as she climbed out of the rack and stumbled towards them. She did her best to regain her dignity by taking a deep breath, straightening up her glasses and posture, and tugging on her jacket hem. She tucked her notebook back in her pocket and took out her press card, which she handed to Frances. "I'd like to speak to Miss Jones, please. Get a quote for the paper."

"No, I'm sorry. We have no time." Frances stepped in between Loretta and Joyce and crossed her arms firmly. "This is a private stop, not for publicity." Frances guided Joyce by the arm to continue on, turning her back on Loretta.

"Oh come on, just a word or two. You know, what brought you to our town, your thoughts on it or even the store," Loretta whined as she trailed behind.

All the while, Joyce Jones stuck to her purpose. While she continued gathering clothes and handing them to Betty, who was running back and forth to the dressing room, she listened to the banter between the whining Loretta and firm Frances. She sighed and remarked, "Frances, I really don't think there's any harm commenting a little in the local paper. I like it here and everyone's been so nice."

Frances stopped and glared at Joyce, arms still folded. "We don't have time," she snarled.

Joyce sparkled with a soft grin aimed at Loretta. "Oh honestly, I'm happy to say a few words. Besides, I can talk while I try on all these lovely clothes." She looked over at Frances and met her gaze, meaning business.

Frances backed down. She took a step backward and slouched as she grumbled. "She should have been at Smart's like everyone else."

Loretta looked startled at Frances. "What did you say?"

"I said that you should have been at the Oldsmobile dealership earlier today," Frances muttered as she flipped through her notepad, checking their agenda.

Betty stopped in midstride going towards the dressing room and pivoted to face them. "Ooh, you were there?" She jabbed an embarrassed Loretta in the arm. "See? I told you it was a big deal. So you must have been the surprise guest. Wow! Did you see my Dwight?"

"Who's Dwight?" Frances snapped.

"My husband. He works there. He's one of their best salesmen." Betty blushed with pride as she accepted another garment from Joyce.

"I don't know, there were a lot of people. Plenty of young men, including one with a camera, snapping a lot of pictures," Frances mumbled.

"Jake? Jake was there?" Loretta exclaimed.

"I don't know, I didn't catch any names. We were up there because Joyce is Miss Starfire, 1957. She's touring all the state's dealerships promoting the car." She pointedly remarked to Loretta. "You're in the press, you should have known that. We had plenty of time for the paper there."

Loretta felt flustered. With the event of Constance's murder, all other stories fell by the wayside. Betty just flitted and grinned, knowing she was the one in the know.

"Never mind. Loretta, I'd be happy to say a few words for the paper." Joyce gently patted her on the arm. Decisively, she stated, "I'll get started in the dressing room and we'll talk while I change outfits."

The staff was kept hopping. As Joyce had covered the whole store, the largest dressing room was filled to capacity. Betty had gone in to assist with the fastenings, while an eager Abigail attended outside the door, bringing other sizes and re-hanging items as needed. Daphne gathered accessories to compliment the outfits and Margot grabbed her sketchpad, as the flurry of activity fired her imagination.

Frances kept an eye on the time and also on Loretta. They stood together on the edge of the waiting area while Frances replied to Loretta's basic enquiries in a bored, impatient monotone. A crowd of women began to gather to watch the impromptu floor show. As word spread, more came in from the market square and created a hubbub of excitement, as the spectators milled around the racks.

Before long, Joyce began to appear in one outfit after another, flitting and twirling out of the dressing room in fitted day dresses and suits, swirling skirts and sweeping evening gowns. Through all the graceful movements, Joyce politely answered Loretta's questions about being Miss Starfire, her two new upcoming movies and various dating adventures with some of Hollywood's leading men.

"Excuse me, pardon me," a youthful male voice came from the crowd, as the women shuffled to make way. "Got your message, Miss Simpson. I'm here. What's the news?"

Loretta, now right by Joyce's side, turned to face Jake. "Why, Miss Joyce Jones, of course. Snap away,

Jake," she said as she posed with her best front-page grin in action.

Jake looked at the subjects and scratched his head. "You mean Miss Starfire? Well, I already took a whole roll of shots at Smart's earlier." His eyes fixed on Joyce and he became bashful. "Hi, Miss Jones. Your pictures look great. I developed them myself this morning."

Loretta's smile fell as she muttered, "Why did everyone know about that except me? How'd you find out about it?"

"Heck, half the town was there. The paper had an ad for it. We were there because my parents picked up their brand new Starfire."

"Oh, never mind. Jake, I want you to get a few more shots of Miss Jones here in the store." She went from her fluttery disposition back to mugging for the camera as Joyce remained posed the entire time.

"Just one minute!" Frances interjected and stepped in between Jake and his subjects and raised her arm to stop him. You've already got pictures from the— argh!" Jake snapped a flash picture at close range, temporarily blinding her. Fortunately, the shattering glass from the bulb didn't hit her. Loretta rushed to Frances, who was grumbly, but basically unharmed.

After a brief discussion, Joyce had persuaded Frances to let them get a couple of pictures. "I know we're on a tight schedule and this stop isn't part of the plan, but I really like the clothes and the shop, and there's just one more dress I would love to try. I'll go slip into that and then we can take the pictures, all right?" Ever the star, she commanded the scene. Floating out in her final garment, an ethereal light blue tulle dress, with a full, crisp, wide skirt and a snug, strapless, straight cut bodice and light blue satin gloves that fit over the elbow, she looked heavenly.

Once Joyce had preened and twirled for the crowd and the camera, she slipped into the dressing room and came out in her original clothing, like the fresh-faced all-American girl she was. After a brief discussion with Betty to determine what she was purchasing and what she was leaving, she walked directly over to Daphne and Margot for a proper introduction. "Betty tells me this is your darling little shop. It's such a wonderful place. I understand these are all your designs?"

"Yes. I'm Margot Williams," she said, pleased as they gently shook hands. "I design the garments and we make them here on the premises." She gestured to her friend beside her. "Daphne Huntington-Smythe, my business partner, purchases the accessories for the store."

The ladies chatted for a few minutes while the spectators watched and listened. Betty took Joyce's new garments to the cash desk for charging and wrapping. Irene had come back from lunch and quietly started filling out the bill of sale, irritated that Mrs. McGillis was still there, by now leaning on the counter, enthralled and oblivious to the fact that she was in the way of their task. Frances kept an eagle eye on the employees, making sure that Betty used enough tissue paper to keep the clothes wrinkle free and that Irene did not trump up the charges.

Joyce then took a few minutes to greet the patient crowd and sign a few autograph books while Frances paid for the garments and gathered up the parcels. "That's enough. Joyce, we have to leave now. We're late already. We still have to get you to the salon before your appearance at the restaurant." Frances turned to address the crowd. "Joyce Jones has a date tonight at the Derby with her latest co-star, Derek Strong. Their movie, *Fall in Love*, will be out in theaters in October." Frances got the reaction she hoped for, a collective, fluttery sigh from the admirers.

As the pair made their departure, the rest of the crowd began to dissipate. Loretta and Jake scurried back to the paper to make their deadline, some curiosity seekers left, while other customers began shopping and trying on the clothes that Joyce had gone through. There was a happy buzz in the air for the first time since Constance's murder.

By the time the girls had rang through all the purchases that Joyce's fashion show had created and began straightening out the store, it was around three o'clock and the market out in the square was beginning to wind down. Hector Avila's son, Juan, a serious boy of eight, came in with both arms loaded down with the bags of Margot's produce. He was beaming from ear to ear.

"My, Juan, what a huge smile on you." Margot returned his grin. "You must have had a fun day."

"Oh yes, Miss Williams. We sold out of everything. Now Papa says we can go buy my new bicycle today!"

"That's wonderful, Juan." She took the heavy bags from the little boy. "Thank you for bringing me my food." She set them down behind the counter and took some change from the petty cash drawer. "Here you go!"

"Thank you!" He looked at the money before he deposited it into one of his bulging shorts pockets. Margot wondered what little treasures he had in those— rocks, shells, gum, anything, knowing an eight year old. As she went to put her bags away in the lunchroom, Juan scampered out the door to get his new wheels. No one noticed that as the bell rang with his departure, another person slipped in.

"There are more pleasurable ways to find out our secrets," Irene purred. She'd slinked up to the counter from the dressing area after she noticed an attractive man curiously rearranging the paperwork at the sales desk. She gently closed the ledger book on his hand. "Now, what do you think you're doing?" she coolly asked as she slid it from the desktop.

"Peter! What a nice surprise!" Daphne came down the spiral staircase from the loft office and greeted him with a smile. "I thought you might be out of town; I didn't hear from you. What brings you here?"

"I decided to stay in town over the weekend. I was wandering around the square and saw the store. I wanted to see your shop." He turned to face Daphne with a huge smile, but not before flashing a glare in Irene's direction.

"Then welcome to Poppy Cove. Let me introduce you to everyone." Daphne took his arm and gave him a tour of the shop, introducing all of the staff. He in turn looked directly into each woman's eyes, repeated their names and took each of their hands and gently kissed them. Abigail and Betty both giggled and blushed, while Margot, on the other hand, felt it was a bit much. Irene, although wary of his motives, nevertheless raised an eyebrow and moved in closer with a sultry smile.

"More than just a casual interest, I'd say," Irene noted with a glance to the desk, then very briefly meeting Margot's eyes, settling back on Peter's.

"Oh that." He turned to face Daphne directly. "Seems I'm caught out," he chuckled. "I hope you don't mind, but I took the liberty to notice you have no more appointments for the day," he commented lightly as he vaguely gestured to the desk. "Maybe we could go for dinner if we can get a reservation at a good restaurant on such short notice. We could even go for a walk, if you're free to leave now."

"Oh, I'm sorry, but when I didn't hear from you, I made other plans for tonight," she hesitated, feeling a little sheepish. "Why don't you come upstairs to the office? I'll make you a cup of tea and we can talk for a while." She gave a little tilt of her head, tossing her curls, eyes sparkling. He agreed and they went upstairs, with nobody noticing Peter and Irene discreetly once again giving each other the once over.

She took him into the office and showed him some of their work—sketches, samples and catalogues—while the kettle boiled. "Have you ever thought of expanding the store, adding more locations? It seems like it may be a great investment opportunity."

"Is that the kind of thing you're interested in? I thought you were here for the resort properties."

"I'm interested in all kinds of things, especially making money." There was a gleam in his eye she hadn't seen before, a little devilish. "You must be interested in that, too."

"Oh, well, I don't give it much thought, honestly. It's there, I spend it, there's more. I like to think about other things." She wasn't sure she wanted to discuss her business with a new boyfriend.

"You must. You're a businesswoman. You own your own store right?" He commented as he watched her prepare the tea.

"I share the store with Margot, we're partners. Besides, my father's accountant takes care of all the money work. Our manager does the daily bookkeeping. I don't care for that sort of thing. I like the buying, accessories and such. To be honest, the business stuff bore me."

Peter was taken aback. "How could you not care? What if that manager—Irene, isn't it?—or Margot was robbing you blind? You have to keep on top of these things. You trust people too much and they'll take you to the cleaners!" There was an aggressive quality to his voice that made Daphne very uneasy.

"It's all just money. They wouldn't do that to me. Besides, I've known father's accountant all my life. He'd tell me if there was anything out of line. Thank you for your concern, but our store is doing very well exactly as we're running it."

Daphne's anxiety was growing, a rarity for her. She stirred her tea absentmindedly to calm down. She didn't like anyone telling her what to do or whom to trust. There was a long pause in the conversation. "Well, this is a first."

"What's a first?" Peter said between sips.

"That any of my dates gave me the third degree about Poppy Cove or my finances."

"What do you discuss?"

"Oh, movies, the weather, tennis, our families, that sort of thing."

Peter looked at her and realized he'd gone too far. "Yes, of course. I'm sorry, it really isn't any of my business. You're right, this is your town and you do things in your own way. Your shop is successful, so you must know what you're doing." He met her eyes. "Is all forgiven?"

She broke into a smile and softened. "Absolutely."

Peter took a sip of his tea and thought he would try treading on thin ice again by asking her, "So what kind of men have you dated? What did they do?"

It wasn't as touchy as he thought it might be. "Mainly local boys, most of them I grew up with." She admitted, "I think you may be the first man I've dated that I haven't known through family or friends."

"Well, here's to the new Daphne!" He raised his cup to toast to her. She clinked it with hers in return. "I promise to remember the lady does not discuss money," he grinned.

She laughed and all was well. He asked her again if she would reconsider about dinner, but she truly was not available and not wanting to change her plans. She was intent on seeing Dan for two main reasons. If he was involved somehow in Con's murder, she wanted to find out soon before she got too interested in him and if he wasn't, well, she liked him. Daphne went downstairs with Peter to see him off. "Since you're not available, I might as well go back to the city tonight. I'll call on you next week," he said when they were in the shop.

"Please do."

He gave a little nod and stepped back slightly, with his hands clasped behind him. "Ladies, a pleasure to meet all of you." Peter turned to leave. "You have a charming little shop. Obviously, I'm dating a smart girl." With that he left Daphne until next week.

Daphne turned to face Margot. "Well, what do you think?"

"He's very charming. Quite handsome." She was a little reserved in her reply, as his continental ways did not appeal to her.

"Very sly, but if you toss him over, throw him in my direction," Irene could make short work of his kind.

Daphne's face puzzled at Irene's reference, wondering if she'd overheard any of their conversation, but she passed it off with a laugh. "I'm glad he met with approval. Well, I'm going back upstairs to finish my order, before the last rush comes in." Although there were no fittings on Saturdays, their clients often came in to pick up their custom garments for that night's parties and events around town, along with the last minute shoppers purchasing off the racks.

Irene set Abigail up to make telephone calls for the upcoming week's appointments, while Daphne had finished her work upstairs and set to reorganize the earrings and other jewelry into new displays for the upcoming week.

Margot went upstairs with the plan to look over her swatches. Sam Goldman of Morgan Imports would be coming back in a little less than a week to pick up his samples, so if she wanted to order any of those prints she should decide soon. But her mind wasn't on the fabrics. She kept thinking that there was something about Peter and his exchange with Irene that bothered her. He was really slick all right, and maybe not to her particular tastes. However, he seemed nice and Daphne liked him a lot. Still, there was something in the way Irene insinuated his presence in the store that made her think twice. But then again, Irene could be a harmless flirt with anything in trousers. She shook the cloud out of her head and decided that maybe she was just reading too much into it and focused in on the fabrics.

As it turned out, it had been a happily distracting day with the surprise visits, making all of the talk of break-ins and murders seem very remote from their world. Everyone pitched in at the end of the day, as they all wanted to be out at five or just after. The atmosphere was charged. Daphne, Margot, and Irene all had dates, while Abigail was going to a summer sock hop at the teen center in the Santa Lucia Community Church Hall. Betty had a meal all planned to cook for her husband— three courses—and she had all the ingredients ready to go at home. Dwight would be home around seven, which gave her plenty of time.

CHAPTER SEVENTEEN

At ten after seven, Daniel sat at the bar at Antonio's, sipping a glass of Valpolicella while he waited for Daphne. He'd been passing the time in conversation with another young man to his left at the bar as he waited. He casually pulled back his shirt cuff and glanced at his watch.

Daphne put things in perspective about what she knew about Dan as she got ready for her date. By the time she arrived at the restaurant, she knew there was no way a man like that could harm a woman—he seemed too caring. She breezed in wearing a fuchsia, duchess, silk dress with a tulip, ballerina skirt, scooping neckline and short, gently overlapping, tulip sleeves. Over her shoulders was a pale pink, cashmere sweater clasped with a pearl chain linked at the neck. She parked herself down beside him at the bar to his right and gave him a once over. She liked what she saw. All his outdoors work and riding gave Dan a fine figure in the dark suit and tie. She noticed he was wearing only the necessary accessories—a tie clip, cufflinks and his watch, with no rings or any pale lines where rings would have been on his fingers. Immediately, Antonio Jr. came over to greet her. He brought her usual, a dry martini. She, like most of the Santa Lucia social set, was a regular and he knew her favorite pre-dinner drink. "I hope I didn't keep you waiting too long."

Dan looked her over from head to toe as well and smiled. He gave her a light kiss on the cheek. "Not at all. You look beautiful." He glanced to his left.

"We've just been talking while I was waiting. This gentlemen's new to town too." He gestured to his companion. "Let me introduce you. Daphne, this is…"

"Peter!" she exclaimed as she looked past Dan to the other man. There was Peter Carson, sitting right beside Dan. *Well,* she thought. *This is a little inconvenient.*

"Oh, you two know each other?" Dan asked innocently.

"We've met briefly, on a couple of occasions," Peter casually replied, looking past Dan at Daphne, and winked at her.

She took a sip of her drink as she flushed slightly. "Um, yes, that's right. I didn't realize you would be around here tonight. I mean, I thought you were going to be in L.A."

"Change of plans. I've decided to stay. I've heard this is one of the places to be on a Saturday night. It turns out to be true," Peter grinned with a good-natured leer.

Daphne really didn't know if Dan had a jealous nature and what he thought of a girl dating more than one man at a time. Feeling awkward, she glanced around and noticed they were both drinking glasses of the house red. Finally, she came up with a topic. "How do you like your wine? All of them come from the family vineyard in central Italy. Antonio and Maria were the first ones from their families to have left the region."

"The wine is very good. They should think about moving more of the family here to produce wine. I've heard that there are some vineyards going up in the hills. They have the right soil and sun conditions. It seems like it may be a great investment opportunity."

"Is that the kind of thing you're interested in? I thought you were here for the resort properties," Dan commented.

"I'm interested in all kinds of things, especially making money. I invest in various world ventures. Natural resources, business startups, stocks. Diversification is the key. If you're ever interested, I'd be happy to advise you," Peter offered.

Dan shook his head. "No, thanks. I've never been inclined to take such risks. I like working with my hands. The land and the horses have always been good to me."

Peter shook his head. "You'll never get rich that way. You've got to make your money work for you." It was obvious from his words that he had no idea of Dan's background.

Daphne sipped her martini and listened to the two of them make small talk, followed by a long period of awkward silence. To her, it seemed that Dan shared her point of view on Peter's ambitious nature. After what seemed to be an excruciating wait, their table was ready. "Well, great meeting you Peter. I'm sure we'll see you around town," Dan reached to shake his hand, while slipping his other arm around Daphne. She nodded quietly and looked in the direction of the dining room.

"Yes, and good to see you, too, Daphne. I'm sure we'll run into each other again," he discreetly chuckled to himself and remained at the bar while the couple departed. By the time they were seated at their table, Daphne was relieved to be in Dan's company alone and had regained her composure. She liked the strong, calm way he carried himself, but she had to admit that she was grateful for Peter's suave discretion.

Antonio's was hopping as usual. There were many full tables and the atmosphere was noisy with plenty of laughter, song and wine flowing. The brick trim and wood plank floors with plenty of leafy, sprawling green plants and colorful travel and food posters decorating the walls made it very charming and homey. Here and there were black and white photos, proudly displayed in wooden frames showing generations of the Chelli family back in Italy, working, celebrating and living their lives. Dan smiled, "It's very nice in here. I could get used to this."

Daphne inhaled and could feel her stomach start to growl. It had been a long time since coffee and muffins. "Maria, Antonio's wife, does everything herself. The girls in the back help her, but she's the one in charge, tastes all the sauces, cuts the pasta. She's her toughest critic." She paused to look over the menu. "Say, why don't we order the antipasti plate and share it to start?"

Dan agreed and signaled to a passing waiter, Luigi, to bring them the antipasti plate and breadsticks. In no time, the waiter had brought the cold plate full of olives, vegetables, salami and cheese. Dan prepared a plate from the platter for Daphne first before helping himself. They ate hungrily and passed their time companionably, discussing movies, horses, the area, and found out they had a lot in common. Every now and then, Daphne glimpsed over Dan's shoulder and saw that Peter was still at the bar, sometimes watching them, sometimes not, marring what would have been a perfect evening. They placed their orders for pasta and gave Luigi their menus. After the starter plates were cleared away, they kept talking and Dan took Daphne's hands in his.

"Your hands are so strong," Daphne mentioned.

"Not too coarse, I hope. The handling can make them pretty tough."

"No, not at all." She played with his hands, looking closer. "No rings, nothing?"

"Nope. Never. They'd get in the way of work."

"Well, what about after work? Something that has meaning for you, a gift, a family heirloom?"

Dan looked confused and gently set her hands down on the table and looked at her straight in the eye. "Daphne, I'm not married. I never have been, and no plans to be in the near future."

Daphne blushed and blustered, "Oh no, no, no! I didn't mean that!" She paused, realizing how her line of questioning sounded like a mantrap. Then she thought quickly back to her discussion with Margot in the morning and tried to sound casual. "I've been thinking about accessories for men in the shop. Rings, tie clips, cuff links, things like that." To her great relief, she felt confident about how she changed the course of their conversation. Also, when she looked over his shoulder she saw that Peter was gone.

Dan chuckled and didn't need to reply. Antonio had personally brought over their steaming plates of pasta. "How is the lovely Daphne this evening?"

She was grateful for the distraction and recovered nicely. "Just fine, Antonio. I don't think you've met my date. Antonio Chelli, this is Daniel Henshaw. He's the riding instructor at Stearns Academy."

Antonio went to shake his hand and a quizzical look crossed his face. "Ah, but I do know you. You've been here before."

"Yes, I have. With Mrs. Montgomery," Dan said it so plainly and casually, Daphne could have sworn she didn't even hear it, but there it was.

Antonio's face relaxed. "Of course. It was the last time she was here, God rest her soul," Antonio lamented, putting his hand on his heart and looking towards the ceiling. He brought his eyes down and his attention was pulled elsewhere in the busy dining room. "Please excuse me," he said as he left the table.

Daphne wasn't hungry all of a sudden and just played with her pasta, twirling the noodles. Her mouth went dry, but she asked meekly, "You were here with Con?"

"Yes, she brought me here after our last meeting at the school." He tried his linguine with clams. "This is great!" he exclaimed as he took another bite, but noticed she wasn't eating. He motioned with his fork to her plate. "I thought you were hungry."

"Umm, yes, I was, I mean, am." She forced a mouthful or two and tried to act as relaxed as he was. "So, you two *were* really close?"

He kept eating. "Well, I knew her, I liked her." He shrugged. "She was an old family friend and gave me a good opportunity." His manner was so open and relaxed that she had nowhere to go with the questions. He made no excuses and basically always said the same things about how they knew each other. It certainly didn't seem like he was hiding anything about a missing ring. She returned to her meal with a bit more interest. Again, they discovered the more they talked, the more they had in common.

The owner returned with the bill at the end of the meal. "Antonio, as usual, the food was superb. I see that Ana and Lorenzo are fitting in nicely," Daphne commented as Dan took out his wallet.

Antonio's niece and nephew had come over from Italy in the spring to help out. "Yes. I am happy to say they both plan on staying." He put his hands behind his back and rocked a little on his heels. He was very proud of his family.

By time they were ready to leave the restaurant, it was clear Dan and Daphne were not ready to say goodnight to each other yet. "I should get back up to the school and check on the horses. Buttercup's left front leg could have a sprained fetlock, or worse. I can make us some coffee at my cabin, if you want to come up."

He had a way of making her calm, but gave her butterflies at the same time. Any idea that he was involved in the murder, however, was right out of her head. "Yes, I'd love to."

"Good. Why don't you follow me up in your car?"

They got up from their table and as they reached the door, they were greeted by a happy couple, Tom and Margot. "Oh, are you two just leaving?" Margot and Daphne gave each other a quick peck on the cheek. "I was hoping that we'd make it in time to have a drink together."

Daphne looked at Dan and then at Margot. "Actually, we're just heading off to go back to the Academy. Dan has to see a man about a horse!" She laughed at her own joke.

Once they all finished smirking, Dan confirmed, "I really do need to check on Buttercup."

"I just need a moment to powder my nose. Want to join me?" Daphne signaled to Margot to come with her.

The men stood and talked, while the women went off to the powder room. After the girls settled themselves in at the dressing table, and Margot made sure no one else was there, she asked, "Well? Did you get any information about the ring?"

"Yeah, I don't think it's his." Daphne took out her compact. "He didn't act like he ever wore one, and then he basically accused me of trolling for a husband!"

Margot stopped applying lipstick in mid pucker. "He did not!"

"He most certainly did! I couldn't ask anything more about it without looking foolish." The girls stopped talking and continued primping while a patron was using the facilities. When she left, Daphne continued, "But you'll never guess who was at the bar, talking to Dan when I came in."

"Who?"

"Peter."

"No!"

"Yes! Let me tell you, it was awkward! Peter covered, though. He said that he knew me very casually. I don't really know if Dan is the kind of man who likes his girl to see more than one man at a time."

Margot looked at Daphne. "So now you're *his girl*?" she queried.

"You know what I mean." The girls began putting away their cosmetics. "And, Dan was the fellow who was here with Constance the last time before she was killed."

"No!"

"Yes."

Margot stood up from the dressing table, closing her purse. "Isn't that curious? Why were they here together?"

Daphne touched up her lip line with her pinkie one more time as she got up. "It was after their last meeting about the horses before the opening. They were friends, so I guess they just decided to have a nice lunch together after finishing up the business meeting. You know, he was pretty forthcoming with all the information; he certainly didn't act like there was anything to hide. I don't think he could have done it."

The girls were making their way back to the lobby. "Well, just be careful, you still don't know him that well," Margot cautioned.

As they approached the men, Daphne changed the subject. "So how was the movie?" Margot had thoroughly enjoyed the book and when she found out

Tom had read *The Sun Also Rises* too, it had brought them closer together.

"It was good. You two should go. It should be playing for the next week."

The couples said good night to each other as Margot and Tom's table became available. Dan and Daphne left the restaurant, with the arrangement that they would each drive their vehicles up to Dan's place on the school grounds for a nightcap.

Margot and Tom were starving after the movie and decided to be seated at a table instead of having a drink at the bar first. As Lorenzo got Margot's chair, Tom draped his jacket over the back of his before he sat down. Margot always thought he looked so handsome in his white shirt and tie and tonight was especially true. As he sat down, she noticed that his shoulders were not so rigid, and his demeanor was more relaxed than it had been since the murder. It made her smile and when she caught his eye he grinned back at her. They ordered large, fresh, mixed green salads right away, big plates of rigatoni and spaghetti with garlic bread to follow and a bottle of the family's Chianti to wash it all down. Tom started talking about the movie, but Margot's mood had shifted, leaving a puzzling look on her face and she didn't hear a word he said.

"What are you thinking about?" Tom looked across the table at her.

"Hmm, what? Sorry. Um, you were saying?" Margot was busy playing with the base of her wine glass, sorting out her thoughts.

"What has you so distracted?"

She hesitated before asking. "What do you think of Dan?"

Tom took a sip of his Chianti before answering. "He's fine, I guess." He looked intently at her, trying to figure out what she was up to. "Why?" he ventured.

"He's seeing Daphne." She wanted to sound casual, but it came out calculated.

"And..." Tom had known Margot long enough to know that there was more to her statement than she was letting on.

Lorenzo had brought their salads. She waited until he had left the table, lowered her voice and looked around to make sure no one was listening. "Well, Daphne told me that he'd been here with Constance, on her last visit here."

Tom said nothing, just started his salad. When she didn't do the same, he commented, "You should have your salad. It's really good. You don't want it to go soggy."

She looked at him and made a face. "Well, what about the ring I told you about last night? You know, the initials—the same as his father's?"

He set his fork down and wiped the corners of his mouth with his napkin, set it down and looked at her again. "It's all been looked after, we've got a handle on the case. Sweetheart, please just enjoy the evening. It's nothing for you to be concerned about; we've looked into all these angles." He grinned at her and gestured with his fork. "If you don't eat your first course, I will!" and playfully made a move for her plate.

"No way, buster!" she laughed as she moved her plate away from his reach and started eating. They looked at each other, grinning, as they ate, happy to be feeling like their normal selves. She decided not to pursue her curiosity further and just have fun.

Antonio came up to the table. "Excuse me, so sorry to interrupt."

Margot turned in her chair to face him. "Hello, Antonio. Busy night!"

"Yes, it is. Tom, there is someone to see you at the door." Margot looked past Antonio and saw Officer Jenkins in uniform waiting in the foyer, looking in their direction.

"Thank you, Antonio." Tom got up and went to see him. Margot turned back around and sipped her wine, as the salad plates were cleared. It was not uncommon for Tom to be tracked down by work while they were out. Margot had to admit she was disappointed; they were just starting to leave the rest of the world behind and hoped it was something he could get others to take care of and not have to cut their date short.

Tom met Jenkins in the restaurant's lobby, where he briefed Tom on the situation. He spoke with quiet discretion. "Mrs. Lewis was causing a disturbance at the Yacht Club—acting irrationally, yelling and swinging out. They had decided not to admit her into the dining room and it made her very angry. She demanded her car from the attendants and sped off up Oceanview Drive. Patrol has her pulled into the school grounds and she seems calm now, but it's been requested that you speak with her. Chief thinks that you may get a confession out of her."

Tom's jaw visibly tightened and his back became more rigid. He spoke briefly with the officer and returned to the table. "Margot, I'm sorry, but I have to go." He grabbed his jacket, took out some money from his wallet and placed it on the table. "That should cover the dinner, in case I don't make it back in time. Have your dinner here, but get mine to go and I'll come by later tonight." He padded his jacket and found his car keys. "I've requested that Officer Jenkins escort you home when you're ready to leave." He gave her a quick kiss and was gone.

Margot signaled to Lorenzo and told him to make both of their orders to go. She didn't feel like eating with Tom called out and Jenkins waiting, albeit patiently, for her to finish her meal. She settled in the best that she could, finishing her wine and playing with the glass after Tom had left. She was used to him being called away during dinner, but she had a sense it was about the case that was now far too familiar to her. The thought gave her a chill on such a warm night.

Antonio personally brought out their packages. "Ah, I know now. That man that Daphne was with."

"Yes, Dan. What about him?"

"No, not the nice one, the other one that was at the bar. I've seen him before, too. I know. I don't think I like him; he lied to me."

Margot felt the hairs come up on the back of her neck. Her mouth got dry. "Oh? What about?"

"He has been here before and he told me he hadn't been when I greeted him tonight. He was also here with Constance, Mrs. Montgomery. Yes. They had lunch here about a week before she died. They sat near the back and he was kissing her hand. A little too friendly, you know?" Antonio had a look of distaste.

Margot nodded, taking the information in. Antonio looked around and then sat down opposite Margot. He continued, in a low tone. "Tonight he was here for hours, drinking at the bar. More and more wine, bought for everyone as they sat down beside him. We left him alone; he was quiet, not causing problems, but..." Antonio shrugged.

"Go on! What else?" she encouraged.

"Someone came in, early, about six. They called him another name. He said that they were wrong and told them to leave him alone. He got a little funny, you know? Maybe pick a fight, but..."

"But what?"

Antonio motioned with his hands and shrugged again, "Eh, they left, he kept drinking. Nothing, but I think he was lying to them, too."

"Really?" Antonio nodded in reply and Margot asked, "Do you remember what they called him?"

"Oh, I don't know, I was busy. Let me think." He paused for a minute, then he grinned, satisfied he remembered the name. "Nestor!" With that triumph, Antonio got up and tugged on his tunic, going to greet other diners.

Margot sat back in her chair. Nestor? What if the person who came in was right and that was his name? He's already lied easily about how well he knew Daphne to Dan, and Antonio's pretty sure that he'd seen him before and denied it. Plus, at the store, Irene seemed to know something about him, too. Her train of thought continued as she downed the last of her wine. Nestor—could that be the $\mathcal{NH}$ on the ring?

She jumped up and looked again in the direction of the bar, double-checking that Peter or whoever he was wasn't still there or hadn't come back. She realized that he was probably on the loose, somewhere in town. He had to be stopped, or at least questioned. She saw Jenkins waiting at the door for her. She grabbed the doggie bags and went swiftly to him. He initially insisted to take her directly home, as ordered, but she stubbornly demanded him to take her to Tom, telling Jenkins she had news that she had to tell Tom herself immediately and it could not wait—it was a matter of life and death. She finally persuaded Jenkins, saying that it was too complicated to just radio it in, it would be more clear if she explained it to him in person. He finally gave in and agreed to take her to the latest crime scene, which happened to be right back at the beginning.

CHAPTER EIGHTEEN

Daphne and Dan arrived at the Academy grounds and swung by the stables. Buttercup was calm and nickering softly, happy with the attention she was already receiving from the stable hands. The couple carried on to his cabin and settled in nicely. It was warm and cozy, so she slipped off her cardigan, sat down on the sofa and removed her shoes. She tucked her legs under her and relaxed while Dan was pouring them a couple of brandies in the kitchen. *Love Letters in the Sand* was playing softly on the radio in the background and she glanced around the small room. It was neat and clean, but already looked lived in, even though Dan hadn't been there very long. There was a big picture window with the drapes closed opposite the couch and a fireplace to the right of where she was sitting. Behind the wall that the couch was against was the kitchen with a little eating nook and to the left of the picture window was the front door. A window was on the left wall and opposite the front door was the doorway to the bedroom and bathroom right around the corner. The whole cottage could fit inside her bedroom at home, but somehow she really liked it. It felt homey.

Dan brought the drinks and sat down beside her. They were very relaxed and talked about nothing. He was just about to lean in for a kiss when there was an urgent knock at his front door. Reluctantly, he got up to answer it. It was one of the stable hands. They spoke briefly and then Dan closed the door and got his denim work jacket that was hanging on a peg behind it.

"I'm so sorry, but it looks like Buttercup might be having some problems after all. I've got to go," he sighed, obviously disappointed to be called away.

Daphne got up. "I'll come with you."

He put his hands on her shoulders and looked in her eyes. "No, really, I won't be long. I'll just get her settled down again. You're not dressed for it. The stables can get pretty messy, especially if she's restless. Wait here; I'll be back as soon as I can. Help yourself to another drink." He smiled at her and left.

Daphne wandered around the room, not knowing what to do with herself. She peeked into the bedroom and bathroom and noticed he was tidy. She was curious about him, but did not want to be a snoop. Sometimes if a person dug too deep, they didn't like what they found and she didn't want to spoil a good time. She went to the fireplace and looked at the pictures he had displayed in frames on the mantelpiece. There were images of Dan at a younger age and a boy slightly bigger and taller than him, who she took to be his brother. There were various other shots of the boys with who she figured were their parents, and a couple shots of the parents on their own and a picture of their farm. Towards the end of the mantel was a photo that she picked up to get a closer look at. There was writing on it and she brought it closer to her face to read it. It was of the parents with the boys and a woman in the center with her arms around the mother and father, and a horse nuzzling over their shoulders. They were all smiling and laughing, and Daphne was surprised to recognize that it was Constance in the middle of the image. She almost dropped the frame when she read the autograph, 'To M. & N. H.—thanks for Shadow. He's made himself right at home! All the best, Con.'

N. H.! As in the *N.H.* they were all looking for? She felt faint and flopped down in the nearby easy chair, drink in one hand, photo still in the other. She looked closer at the picture, trying to see if anyone was wearing the signet ring, but she couldn't get a good look at the hands. Her mind was going a mile a minute, realizing that it truly could be Dan or even his father who could have been the killer. She got up and replaced the photograph carefully, set down her drink on the nearby end table, slipped on her shoes and grabbed her purse. When she got to the door, she peered around carefully and saw no one. The lights were on in the stable and she could hear voices, but they seemed very preoccupied. Other than that, she could hear nothing over her thudding heart as she shut the door and made a run across the school grounds to get to her car as fast as she could. She had to tell Tom what she knew and, moreover, she didn't want to be left alone with a killer—no matter how nice his manners were.

Daphne was briskly half running, half walking in her heels across the unlit athletic fields. It was slow going. Her high heels were digging into the grass, no matter how hard she tried to stay on the balls of her feet. She decided that she'd make faster progress in her stockings, so she stopped and slipped off her shoes. She looked around in the dark and to her left she saw a few lights on in the teachers' residences and wondered if she should simply call the police from there, but the only person she knew was Mrs. Peacock, and she had no idea where she lived, or who else she could trust. On the other side of the field, the outdoor lights of the administration buildings of the Academy shone like a beacon. They looked deserted, like something out of a gothic novel, tall with brick and stone and huge paned windows, but she guessed they were locked up tight, and thought it would be safer to be in the illumination to get to her car, even if it did add a few feet to her path. She continued on, realizing she was half way to the parking lot now with a good head start before Dan could catch up with her by the time he realized she was gone. When she got to the concrete walkways, she stopped between lampposts to pop on her shoes. She kept out of the full light, frightened and alert, frozen to watch for movement and not wanting to be seen by Dan or any of his men. She had no idea how much they knew about him or if they were involved in the murder. Then she thought she saw a blur of a shadow and could have sworn she heard branches crackle and footsteps near the doors between the first and middle structures. She double-checked that she was still in the dark and was so scared she wasn't sure if she was even breathing.

The figure, lean and lithe, in dark, close-fitting top and pants stopped in mid-motion, slightly crouching and putting arms out, like a caught tomcat on the prowl. It jumped back out of its own lit circle and peered around to see if it had been seen.

Daphne bristled for a moment, thinking Dan or one of his henchmen had come out of the woodwork. She squinted and panicked as the figure stood up straighter and strode closer to her in the dark, between the buildings. With a flood of relief, she realized who it was and positioned herself under the nearest lamplight. "Oh, Peter! I'm so glad to see you. You've got to help me get out of here!"

"Daphne, is that you?" Peter remarked in his strong male voice as he approached her.

"My car's down at the parking lot, just over there." She continued and then paused, asking, "What are you doing here?"

"Andrew said these were the best made new buildings in town and suggested to me to check out the construction when I had the time. My best girl turned me down, so here I am," he remarked with a surly grin. "What are *you* doing? Did your hot date cool down?" As he put his hands on her shoulders and looked her square in the eye. He noticed she was shivering, but the breeze was not cold. "What happened?"

"Oh God, Dan!" she exclaimed. She was so startled about her discovery that she almost forgot that she'd been on a date. She leaned on Peter. "You have to help me get to my car. I need to leave right now. I think I'm in danger!"

"Are you hurt? Did that jerk hit you?"

"No, no, it's not that. I just figured something out. I've got to get to Tom."

"That detective? Must be serious." Peter looked her in the eyes, judging her fear. "Look, I understand you're upset, but maybe you should just calm down and tell me what has you so frightened." He glanced around and saw a nearby bench. He guided her to sit down and watched her.

Daphne took a couple of deep breaths and regained her composure, still not wanting to reveal her findings to anyone but the boys in blue. She huffed up again. "There's no time to waste! I might have put you in danger too! We've got to find Tom, or get to the station." She tried to bolt to her feet.

Peter remained calm and held his grip on her arm, keeping her seated. "Why don't you tell me what's going on? You can sort out your thoughts, so you can give a straight story to the police." She motioned to get up again, but he stayed firm. "I'll keep you safe."

She finally released a heavy breath. "I think I know who killed Constance. I'm sure of it." At least, she thought she was sure. She didn't want to say Dan's name out loud until she spoke it to Tom first.

"Nancy Lewis," he stated flatly. "The police have evidence. They think she did it."

"No! Not Nancy. It was someone else."

He paused for long moment. "Really?" he finally asked.

"Yes. Now I'm sure of it. The more I think about what I saw…"

"What did you see?" he snapped as he interrupted her.

"The initials, the photo, knowing Con," she rambled.

Peter looked bewildered. "What are you talking about?"

"I've got to tell them. They're going after the wrong person! She didn't do it!" She tried to stand up; he firmly held her down by her arms.

"You're not making sense. Slow down and tell me what's going on."

Daphne took a deep breath and saw there was still no one else around and settled in, feeling a little safer with Peter keeping her protected. She sighed and began to tell him her theory. "Nancy Lewis didn't do it."

"Really, who else has such a strong motive?" He let go of his grip on her and crossed his arms as he sat back, scoffing at her. "The police think it's the Lewis woman. They say an arrest is imminent. Leave it alone."

"No, it's someone else!" Daphne repeated. "Look, I've got to go. I think the murderer is nearby. You've got to help me!" She tried to get up, but he again held her down with one arm pressing around pressing her shoulder and the other gripping her arm between them, in a quiet, eerily calm demeanor. "I've got to get to my car."

"And I think you should leave it alone," he said through firmly, gritted teeth. He kept his grip on her. He was silent for a long time and Daphne watched him, still terrified, but becoming mesmerized by his odd behavior. He was acting in a way she'd never seen and she wasn't too sure of him. He relaxed a little when he could read her reaction and relented. "Okay, but you're in no shape to drive. I'll take you. In a moment."

Daphne continued to watch his mood. She stayed quiet. Was he in on it too? How well did he know Dan? Did they really just meet that night at the bar?

Eventually he spoke again. "This is where the murder took place, right?" Peter looked around his surroundings.

She was stunned. Yes, there they were, sitting on a bench very near where Constance had been killed. She didn't know how to answer, but was getting the sense that if she stayed calm and played along, it may be her best defense. She remained quiet and let him take the lead.

"Strangled in the rosebushes," he stated, his eyes glued to the spot.

It was as if he was in a trance. She started noticing things about him. She couldn't believe that in all of her worry, she'd never noticed that he was not in the same clothes from dinner. He was head to toe in black—t-shirt, chinos, shoes. She didn't buy his story as to why he was up there in the first place, and wondered what was his real reason, but didn't think she could ask him. Her murderer theory may have been wrong after all. She brought the conversation back to Nancy, thinking that may be the best way to get to safety. "You know, I think you're right after all. I've also read that the police think it's Nancy Lewis."

"Anyone could be pushed to murder if they had to be," Peter remarked.

"Not me. I couldn't imagine that," she blurted out. Daphne didn't mean to antagonize or disagree with him, but it was a gut response.

"What if someone tried to kill you—it was kill or be killed?"

Daphne said nothing. Peter continued. "What if someone threatened everything you've made for yourself?"

He turned to face her and looked directly in her eyes. "You didn't answer my question, Daphne. What would it take for you to take another life?" He stopped and demanded an answer.

"Nothing. I mean, I couldn't," she stammered. After a pause, she added, "I don't think you could either." Even after she said it, she didn't know if it was true, but felt it bought her some time.

"But what if I could," his grip relaxed a little and slumped his shoulders. "I didn't mean it."

"That's okay, it's just an odd conversation. Let's be more fun." Daphne thought that if she could make him think she took it lightly, they could get out of there. Still, she could barely breathe and couldn't tell if her heart was still beating.

"I mean I didn't mean to kill her."

Daphne's worst suspicion of the moment came true. "You killed Constance?"

"I didn't mean to," he repeated. "It was her or me— my life."

"The affair," the shock left her voice flat.

"It's always harmless, but this one was going to spoil things for me, turn me in."

"So there was a mystery man. It was you."

Peter carried on with his confession, oddly relieved. "It was usually so simple. They always gave me money as soon as I threatened to expose them, but she didn't care."

"They?"

"The others." He was exasperated, tired of running. "I made so much off of these lonely dames. I treated them well and was amorously attentive to their needs and then when I told them their town would know all about it, they just paid me off and I left."

"Constance was different," she added. The longer he kept talking, the safer she felt. He seemed less dangerous, deflated as he told his story. If it kept up this way, she felt she might be able to make a break for it.

"She fell as hard as the others at first, but she figured me out when she saw my notebook and stole it."

"Your notebook?"

"I kept clippings and notes, so I wouldn't cross women too closely connected to each other and have the goods on them. She stole it from my room. I only wanted it back. I was going to leave her alone and walk away from the whole thing, but the book was damning."

"Are you sure Constance had it?"

"Yes. It went missing right after she came to see me last Thursday. I went to go have a shower and when I came out, she and my book were gone."

"What did you do then?" Daphne's mind was reeling but she was getting caught up. She was trying hard to put her fear behind her and pay attention to what he was saying so she could repeat it to the authorities. She knew she was going to get away. She had to.

"I came up to the school. I had to speak to her. I snuck onto the grounds and posed as a waiter."

"Oh my God! That was you!" Daphne remembered the clumsy waiter who almost ruined Loretta's new silk dress.

"Yes. I tried to talk to Constance, but she was furious. She was going to the police right after the ceremony. She wouldn't tell me where the book was. I grabbed her and she brushed me off. I took the scarf, found the other end and pulled. She was caught by surprise. It happened so fast, and she was on the ground. I didn't even know if she was dead or just passed out. I looked around. For so many people there, no one paid any attention. I was lucky. Then I ran."

"I read about her death in the paper," he continued. "And that damn kid taking all the snaps. The article said the police were keeping them as evidence. I was in shock, but I still hadn't found the book and I needed to get hold of those photos too."

"You took the pictures from the police station and broke into the house," Daphne deduced.

"Yes. I wasn't in any of the pictures and the book wasn't in her house."

Daphne's anger was getting the better of her fear. "You were going to let Nancy Lewis take the blame for this!"

"I still am. What else can I do?" By now, Peter was no longer gripping Daphne. He was sitting on the bench, facing forward and head down, while Daphne stayed seated, beside him, thinking she could bring him around to doing the right thing.

"Confess! If you truly feel that bad about it, take responsibility for it," she put her arm around his shoulder.

"Look, just help me find the book, and I'll leave," he resigned. "It seems that Nancy has done enough wrong deeds to merit prison."

Daphne removed her arm and stared at him. "Why did you date me?"

"You were pretty." She rolled her eyes. "Okay, and you might have known something, where I could find the book. Constance had raved about you and your shop, her new dress, which I still think did wonders for her."

As Peter sat silently in his reverie. Daphne slowly glanced around, trying to find her best way out of the situation. She thought she heard footsteps in the distance and a faint cry. Then the noise was louder. It was Dan, calling out her name. He found her! She couldn't believe how happy she was to see him and tried to call out, but Peter started around wildly as he heard him too and gripped her again, and with a hand clamped over her mouth, he was back in control. "Don't make me hurt you too. I killed once, I can do it again," he hissed as he pulled her off the bench and into the darkness.

CHAPTER NINETEEN

Officer Jenkins drove the squad car at a leisurely and cautious pace. By the time he and Margot were winding up Oceanview Drive, she was impatient and irritated. There had been nothing she could say to Jenkins to make him understand that the matter was urgent. Jenkins treated her like just another cop's ditsy girlfriend and that didn't sit well with her. Margot put her feelings about him aside and thought clearly about what she needed to tell Tom. She wanted to recall all that Antonio had said as accurately as possible and wondered about Peter/Nestor being at the restaurant, both tonight and with Constance on an earlier occasion. Also, in her own limited contact with him at Poppy Cove, she noticed he was very slick and there was that strange exchange between him and Irene that she never questioned her about. There was definitely something odd about his character and the sooner the police tracked him down, the better. She didn't want to cloud the details with too much personal speculation. Tom would want just the facts, like they say on television. That was Tom.

She was just about to ask Jenkins again where they were going and how long it was going to be before they got there when she was surprised to see them turn onto the wooded driveway of Stearns' Academy. There were a couple of black and white squad cars and a few of the men standing about, just a few feet off the road. Her surprise grew even deeper when she saw Nancy Lewis with her head down and hands shackled behind her back, sitting in the back of one of the cars. Tom was leaning over talking to her. As Jenkins barely came to a rolling stop, Margot jumped out and ran to Tom.

"Tom! I've got to tell you something!"

He was startled and looked over to her. "What are you doing here?" He glanced behind her towards Jenkins as he was getting out of the car. "Why did you bring her up here? We're on a case!" he snapped.

"She insisted." Jenkins sheepishly shrugged, as he sauntered over to where the rest of the officers were, hovering around Tom.

"Yes, I did. Listen, Tom. There's this man, going by the name of Peter, saying that he's an investor…"

"Oh, so now you're going to slander him, too! Don't listen to anything she says! Peter's a fine man," Nancy interrupted from her seat in the patrol car.

Margot shot an irritated glare at Nancy and grabbed Tom by the arm, gently pulling him out of hearing range from the others. "He's not who he says he is. He's been charming his way around town, specifically to Daphne, Nancy and apparently Constance, too. Antonio recognized him and said that someone else in the restaurant identified him as Nestor. He tried to deny it and hush them up. He's a sly one, Tom, and I have a hunch he might be the $\mathcal{NH}$ that you're looking for."

"This is ridiculous! Are you going to take me down to the station or let me go?" Nancy was starting a new tear on her tantrum, kicking the back of the driver's seat with her pump. "I want my lawyer!"

Margot glanced in her direction. "What happened to her?"

"Disturbance at the yacht club, reckless driving and given that she is still under suspicion, we're taking her back in," stated Tom. "You can call your lawyer as soon as we get there." Tom closed his notebook as he wearily addressed her.

"Ooh, you just wait 'til Andrew gets back. When you need a loan, he'll fix it so you'll never get one in this town!" she threatened.

Tom smirked and shook his head. "Curtiss, get Mrs. Lewis comfortable in the car. We need to keep you here until we sort out the details."

Nancy protested again and then slumped down dejectedly in the back seat while Officer Curtiss closed the door. Tom focused on Margot. "So what else can you tell me about this man?"

Dan stopped mid-field and looked around. After he'd called out for Daphne, he could have sworn he heard something—a call back or a yelp, but he couldn't be sure. It was dark around him and when he looked towards the lit buildings, he saw nothing. He figured it must have been a hawk or another night creature and kept walking towards the parking lot.

He was surprised to find her gone when he returned to the cabin. She left in a hurry, her drink only half finished and she'd forgotten her sweater on the couch. He thought everything was going well; he knew he'd been enjoying himself and he thought she had been too. He hadn't been gone that long, where could she be? Dan felt panic rise as he noticed all the police around the cars. He made a beeline to a couple of familiar faces.

"Margot, Tom? What's going on?" he asked as he approached the couple. "Is it Daphne?"

"Daphne? Isn't she with you? Didn't she come up here with you?" Margot was startled. She thought Daphne was with Dan and never gave her a second thought.

"Yes, she did, but I had to tend to one of the horses and when I came back, she was gone. She left so fast she forgot her sweater. Why are all of you here? What's happened? Is it Daphne?" He repeated, growing more concerned.

"No, it's a different matter," Tom stated. "We haven't seen her."

"Why would Daphne leave? It seemed like you two were having a good time at the restaurant," Margot noted. "Did you have a tiff or something?"

"No, I think something must be wrong. I was really surprised. We were having a great time. Is that like her, to just leave when she wants to?" Margot shook her head in answer. "I didn't think so," he continued. He glanced around. "Her car's still here, so she must be somewhere around. I called out to her, but she never answered. Do you know any reason why she'd do that?"

Margot's eyes widened and she bit her top lip. "Well, there was a time where we wondered if you'd been the one having the affair with Constance and was her killer."

At first, Dan was embarrassed, then mad, then flabbergasted, then hurt. "I've known Constance almost all my life; she's like family. I could never have an affair with her and certainly not kill her or do her any harm! Did you really think I could do such a thing?"

She blushed, considering how to continue, especially with Tom giving her *that* look as she said it. "Well, sorry; it's just a bad time and we didn't know you very well. There's the whole thing with the initials and all…" she trailed on, awkwardly. "I mean, I don't think so now, but do you think Daphne could have seen something at your place that made her think that was possible?"

Past Dan's shock, he gave some thought to the group picture with Constance that he had briefly noticed was out of its usual place. "Maybe. There was a photo of our family with Constance that had been moved. Daphne could have seen that."

"Daniel's been checked out and cleared of any suspicion." Tom met Dan's eyes and then looked at Margot sternly. "We'll discuss this later." Tom's instincts took him in a new direction. "What can you tell me about this Peter?"

Margot and Dan both told Tom a brief but detailed description of the man they knew as Peter Carson, realizing they did not know very much about him at all. Margot also revealed that Daphne had gone on a date with him and he'd been at the shop and at Antonio's bar that night. Margot couldn't read Dan's expression regarding the news that Daphne was seeing both of the men. He seemed fine, comfortable enough with it to talk about the conversation they'd had that evening. Nancy chimed in on how she thought he was such a marvelous man and could have nothing to do with this. Tom scanned around the parking lot, sizing up his available manpower. "Curtiss, keep an eye on Mrs. Lewis. Riley, call in an APB for a Peter Carson. Jenkins, organize a search for Miss Huntington-Smythe. Her car's still here, so she must be somewhere on the grounds."

Margot was shocked at the idea that they had to search for Daphne. "Tom, do you think she's in trouble?"

"We're not taking any chances. Both Carson and Daphne are unaccounted for. Margot, I need your help. Call for her in a friendly tone. She may still be up here, and if Carson's been following her, he may have her. If that's the case, then we don't want to alarm him."

Everyone stood still as she met his eyes and took a deep breath. "Hey Daphne! Are you up here?" Her voice started out as a quiver, but finished out in its usual warm tone.

But it was met with a shriek and a sickening thud. It echoed off in the night, bouncing off of the buildings and pavement. Margot felt lost as she tried to concentrate where the sound came from, but the trained police zeroed in on one direction.

Jenkins and another officer led the way, running to the buildings with Tom, Dan and Margot in quick pursuit. The race ended near the steps and rosebushes where Constance had been found only days earlier. One person was crouched over a figure lying crumpled on the ground—the head at a funny angle on the steps and the legs sprawled towards the shrubbery. The moon rose over the tops of the buildings and cast a glow, revealing the two figures—Daphne beginning to stand up and Peter, motionless on the ground. Daniel and Margot rushed to comfort and embrace their friend, while the officers dealt with the second death at Stearns' Academy.

EPILOGUE

On Monday, September 16, Stearns' Academy for Girls officially opened. It was two weeks late and a very low-key ceremony with just the local press, staff and families present. Reginald and Charles each gave short speeches and a tearful but quietly composed Headmistress Larsen cut the ribbon at 9:05 a.m., just before classes started. Constance had been laid to rest as well as her murderer—Nestor Hernandez. During the struggle after his confession to Daphne, he'd tried to escape and slipped and fell, hitting his head on the steps, inches away from where he had strangled Constance.

The details to why he would murder Constance in the first place were generally unknown to the close-knit community. The police had kept mum about the situation, only revealing the basic facts to the press, but the events the night of his death were permanently etched in Daphne's mind. She told the police how "Peter" had confessed to her that he had killed Constance, his claim to past dalliances and references to some kind of a notebook. It was something Constance had taken from his room and it would have exposed him for the shyster he was. But so far, the book had not shown up during the police searches of the Montgomery estate, Constance's car or the Academy. He died leaving many unanswered questions, but at least after a thorough search of his belongings, the police were able to establish his true identity—Nestor Hernandez of Los Angeles. Any requests made to the general public had turned up nothing concrete regarding the man or the notebook.

Miss June Clark was getting ready for her basic bookkeeping class early that Monday morning. Just before she headed out to the garden for the official opening, she had gone to the supply room and got out twenty-one black ledger books, one for each of her first period students and one for herself. She laid them out on the desks, shut the door and joined the rest of the faculty.

The classes started immediately following the ceremony and the teachers were eager to get to business, having missed two weeks of classes. She introduced herself to the students, took the role call and instructed them to open their books and write the headings in the columns, as she would do on the board. A curious sound of flipping pages and girlish gasps caught her attention. As she turned around, she saw that one of the young ladies had a scrapbook of sorts, instead of a columned ledger. Rapidly, the rest of the girls got up and hovered at the desk.

"What's that? Hey, he's kinda cute."

"These are weird, they're in French and Italian, I think."

"This one's from the *New York Times*."

"Ladies, please." The girls grew silent as Miss Clark went to have a closer look. She walked up to the blonde girl's desk. "Everyone sit down. Young lady, what do you have there?"

The group went back to their seats as the girl reddened and seemed flustered. "I don't know. I opened up the book on my desk, but I think there's been a mistake."

Miss Clark quickly glanced at the open page and closed the book. From the outside it looked like the rest of the ledgers, albeit a little lighter in color and slightly scuffed in the top left corner. "Thank you. I'll take this and get you a new one. The rest of you, copy what I've written and sit quietly. I'll return shortly." She picked up the book calmly, opened the door and left the classroom. As her hand lifted from the doorknob on the other side, she began to tremble when she knew what she had.

Loretta burst into Poppy Cove, flush-faced and larger than life. "You won't believe what happened today at the school!" Jake, as ever, was in tow, laden down with a couple of heavy cameras around his neck and dragging a tripod behind him.

Margot was in the middle of a fitting. She had three pins in her mouth and Mrs. Falconer standing stock still on a wooden stool. Marjorie looked up from her clipboard, pen in hand and glared over the top of her glasses. For a split second, Margot paled. She took the pins out of her mouth. It seemed that every time something happened at the school grounds, a person perished. "Please tell me nothing bad," she sighed.

"No! Just the opposite. They found the notebook!" Loretta's eyes glittered.

"Really! Where?"

"It ended up in a classroom. One of the girls found it. I was just on my way to hand in the story to my editor. Deadline's at three. I've got to make sense of my notes. Had to tell you, though. Listen, what are you doing tonight?"

"Tom and I had plans for dinner, but if there's been a break like this, he'll be busy. What about you?"

"Oh yeah, he'll be busy with this one tonight. Since you'll be free then, let's go for a drink, maybe some dinner. I'll give you the scoop, on the sly. Once it's in print, it's out. Think Daphne's up to joining us?"

Margot was unsure when it came to her dear friend. Ever since that fateful night, Daphne hadn't been around much. There was the police investigation and when Peter's death had been ruled to be accidental, she was taking a well-deserved break. Even Margot, her closest companion, hadn't seen her in days. "Leave it to me, 'Retta. I'll call the house and see how she's feeling. As for me, I'd be happy to join you. Why don't you come by here at six and we'll take it from there."

"That's an super idea. Later, gator!" Loretta turned on her heels with Jake following as usual.

Margot was locking the door as Loretta showed up in the evening. "I spoke with Mrs. Huntington-Smythe earlier. She said that Daphne was almost like her old self and thought it would be a great idea for us to see her."

Loretta grinned. "Wait till she gets an earful of the news! It'll knock her socks off!"

Margot lightly grasped Loretta on the arm. "Just remember that the whole Peter/Nestor situation has been really difficult for her. Try to keep it down to a dull roar, okay? She was there when he fell. Think about how you felt when you found Constance."

"Oh, right. Sorry, I just get so excited with the news. I'll go slow." The girls took off in Loretta's brown sedan up to the Huntington-Smythe estate.

"Oh Miss Margot, you are a sight for sore eyes!" Eleanor, the housekeeper, was glad to be greeting her. "You too, Miss Loretta. Our Daphne could use some refreshing company." She led them to the sun porch where they could see Daphne with her back to the door, staring off to the ocean view.

"Miss Daphne, you have visitors," Eleanor said as she ushered the girls in and left, shutting the door behind her.

Daphne looked back and her eyes immediately brightened. A grin broke on her face. "Hey, thanks for coming! It's so good to see you both. Sit down!" She hugged the girls. She was so glad to see them she almost cried. They all sat down and she called back to Eleanor and asked her to bring in a pitcher of martinis.

All of them began to talk at once and laughed. There was so much to say, really it was about nothing, but it felt good to be in the company of each other. The drinks came and there was an awkward lull.

Margot spoke first. "We miss you terribly at work. When are you coming back? Irene's hard for me to take without having you to smirk to behind her back."

Daphne sighed. "Soon, in a couple more days. I can't seem to stop replaying that night. I know I should come back, but I just can't concentrate."

"It would be so good for you," Margot encouraged. "It'll take your mind off things."

"I know," Daphne slouched, sheepish that she still felt down.

Margot took a sip of her drink and set it down on a small napkin. "Well, maybe this will help. There's been a new twist in the case. Loretta has some news."

Both of the women looked at Daphne. She cringed slightly, but said, "Go on. The sooner we put this behind us the better."

Loretta cleared her throat and began. "Remember that Peter had said to you that Constance had taken his book and it would be the end for him if it was ever read?"

"Yes, but we didn't know where Constance had hidden the book, or what was in it."

"We do now. It was found today at the school, during one of the first classes. She must have left it there for safekeeping until after the original opening night's event. Didn't Peter say it disappeared that day?"

"Yes and it sounded like Con had gone straight from Peter's to the school. She must have hidden it there after all."

"It was in a pile of similar looking books in the supply room," Loretta reported.

"That's why he'd been up there looking for it that night."

Loretta nodded. "It was quite the eyeful for a group of young ladies."

"Did you actually see it?"

"I did. Jake and I were there covering the Academy opening today, and while we were finishing up, a teacher brought the book to the office. They were calling the police. We caught a quick look before Headmistress Larsen snatched it out of our hands. Then we had a better look when Santa Lucia's finest held a press conference at noon and I got a good read of it. We're printing some excerpts of it in tomorrow's paper. He was a real gigolo, that one!"

"Really? What was in there?" Daphne's curiosity was replacing her melancholy in leaps and bounds.

"Proof that he'd scammed women all around the world. Dowagers in Denmark, spinsters in Sweden, nervous Nellies in New York. He seduced them all under various names, too. Peter Carson was the latest of many. He kept clippings of it all, like notches on a bedpost. He would take what they had and leave them."

"So were his own true initials NH?"

"Yes. Nestor Hernandez was his true name, born and raised in Los Angeles. His father was a ladies' man and small time lothario. Taught his son all he knew and Nestor added a few new tricks, from what we can gather."

"Unbelievable. How could he get away with it all?"

"He was slick, really made the women believe he loved them. They were flattered and then humiliated. According to the clippings he kept, he was never discovered. Sometimes family members or accountants noticed large sums of money missing and reported it to the authorities long after he left town. By then, he would have moved onto the next town, next woman."

"It surprised me that Constance was taken in by a man like that," Margot commented.

"Right time, right place," Loretta shrugged. "I hate to speak ill of the dead, but let's face it, Constance was not a raving beauty or had that many admirers. Maybe with Reggie being so busy, a little extra attention made her feel special. This creep snuck in, told her just what she wanted to hear. Nestor did his research, too. He studied the social scene for weeks before he would come into town, noticing who appeared to be lonely and rich."

"Oh great! So I looked like an old spinster to him?!?" Daphne was mortified.

"No, I don't think so. Yes, he was always after money, but by the time he met you, he was already trying to get the scoop on Constance and where she'd hide his book. And because of your partnership with a police detective's girlfriend, he might stay one step ahead of the game in her murder investigation."

"Ooh, and all that time, I wondered if it could have been Dan! He hasn't been around much since that night. He said that he wanted to give me some time and that he would be really busy with the school for the next few weeks, but I'm sure he wants nothing to do with me now. He must have thought the worst of me." Daphne wailed.

"I wouldn't be so sure about that." Daphne's mother walked in with a huge bouquet of red roses and white daisies. She was grinning from ear to ear.

Daphne laughed as she took the card. "They're from Dan! He wants to know how I'm doing. He wants to see me again when I'm ready!" she read.

"That's that. Nothing can keep our Daphne down for long," Margot smiled. "Listen, we have a fashion show to get ready for in less than two weeks. I need you in the shop! There are a million things to do. Can you be ready now?"

Daphne looked at her friends, her mom and her beautiful flowers. "I'll be there tomorrow. After all, I need to go shopping. I've got a hot date waiting for my call!"

Barbara Jean's Fabulous Fashion Tips for the Modern 1950's Woman

When heading out on a picnic, choose a sleeveless shirtdress style with a fitted bodice to emphasize your shapely figure, but full skirt to allow for modesty and coverage as you nosh on the lawn. Try one of the new mod cotton prints for fun and avoid gingham, as it may make you look like the tablecloth.

Out for a swim? Why not be daring and try one of the new two-piece suits. Be sure it has a fully supported top and skirted bottom to show off just the right amount of feminine assets.

Gloves are a must for social events—day or night. Wrist-length cotton are perfectly acceptable for daytime, in white or pale dove grey to best complement your ensemble. For evening, select satin or velvet, in black, white or the same color as your gown. Not only do they protect your delicate hands, but as a single girl, casually dropping one accidentally in the presence of an eligible bachelor could gently start the chase. The same application can be used with married couples, to help the wife gauge if her husband is paying enough attention to her.

Is the man in your life charming, but short on stature? Not to worry, the new fashionable ballerina flats are becoming just as popular as stilettos.

And, speaking for the men, why not help him relax and break out of his gray flannel work uniform on the weekend? Surely the man in your life—albeit boyfriend, husband or father—would certainly appreciate the weekend backyard barbeque more wearing the new modern casual look of Hawaiian prints and Huarache sandals. Be sure to inform him that socks are not part of the new look.

The lovely new Bakelite and cut-glass bijoux brooches are very versatile. Not only do they complete your look, but if you happen to spill a little on your lapel or collar, just strategically place to cover your minor inconvenience.

Dorothy Parker is very clever, but men do make passes at women who wear glasses—horn rimmed with rhinestone cat-eyes, that is. They give a certain perkiness to a girl. Just for a blast, try a pair with plain glass in them if you have perfect vision and practice making eyes over the top. It'll send them!

Always leave the house in full control of your appearance. Place a mirror just inside your front door to give yourself the once over. Is your lipstick in a bright and even coat? Powder giving you a natural glow? Eyeliner and shadow smudged in that perfect way?

Don't forget, that as you give your hair the last coat of lacquer, a quick spritz over the face sets your make-up for the day. Be sure to close your eyes first.

Scent makes the woman. Many new fragrances have such wonderful layering complementary products. Before an important night out on the town, pamper yourself in a warm scented bath, followed by talcum powder and *eau de parfum* in the same aroma. The men will be left breathless as you waft around the room.

Never forget your foundations. A simple combination of the new cantilevered brassiere, girdle, garter, full, camisole or half slip, (crinoline for a full skirt) and stockings will make any modern girl look trim and carefree.

ABOUT THE AUTHORS

Barbara Jean Coast is the pen name of Andrea
Taylor and Heather Shkuratoff.

Andrea Taylor always imagined
herself being a super sleuth girl
detective and writing adventurous
stories, full of mystery and intrigue
since she was old enough to hold a
pencil. She resides in Kelowna, BC,
Canada, where she writes under the pen name of
Barbara Jean Coast with her co-author friend, Heather
Shkuratoff. She travels often to California to further
develop the stories and escapades of the Poppy Cove
Mystery series. STRANGLED BY SILK is her first
novel. Andrea has also published freelance articles
about fashion, current events and childcare, and is
currently blogging on Wordpress about creativity and
poetry, as well as researching for her own literary
novels.

Heather Shkuratoff, an avid mystery
reader, joined lifelong friend Andrea
Taylor to create STRANGLED BY
SILK, the first novel in the Poppy
Cove Mystery series, written under the
pen name of Barbara Jean Coast.
Growing up in a family of talented crafters and sewers,
Heather developed her own skills to become a
dressmaker and designer, which helps to give rich detail
and character to their stories. She lives in Kelowna, BC,
Canada, but spends much time in California,
researching for the novels and doing her best to live like
Barbara Jean.

CPSIA information can be obtained at www.ICGtesting.com
Printed in the USA
LVOW06s1611211015

459180LV00002B/438/P